A LOW BLOW

"Where in the hell can he have gotten to?" He pointed at the sibling with the Winchester. "Zeb, you go check the outhouse. Barnabas, sit out front and keep an eye on the gruella. Sooner or later Frost is bound to show."

"Sooner rather than later," came a voice from under the table.

Startled, Temple Blight straightened and whirled. He was not quite all the way around when a pistol barrel poked from under the table, pointed at his groin. The pistol cracked, and Temple shrieked and clutched at himself, dropping his Remington. The next shot caught him smack in the center of the forehead and blew out the rear of his cranium in a spray of hair and gore.

By then Zebulon and Barnabas Blight were rushing to their brother's aid. Zeb jerked his Winchester to his shoulder, but he did not quite have it level when the pistol under the table boomed a third time and Zeb's left eyeball dissolved. . . .

Ralph Compton

Blood Duel

———

A Ralph Compton Novel
by David Robbins

A SIGNET BOOK

SIGNET
Published by New American Library, a division of
Penguin Group (USA) Inc., 375 Hudson Street,
New York, New York 10014, USA
Penguin Group (Canada), 90 Eglinton Avenue East, Suite 700, Toronto,
Ontario M4P 2Y3, Canada (a division of Pearson Penguin Canada Inc.)
Penguin Books Ltd., 80 Strand, London WC2R 0RL, England
Penguin Ireland, 25 St. Stephen's Green, Dublin 2,
Ireland (a division of Penguin Books Ltd.)
Penguin Group (Australia), 250 Camberwell Road, Camberwell, Victoria 3124,
Australia (a division of Pearson Australia Group Pty. Ltd.)
Penguin Books India Pvt. Ltd., 11 Community Centre, Panchsheel Park,
New Delhi - 110 017, India
Penguin Group (NZ), 67 Apollo Drive, Rosedale, North Shore 0632,
New Zealand (a division of Pearson New Zealand Ltd.)
Penguin Books (South Africa) (Pty.) Ltd., 24 Sturdee Avenue,
Rosebank, Johannesburg 2196, South Africa

Penguin Books Ltd., Registered Offices:
80 Strand, London WC2R 0RL, England

First published by Signet, an imprint of New American Library,
a division of Penguin Group (USA) Inc.

First Printing, December 2007
10 9 8 7 6 5 4 3 2 1

THE IMMORTAL COWBOY

This is respectfully dedicated to the "American Cowboy." His was the saga sparked by the turmoil that followed the Civil War, and the passing of more than a century has by no means diminished the flame.

True, the old days and the old ways are but treasured memories, and the old trails have grown dim with the ravages of time, but the spirit of the cowboy lives on.

In my travels—to Texas, Oklahoma, Kansas, Nebraska, Colorado, Wyoming, New Mexico, and Arizona—I always find something that reminds me of the Old West. While I am walking these plains and mountains for the first time, there is this feeling that a part of me is eternal, that I have known these old trails before. I believe it is the undying spirit of the frontier calling, allowing me, through the mind's eye, to step back into time. What is the appeal of the Old West of the American frontier?

It has been epitomized by some as the dark and bloody period in American history. Its heroes—Crockett, Bowie, Hickok, Earp—have been reviled and criticized. Yet the Old West lives on, larger than life.

It has become a symbol of freedom, when there was always another mountain to climb and another river to cross; when a dispute between two men was settled not with expensive lawyers, but with fists, knives, or guns. Barbaric? Maybe. But some things never change. When the cowboy rode into the pages of American history, he left behind a legacy that lives within the hearts of us all.

—*Ralph Compton*

Chapter 1

The man who rode into Coffin Varnish did not look like a killer. If anything, he had more in common with a mouse. He was small like a mouse, not much over five feet, with stooped shoulders that gave the illusion he was hunched forward in the saddle when he was sitting as straight as he could sit. He wore a brown hat with so many stains that a person could be forgiven for thinking he used it to wipe his mouth. His buckskins were a mousy brown, and his boots had holes in them, one at the toe, the other above the heel.

The man rode a gruella, which was fitting, since a gruella is a mouse-colored horse, a sort of gray-blue more commonly called mouse dun. The horse, like the man who rode it, was weary to its core, and like as not would not have minded being put out to pasture, if only the rider owned a pasture. But all the rider owned were the clothes on his back and the gruella and a few odds and ends in his saddlebags, and that was it.

The other thing the rider owned was a revolver. It was the one thing about him that was not ordinary. No common Colt, this was a Lightning, with a blue finish and pearl grips. The man had spent extra money to have it engraved. He had also filed off the front sight and removed the trigger guard. Since it was in a holster high on his right hip, no one noticed the modifications he had made to his hardware when he rode into Coffin Varnish. If they had, they would have known right away that he was not the mouse he appeared to be.

The single dusty street was pockmarked with hoofprints and rutted by wagon wheels. Horse droppings were conspicuous, and other droppings were almost as plentiful. A couple of chickens were pecking at the dirt near the water trough. A dog lay in the shade of the general store. It raised its head but did not bark. When the rider reined to the hitch rail in front of the saloon, the dog lowered its head and closed its eyes.

The rider stiffly dismounted. Putting a hand at the small of his back, he arched his spine, then looped the reins around the hitch rail. "Not much of a town you got here."

The two men in rocking chairs under the overhang regarded him with no particular interest. They had not yet seen the Colt; its pearl grips were hidden by the man's arm.

"More of a town than you think," Chester Luce replied. He was a round butterball whose head was as hairless as the rider's saddle horn and shaped about the same. His suit was the one article in the whole town that did not have a lick of dust on it because he constantly swatted it off.

The rider studied him. "You must be somebody important hereabouts."

Chester smiled and swelled the chest he did not

have, and nodded. "That I am, stranger. You have the honor of addressing the mayor of this fair town."

"Fair?" the rider said. He had a squeaky voice that fit the rest of him. "If this place was any more dead, it would have headstones."

From the man in the other rocking chair came a chuckle. He had white hair and wrinkles and an unlit pipe jammed between his lips. He also wore an apron with more stains than the rider's hat. He did not wear a hat, himself. "You do not miss much, do you?"

"I live longer that way," the rider said, and went under the overhang. He pointed at the apron. "If you're not the bar dog, you are overdressed."

Again the white-haired man chuckled. "I do in fact own this establishment. My name is Win Curry. Short for Winifred." Win stared at the rider expectantly, as if waiting for him to say who he was, but the rider did no such thing. Instead, he nodded at the batwings.

"This saloon of yours have a name, too? There is no sign."

"No sign and no name. I couldn't think of one I liked, so it is just a saloon," Win explained.

The rider arched a thin eyebrow. "All the words in the world and you couldn't come up with one or two?"

Win defended the lack. "It is not as easy as you think. Do you name everything you own?"

The rider looked at the gruella. "I reckon I don't, at that. Anyhow, I'm not here to jaw. I'm here to drink in peace and quiet."

"Go in and help yourself. I'll be in directly."

"Right friendly of you," the rider said.

"Coffin Varnish is a right friendly place," Win told him. "Not a grump in the twelve of us." His eyes drifted toward Chester. "Well, leastways most are daisies."

"Twelve, huh?" the rider said. "Must make for long lines at the outhouse." The batwings creaked as he pushed on through.

Chester Luce frowned. "I don't know as I like him. He poked fun at our town."

"Hell, can you blame him?" Win responded. "As towns go it would make a great gob of spit."

"Be nice."

"We have to face facts," Winifred said. "Another five years and Coffin Varnish will be fit for ghosts."

"Five years is stretching," Chester Luce said gloomily. "I will be lucky to last two." He gazed across the dropping-littered street at the general store. "I haven't had a paying customer in a month."

"I've got one now," Win said, and went to stand. He stopped with his hands gripping the rocker's arms and squinted into the heat haze to the south. "Glory be."

"What?" It was no small source of annoyance to Chester that the older man's eyes were twice as sharp as his.

"There are more riders coming."

"You're drunk."

"The hell I am. I haven't had but one drink all morning and that was for breakfast." Win's brown eyes narrowed. "Two of them, by God. One isn't much of a rider. He flops around something awful."

"Three visitors in one day," Chester marveled. "We

haven't had this many since I can remember." He pried his round bulk from his chair and ran his pudgy hands down his jacket. "I better go to my store in case they want something. I would hate to lose a sale."

"More than likely they won't even stop," Win said. "We're not far enough from Dodge for them to have worked up much of a thirst."

Chester scowled. "Don't say that name. You know I hate it."

"Don't start," Win said.

"I will damn well do as I please," Chester said heatedly. "And if I damn well happen to hate Dodge City for what it has done to us, you can damn well show me the courtesy of never mentioning that damn vile pit in my presence."

"You are plumb ridiculous at times. Do you know that?"

"I know Dodge stole the herds from us. I know Dodge stole the railroad and the wagon trains and all the trade that goes with them."

"Dodge stole nothing. It just happened," Win argued.

"When will you admit the truth?" Chester demanded. "Dodge has had it in for Coffin Varnish from the beginning."

Win sighed. "Keep this up and folks will think you are touched in the head."

Chester's pie face became cherry red. He stabbed a pudgy finger at the saloon owner and snapped, "How come you always take their side? How come you never stand up for the town you helped found? You're the one who named it."

"I was drunk. We were all drunk. If we hadn't been, maybe we would have come up with a better name than Coffin Varnish."

"It is original. You have to give us that much. But there is nothing original about Dodge. And the gall, to call themselves a city when they are hardly a big town."

"Damn it, Chester, stop." Win bobbed his chin at the stick figures. "Not with them almost here."

"It will be minutes yet," Chester said. He stepped to the edge of the overhang. "You can't blame me for feeling as I do. No one can. I had high hopes for Coffin Varnish."

"Oh, hell. When you get formal I am in for a speech."

"Mock me all you want," Chester said. "The facts speak for themselves. Dodge City and Coffin Varnish started about the same time. We can thank Santa Fe traders for that. Dodge and Coffin Varnish were a bunch of shacks and tents. Then you built your saloon and I built my store and for a while there, we were bigger than Dodge and—"

"Before you prattle on," Win interrupted, "I have heard this probably a million times and I do not care to hear it a million and one. We both know what did Coffin Varnish in. The Santa Fe Railroad decided to run through Dodge and not through us. Dodge prospered and we withered. It is as simple as that."

"I hate trains to this day," Chester said vehemently, and shook a pudgy fist at an imaginary rail line. "I will walk before I will take a train. I will crawl!"

"Here we go," Win said.

"It's just not fair," Chester lamented. "I put all I

had into my store, stocked it so I could outfit traders and emigrants and anybody else under the sun. And what happened? People stopped coming. They went to Dodge." He glowered in the general direction of the offending municipality. "Want to know what my mistake was?"

"God, not that again."

"My mistake was in not blowing Dodge to bits and pieces. I could have, back when they were the same size as us. I could have bought a wagonload of powder and snuck into Dodge one night and blown it to Hades and back."

"You can't sneak around in a wagon," Win said.

Chester did not appear to hear him. "I could have disguised myself as a trader and they never would have suspected. I'd have waited until they were all abed, then lit the fuse and got out of there." Chuckling, he rubbed his palms together. "Oh, to see the looks on their faces when their precious town was in ruins!"

"You worry me sometimes, Chester. You truly do."

"Dodge would have been no more. Coffin Varnish would be what Dodge is today. Prosperous, booming, with a stage line and the cow trade and more customers than a store owner can shake a stick at."

Win sadly shook his head. "You could move to Dodge City and open a store and have all the customers you would want."

Chester turned, his pie face mirroring shock. "Move to *Dodge*? Are you addlepated? After what they did to us?"

"You take things much too personal," Win said.

Sniffing, Chester hooked his thumbs in the pockets

of his vest. "And you don't take them personal
enough. As your mayor, I can't say I am pleased by
your lack of civic devotion."

Win sat up. "Don't you dare take that tone with
me. If that means what I think it does, I have as much
devotion as the next gent."

"Who are you kidding?" Chester rebutted. "You
are perfectly content to laze away the rest of your
days in that rocking chair. You don't care one whit
about making money."

"I am not as devoted to being rich as you are, no,"
Win conceded.

"Where is the sense in starting a business if you are
not out to make a profit? It is blamed silly."

"I won't be insulted."

Before Chester could respond, hooves drummed.
Into Coffin Varnish trotted the two newcomers. They
were not dressed as cowhands or farmers but in the
dandified attire of city dwellers. The taller of the pair
had on a fine blue coat and white pantaloons; the
other's suit was gray. Both wore derbies. They came
to a stop near the hitch rail and the tall man gave the
mouse dun close scrutiny. "Where is he?"

"Where is who?" Winifred asked.

"The rider of this animal," the tall man in the white
pants said with a jerk of his finger at the gruella.

"You are from Dodge, aren't you?" Chester inquired.

"Oh Lord," Win said.

The tall man glanced from one to the other in some
annoyance. "What of it? I happen to be Edison Farnsworth." He waited, and when he did not get a reac-

tion, he snapped, "Surely you have heard of me. I write for the *Dodge City Times*."

"The what?" Chester Luce said.

Edison Farnsworth jerked back as if he had been slapped. "What foolishness is this? You can't stand there and tell me you have never heard of it, either."

"Why can't I?"

"For one thing, this dreary hamlet of yours is only a two-hour ride from Dodge City," Farnsworth said. "For another, the *Times* is the leading newspaper in the entire county, if not all of Kansas. There isn't a living soul within five hundred miles who hasn't heard of my newspaper."

"You own it, then?" Winifred asked.

Farnsworth shook his head. "Didn't you hear? I said I write for it. I am the best journalist on their staff."

"We haven't heard of the *Times* here," Chester assured him. "And Coffin Varnish is a town, not a hamlet."

Farnsworth shifted in his saddle toward his younger companion. "Do you believe what you are hearing, Lafferty?"

"If I hear it, I guess I do."

"Pay no attention. Go inside and confirm he is in there and let him know I will be conducting an interview."

Lafferty started to climb down.

"Hold on there," Winifred said. "What is this about? I won't have my customers bothered."

"I plan on writing an article about the gentleman in there for the *Times*," Edison Farnsworth replied. "I tried to interview him in Dodge but he slipped away and left town."

Chester snickered. "Anyone who wants to be shed of Dodge has my blessing. What has he done worth an interview, anyway?"

Farnsworth leaned on his saddle horn. "Can it be? You have no notion of who he is?"

"He's not the governor," Win said, and turned to Chester. "Who holds the office these days? Is it Anythony? Or did St. John beat him in the last election? I don't pay much attention to politics."

"Which is fine by me or you might take it into your head to run for mayor." Chester stared at the newspaperman. "What was that about the runt inside?"

"I would not let him hear you say that," Farnsworth advised. "That runt, as you call him, is one of the deadliest killers alive."

Chapter 2

Winifred Curry and Chester Luce stood in the doorway and peered over the batwings at the small man sipping whiskey at a corner table and listening to young Lafferty.

"You're joshing," Chester said. "He doesn't look any more deadly than a minnow."

Farnsworth, smoothing his sleeves, came up behind them. "Shows how deceiving looks can be. That there is Jeeter Frost."

"The name does not mean a thing to me," Chester said.

"Frost?" Win repeated. "There was a curly wolf with that handle who made a reputation for himself maybe seven to ten years ago."

"One and the same," Farnsworth confirmed. "With a tally of seventeen kills to his credit."

"And he is still breathing?" Winifred marveled. "It has been so long, I figured he was worm food."

"Not Jeeter Frost," Farnsworth said. "The worms would spit him back out. He is too mean to die. They say he once shot a man for snoring."

"I can't blame him there," Win said. "My first wife snored. She sounded like an avalanche. I couldn't sleep unless I plugged my ears with wax, and even that didn't always shut out the racket she made. Then one day in Kansas City we came across a patent medicine man selling a cure for snoring."

"A cure?" Farnsworth said skeptically.

"I bought six bottles on the spot," Winifred related. "I don't know what was in them. He claimed it was rare plants and such. I had my suspicions it was opium and whatever else he had handy."

"Did it cure her?" the journalist asked when the saloon owner did not go on.

"Hell no. But she got addicted to the stuff. Couldn't go a day without a spoonful of her precious bitters, as she called it. Before long she went from a spoonful to half a bottle and from half a bottle to a full bottle. Then she died."

"The cure killed her?"

"No, a tree I was chopping down fell the wrong way and crushed her," Win said. "Her busted bones were sticking out all over."

"You have a frivolous nature, sir," Farnsworth stated in mild disgust and shouldered past them. "Excuse me while I conduct my business."

Win nudged Chester. "He sure is prickly."

"It comes of being from Dodge," Chester said. "People there have no manners."

"Are you still going over to your store?"

"I've changed my mind," Chester answered. "I think I would like to hear this. It could be entertaining."

Lafferty was hurrying toward Farnsworth. His expression did not bode good news. "He says he does not want to talk to you. He says you would be well advised to turn around and leave."

"Oh, he does, does he?" Farnsworth drew himself up to his full height, adjusted his derby, and strode toward the corner table with a confident swagger. If he noticed the small man's glare, it did not deter him. "Jeeter Frost," he loudly announced. "I mean to have your life story."

"You are not one for hints," the notorious leather slapper rasped. "I thought I made it plain in Dodge I do not want to talk to you."

"But *I* want to talk to *you*," Farnsworth said. "You are news, sir, whether you like it or not. And I, sir, have a duty to my readers to present them with the news. I am a journalist, and a good one, if I do say so myself."

"If I am news," Jeeter said, "it is old news, and no one but you is interested. I told your boy and now I am telling you: Go away and leave me be or you will not like what happens."

"Was that a threat, sir?" Farnsworth asked.

"Mister, I am trying to be polite," Jeeter Frost replied. "But you can take it as a threat if you want if it will persuade you to pester someone else. I am not in the mood for your brazen antics."

Lafferty cleared his throat. "Maybe you should listen to him, Mr. Farnsworth. He has the right not to be interviewed, doesn't he?"

Farnsworth dismissed the legal quibble with a wave of his hand. "He is *news*, I tell you, and good journalists, those who make their mark as I have, go to whatever lengths are necessary to see that the news is printed. His own wishes do not enter into it."

"So you say," Jeeter Frost said. "Mister, stick your nose where it is not wanted and you are liable to find yourself without one."

"Oh, please," Farnsworth said. "Spare us the melodramatics. They might scare my assistant but they do not scare me." He pulled out a chair. "Now then, I would like to begin with the first man you ever killed and take it from there."

"I have a better idea," Jeeter Frost said.

"Hear me out. I will begin with an account of one of your triumphs," Farnsworth said. "Then I will delve into your past. What it was like growing up. Did you love your parents? Did they love you? Who was the first person you ever killed? Did you tingle at the deed or were you filled with revulsion?"

The journalist might have gone on endlessly had it not been for the metallic ratchet of a hammer being thumbed back. Farnsworth glanced up into the muzzle of the Colt Lightning. "What is this?"

"A pistol. A six-gun. A hog leg. A man-stopper. A smoke wagon," Jeeter quickly recited. "I am surprised a good journalist does not know what they are called."

"You are not amusing," Farnsworth said.

"Oh, *I'm* amused," the killer said, and then mimicked the other's manner and previous statement, saying, "Your own feelings do not enter into it."

Farnsworth had no shortage of bluster. "You do not scare me, sir. I know you will not shoot. I know it as truly as I have ever known anything."

Jeeter Frost cocked his head and studied the newspaperman much as he might a new kind of toad. "How some folks cram so much stupid between their ears is a wonderment." And then, without so much as a bat of his eye or a twitch of his mouth, Jeeter Frost squeezed the trigger.

The blast and the belch of smoke were simultaneous. So, too, was the derby's remarkable feat. It took wing, performing an aerial somersault that ended with the bowler on the floor at its owner's feet, a hole in the crown.

Jeeter snickered and twirled the Lightning and neatly slid it back into its holster. "Now take your pot and skedaddle, you damned nuisance."

Win Curry and Chester Luce tried to smother grins but did not succeed. Even young Lafferty was on the verge of guffaws but trying mightily not to give in.

To their considerable amazement, Edison Farnsworth calmly picked up his derby, calmly replaced it on his head, and calmly sank into the chair across from Jeeter Frost. "If you are done with your theatrics, may we begin?"

About to take a swig, Jeeter lowered the bottle to the table with a loud *thunk*. "You beat all, scribbler."

"I only do my job as best I am able," Farnsworth said. From under his jacket he produced a pencil and a few folded pieces of paper. He unfolded a sheet and spread it on the table, then wrote the date at the top. "I am ready when you are."

Jeeter Frost looked from the journalist to the sheet of paper and back again. "You are like a tick I can't pry out."

"Is it true you were born in Missouri? And that you killed your first man at fourteen when he insulted your sister?"

"Where in God's name did you hear such foolishness?"

"In a penny dreadful," Farnsworth said.

"A what?" Jeeter asked.

"A penny dreadful," Farnsworth repeated. "They have been all the rage for close to ten years now. Most are published back East. They recount the life stories of famous frontiersmen like Davy Crockett and Daniel Boone, outlaws such as Jesse James, and desperadoes of lesser notoriety, such as yourself."

"Are you saying it is some kind of book? Someone went and wrote a book about *me*?" In his astonishment Jeeter needed another healthy swig.

"Not a book, exactly," Farnsworth said. "They are not quite as long and the binding is not as permanent." Stopping, he turned and snapped his fingers at young Lafferty. "Fetch my saddlebags. Instead of telling him I will show him."

His assistant wheeled and hurried out.

"You must be mistaken," Jeeter said. "I never talked to anyone about my life. How can there be a story about me?"

"Quite often those who compose them make up the tale as they go," Farnsworth elaborated. "Writers never let facts stand in the way of a good yarn. Which is all the more reason for me to do an account of your life based on the truth and not make-believe."

"About me, by God?" Jeeter snorted and swallowed more red-eye.

"I can't believe you have never read one," Farnsworth said. "They are hugely popular. You can find them practically everywhere."

Jeeter Frost looked down at the table and said something that came out barely more than a mumble.

"I didn't catch that."

"I can't read."

Farnsworth removed his derby and set it in front of him. The sight of the hole caused his jaw muscles to twitch.

"Did you hear me?" Jeeter asked.

"Yes. You can't read. A not uncommon condition," Farnsworth said with the air of a man addressing an imbecile. "Yet another contributing factor to the widespread ignorance of the lower classes. Into this darkness I cast my shining light of truth."

"Is it me or do you talk peculiar?" Jeeter reached for the bottle again. "Wait. What was that about lower classes?"

"Some say that society is divided into those who have and those who have not but wished they had. I believe a more fundamental division is between those who know and those who do not know and have no idea they do not know."

"What in hell did you just say?"

"The important point is that this ignorance must be alleviated," Farnsworth continued. "Newspapers perform an invaluable function in that regard, wouldn't you agree?"

"Mister, you lost me back at penny dreadfuls."

"I will remedy that momentarily. Ah, here he comes now." Farnsworth accepted the saddlebags from Lafferty and placed them on the table. He began opening one. "I brought yours with me to use as reference material."

Lafferty cleared his throat. "Mr. Farnsworth, sir?"

"Not now, boy. Can't you see I am working? What

have I told you about disturbing me when I am interviewing someone? Whatever you have to say can wait."

"Very well," Lafferty dutifully responded.

Farnsworth rummaged in the saddlebag and brought out half a dozen of the publications in question. He sorted through them and smiled. "Here it is. This is you on the cover, with your arm around a fair damsel in distress, brandishing a bowie knife at a horde of red savages."

"Dear God," Jeeter said.

"I assure you the story is quite flattering. It paints you as a desperado with a heart of gold."

"From the looks of this, I am seven feet tall. And why is my hair down past my shoulders? I've never worn it that long in my life."

"The woman is Sagebrush Susan, your sweetheart. She figures prominently in your adventures."

"But I never met a gal by that name." Jeeter held the penny dreadful out to Farnsworth and tapped the cover. "What does it say there? All these big black letters?"

"Jeeter Frost, the Missouri Man-Killer," Edison Farnsworth read. "His thrilling escapades. His narrow escapes."

Jeeter's mouth fell open.

"I can tell you are impressed. Here. Let me read a bit more." Farnsworth opened to the first page. " 'The waterways of Missouri were frozen solid the morning Jeeter Frost came into this world. None could have guessed from his squalling debut that he would grow to lead a life of mayhem and debauch, yet in the end

find true love and the happiness that so eluded him.' "
Farnsworth looked up. "What?"

Jeeter Frost's mouth was moving, but no words
were coming out.

"Here. Let me read more." Farnsworth flipped
pages until he found the one he was looking for. "This
next part is one of my favorites. The author, Cooper
Fenimore, has a flair. Although I warrant he used a
pen name and not his real name." Farnsworth raised
his voice and read, "Into the saloon swaggered the
Walker brothers, all nine of them, as vile and despicable a brood of vipers as ever trod this earth. The oldest, Wolf Walker, leered at Sagebrush Susan, who
stood at the piano practicing for her next rendition of
'How Sweet Is Our Valley.' "

"Hold on there," Jeeter Frost broke in. "I never
heard of any Walker brothers. The Blight brothers,
yes, but no Walkers."

"Who are the Blight brothers?" Farnsworth asked,
reaching for his pencil and paper.

"There used to be four but I killed one about a
month ago over to Topeka, so now there are three.
The others have been after me ever since. They're the
reason I lit out of Dodge like I did."

"You didn't leave to avoid talking to me?"

"Hell no. You showed up as I was fixing to light
a shuck."

Young Lafferty coughed to get their attention.
"These Blight brothers ran into you in Dodge, Mr.
Frost?"

"That's right, boy. Wearing an armory and out for
my blood."

"Is it possible they are still after you?"

"They won't likely give up this side of my grave," Jeeter Frost said. "The Blights are big on the feud. Kill one and the rest won't rest until they have had their revenge."

"Does one ride a pinto, would you know?"

"The oldest. Temple, his name is."

Farnsworth turned toward Lafferty in irritation. "Why are you asking all these questions, Frank?"

"I tried to tell you when I came in with your saddlebags. Three riders are headed this way, and kicking up a lot of dust. They should be here any second." Lafferty paused. "And one of them is riding a pinto."

As if on cue, Coffin Varnish thundered to the drum of heavy hooves.

Chapter 3

The first fifteen years of Winifred Curry's life were spent on the family farm in Pennsylvania barely eking out an existence. Milking cows and plowing fields never appealed to him, so he struck off to see the world. He dug ditches, he drove freight wagons, and tended bar in St. Louis, Santa Fe, and Houston. He found he liked tending bar, chiefly because he liked drinking even more; the occupation fit him like a liquid glove. When, in a whimsical course of events, he won a few thousand in a poker game, he hoarded the money and eventually used it to start his own saloon in Coffin Varnish. At the time it seemed a fine idea. Coffin Varnish was growing and bound to grow more, or so everyone thought.

But now Coffin Varnish was slowly dying, and with it Winifred's dream of prosperity. He was getting on in years and was too old to start over. When he was forced to close, he would be adrift with no money and no prospects. He figured that everything that could go wrong had gone wrong. He should have known. Life had a way of kicking people in the teeth just when they found their smile.

Winifred stood flat-footed with astonishment as a

horse nickered outside and someone gruffly declared, "That there is his gruella. We've caught up to him."

Winifred glanced at Chester Luce. "What should we do?"

"Why ask me?"

"You are the mayor."

There were days, many days, when Chester Luce wished he wasn't, when he wished he had never set foot in Coffin Varnish and never spent every cent he had to build and furnish the general store. At the time, he had thought it was the right thing to do. His wife said it was, anyway.

The mercantile profession was in Chester's blood. His father had run a general store, and his father's father before him. The Luces prided themselves on their head for business.

By rights Chester should have taken over the family store in Buffalo, New York. He was the oldest son. His father had come right out and told him it would be his one day. But that was not enough for Chester. He did not want his life handed to him. He wanted to strike off on his own, to make something of himself through his own sweat and brain. That, and his wife had a yearning to see the West.

So one day Chester rode into the collection of huts and tents that was to become Coffin Varnish, and when he assessed the situation, when he carefully weighed all the factors a good businessman had to consider, and his wife gave her opinion, he concluded he had found that ideal prospect. It never occurred to him that Coffin Varnish might wither and die. He never conceived he could end up a penniless failure.

Or dead. Chester had never witnessed a saloon shoot-out, but he had heard enough about them to know that bystanders as often as not fell victim to stray lead, and in his estimation dying by accident had nothing to commend it over dying by design. Dead was dead.

"We should get out of here," Chester said to Win.

Together they turned toward the batwings and together they froze.

Filling the doorway was a bear of a man with a bristly black beard and an unkempt mane of black hair that spilled from under a floppy hat. His home-spun clothes were rumpled and in need of washing, his boots badly scuffed. He shoved on through, nearly tearing the batwings from their hinges, and glared about him. "Where is he?" he demanded. "Where is that mangy son of a bitch?"

Win and Chester glanced toward the table in the far corner and were struck speechless.

Edison Farnsworth still sat in a chair, the saddlebags in front of him. Near him stood Lafferty. But the chair across from Farnsworth, the chair in which Jeeter Frost had been sitting not twenty seconds ago, was empty.

"Didn't any of you hear me?" the man demanded. "Where is the owner of that gruella at the hitch rail?"

"I honestly don't know," Chester said in bewilderment.

"Me either," Win said.

"My name is Temple Blight," the man said, moving warily toward the bar, one big hand on a Remington revolver tucked under his wide black leather belt.

"These here are my brothers, Zebulon and Barnabas. The bastard who owns that gruella killed another brother of ours and we aim to make him pay."

The other two Blights were slightly shorter but equally scruffy versions of Temple. One had a Winchester, the other a shotgun.

Temple drew the Remington and cocked it. Ever so carefully, he leaned over the bar so he could see the other side. "Damnation. He's not here." Wheeling around, he stalked toward the newspapermen. "Who are you two and what are you doing here?"

Edison Farnsworth sniffed in indignation. "I don't see where it is any of your concern, but if you must know, my assistant and I work for the *Dodge City Times.*"

"Did you see a man come in here? A runt in buckskins wearing a pearl-handled Colt?"

"You say he killed your brother?" Farnsworth asked.

Temple Blight scowled. "The youngest of us, Simeon. Shot him for no reason. Me and my other brothers were upstairs with doves or we'd have bucked him out in gore then and there."

Young Lafferty indulged in his habit of clearing his throat before he spoke. "This Frost shot your brother without cause?"

"They were arguing over cards," Temple said. "Hardly enough cause as far as I am concerned." He turned his back to the table and leaned against it. "Where in hell can he have gotten to?" He pointed at the sibling with the Winchester. "Zeb, you go check the outhouse. Barnabas, sit out front and keep an eye on the gruella. Sooner or later Frost is bound to show."

"Sooner rather than later," came a voice from under the table.

Startled, Temple Blight straightened and whirled. He was not quite all the way around when a pistol barrel poked from under the table, pointed at his groin. The pistol cracked, and Temple shrieked and clutched at himself, dropping his Remington. The next shot caught him smack in the center of the forehead and blew out the rear of his cranium in a spray of hair and gore.

By then Zebulon and Barnabas Blight were rushing to their brother's aid. Zeb jerked his Winchester to his shoulder, but he did not quite have it level when the pistol under the table boomed a third time and Zeb's left eyeball dissolved.

Barnabas did not bother with aiming. He simply trained his shotgun at the table. But he had to thumb back the hammers before he could fire. It only took a second and a half, which was long enough for the pistol under the table to go off twice more. Slugs smacked into Barnabas and he staggered back, swearing. He had been shot through the heart. Gamely, with his final flicker of life, he squeezed both triggers.

The shotgun was not pointed under the table. It was pointed at the chair in which Edison Farnsworth sat. Farnsworth was starting to rise when it went off, and the full force of both barrels, loaded with buckshot, caught him in the chest. His chest exploded like so much melon and the impact lifted him off his feet and flung him onto his back on top of the table.

In the silence that ensued, none of the living moved. Lafferty lay on the floor where he had dived when the first shot rang out. Winifred and Chester were rooted in shock.

A foot slid out from under the table, and another foot, and then the rest of Jeeter Frost. He stepped clear of Edison Farnsworth's dangling legs and calmly commenced reloading.

"You shot them!" Chester Luce blurted.

"I sure as hell did," Jeeter Frost agreed.

"You killed them!"

"Generally when I shoot it is to kill," Jeeter said. "They were close enough. It was easy."

Winifred found his voice. "But you shot them from under the table! They didn't stand a prayer."

"And how much of a chance do you reckon they'd have given me?" Jeeter rejoined. "What did you expect? That we'd go out in the street and stand back to back and take ten steps like in a duel?" He laughed.

"No, no," Win said, gaping at the bodies. He had seen men shot before but never like this, never so abruptly, so methodically, so—so—coldly, as if they were targets in a shooting gallery. Most of the shootings he witnessed were drunken affrays waged in the heat of anger and under the influence of liquor.

"Four men dead!" Chester exclaimed. "Just like that!" He snapped his pudgy fingers.

"They were lying about me not having cause," Jeeter said. "That brother of theirs, the young one, was cheating at cards. I caught him and he pulled his iron on me." He leaned toward the table and examined the hideously huge cavity in Edison Farnsworth's chest. Rib bones gleamed, framing internal organs. "Too bad about this fella. I was just getting used to his airs." He turned. "How are you doing down there, sonny? Were you hit?"

Frank Lafferty had sat up and was groping himself. "Apparently not," he said in amazement. "I am unscathed." He slowly rose, his horrified gaze glued to the remains of his associate. "I never saw anyone move so fast as when you ducked under that table."

"It always pays to have an edge, boy," Jeeter Frost said. "Take that brother of theirs who cheated. I let him start to walk off before I shot him."

"In the back?"

"He had his pistol out."

"But in the *back*!"

Jeeter finished reloading and slid the Colt Lightning into his holster. "I would take exception if you weren't so green behind the ears. He cheated, boy. He had it coming. Whether I shot him in the front or the back doesn't much matter, but the back is always safer."

"What kind of killer are you?" Lafferty asked.

"The kind who likes to go on breathing." Jeeter reclaimed his bottle and gulped, whiskey dribbling over his lower lip. Wiping his mouth with his sleeve, he made for the door, saying, "It has been interesting. But I reckon I'll mosey on before more trouble shows up."

"Wait!" Lafferty cried.

Jeeter stopped, his right hand straying to the Lightning. "What is it, boy? You sound like a girl when you screech that way."

Frank Lafferty stepped to the table and gingerly pulled the paper and pencil from under Farnsworth. The paper was spattered with scarlet drops. "I want to do the interview."

"How's that again?"

"The interview Mr. Farnsworth wanted with you. He's gone, so it is up to me."

"Hell, boy. His body ain't cold yet and already you want to fill his boots?" Jeeter grinned. "You are my kind of hombre."

"Frank," Lafferty said. "You can call me Frank. And yes, I want to. I can write up the interview and then write about the shooting. Every paper in the state will carry it. Even some out of state will pick it up. I will go from a nobody to a somebody overnight." His face positively gleamed. "I can ask for more money. A lot more money."

"If it means that much to you, and because I have a generous nature," Jeeter said, "I will give you five minutes and only five minutes for twenty dollars."

"Five minutes isn't much."

"It is more than your friend got."

"And I don't have twenty dollars. All I have is—" Lafferty shoved a hand in a pocket and happened to gaze down at the former leading light of Kansas journalism. A new gleam came into his eyes and he quickly bent and went through each of Edison Farnsworth's pockets. "Ah!" he cried, and flourished a wallet. Opening it, he counted aloud, "Ten, twenty, thirty, why, there is over sixty dollars here." Beaming, he strode toward Frost. "Here you go." He held out twenty dollars.

Jeeter accepted the bills. "Forty more and you can ask me any questions you want."

"But you said twenty and I gave you twenty."

"That was before I knew you had sixty." A sly grin

curled Jeeter's mouth. "Besides, how much is being somebody worth to you?"

Frank Lafferty laughed. "Point taken. Here. Have it all." He shoved the wallet at Frost. "But I expect my money's worth. Five full minutes, and you will answer every question truthfully."

"As best I can, boy, but my memory ain't all it should be."

They went out. Chester and Winifred swapped looks and Chester asked, "What in God's name just happened?"

"You saw it all the same as me," Win said. "You were right next to me the whole time." He swore. "There are four dead men here. Why couldn't they be dead in your store? Who is going to clean up all this blood and whatnot? I shouldn't have to. I didn't shoot anyone."

"I wouldn't count on Jeeter Frost volunteering," Chester Luce said.

"I have half a mind to march outside and demand he do it."

"Go right ahead," Chester said, "and there might be five bodies to bury instead of four."

"Hell in a basket." Win stepped to the fallen form of Zebulon Blight and started to go through the dead man's pockets. Suddenly he stiffened and held up a fat poke. He shook it and coins jingled. Loosening the drawstring, he whistled. "Land sakes. There must be thirty dollars."

Chester went to Barnabas Blight and squatted. He patted each pocket. "Look at this!" The poke he found had twenty-four dollars in it. "Where do you suppose they got all this money?"

"Maybe they sold some stock."

"Rustled stock is more like it. Or else robbed a bank."

"No, we would have heard if they did that."

Win hurried to Temple Blight, Chester at his elbow. The poke was inside Temple's shirt, above the right hip. Fatter than the others, it contained eighty-six dollars in coins and banknotes.

"What should we do with all this?" Win wondered.

Chester glanced at the batwings. "Fifty-fifty sounds fine to me." He fondled Temple Blight's poke, and smiled. "There is more to this killing business than I ever imagined. It is food for thought."

Chapter 4

Not two hours later Mayor Chester Luce called a special meeting of the Coffin Varnish Town Council. It was the first time the council had met in over six months. He did not have to go to any special effort to get them together; everyone in Coffin Varnish converged on the saloon to find out what the shooting was about. Or nearly everyone. The Swede and his wife, who lived a mile north of town but were considered residents anyway, did not hear the gunshots.

Chester sent one of the Mexicans, as he always called them, to fetch the Swede, as Chester always called him.

The Mexicans had names. One was Placido, the other Arturo. They had shown up one day shortly after the saloon and the general store were built, and for reasons of their own decided to stay. They erected and ran the livery, and lived together in a room at the back. They kept to themselves and were seldom seen. When they were seen they were always together. On several occasions they were observed holding hands, which Chester thought a damned silly custom for grown men, but he always tried to be tolerant of those unfortunate enough not to be born white, and he did not say anything. Little was known about their past. Gossip had it they were from a small village somewhere in the mountains of northern Mexico and had to leave when they got into some kind of trouble.

The source of the gossip was Sally Worth, a dove well past her prime. She lived above the saloon. Rented a room, although the rent was not in the form of money. She was an old friend of Win's who had appeared out of the dust one day, worn and beat and just looking for a place to stay for a week or so while she pulled herself together. The week became a month and the month became a year and she never left.

Coffin Varnish boasted two other women. One was Chester's wife, Adolphina. The term most used to describe her was formidable. She was big, a lot bigger than Chester, with big bones and big shoulders and a disposition that Winifred Curry once compared to a grizzly in a bad mood. She was the only female on the town council. She had not been elected to the post. She just came to the meetings and no one dared object.

The third female was the Italian's wife, Gemma. The Italian was Minimi Giorgio, a native of Naples. They had two sons, seven-year-old Angelo and twelve-year-old Matteo. They lived in a cottage at the north end of the street. A real cottage, not a cabin or a shack, built by Minimi. Like nearly everyone else in Coffin Varnish, they tended to keep to themselves. No one knew much about them. They were secretive about their past and, it was noticed, wary of strangers. Every now and again a letter arrived from Italy, and for days afterward Minimi and Gemma would walk around with sad faces.

That left the Swede. Dolph Anderson and his wife, Filippa, wrested a living from a one-hundred-and-sixty-acre farm. They had a big white frame house and a big red barn and a chicken coop and pigs and a team of horses for plowing and four cows, and without a doubt were Coffin Varnish's most prosperous citizens. They were also its most industrious. The big Swede worked from dawn until dusk six days a week. On the seventh day they observed the Sabbath. A stream bordered their property, and thanks to the irrigation ditches the Swede had dug and maintained, he grew corn and wheat and barley and had a small orchard. He sold his surplus in Dodge City—much to Chester's annoyance.

The Andersons did not come into town all that often. Adolphina blamed it on uppity Swedish airs. Chester was of the opinion they were kind, gentle folk who simply could not take much time away from their daily toil, but he did not offer his opinion to Adolphina. She generally disliked opinions that were not her own.

Twelve people. The total population. All that remained of the four score who once called Coffin Varnish home.

The dust from the departures of Jeeter Frost and Frank Lafferty had not yet settled when Chester and Win came out of the saloon. Lafferty had galloped south toward Dodge. Frost had ridden west toward God knew where. The bodies, and the blood, had to be dealt with, and Chester and Win were arguing over whether Chester should help clean up the mess when the Giorgio family came from their cottage and Placido and Arturo hurried from their livery, all with worried expressions. Gunfire in Coffin Varnish was unheard of.

"Everything is all right, folks," Chester cheerily assured them. "There has been an incident but it is over."

Minimi Giorgio, at a nudge from his wife, came closer. *"Per favore, signore. Non capisco. Che cos'e quello? Incidente?"*

"Damn it, Mini," Chester testily responded. "I have just been through hell and you stand there chirping at me. How many times have I told you to speak American or don't speak at all?"

"I am sorry, signore," Giorgio said politely. "I always forget. But what is this incident you make mention of?"

Win answered him. "In this case four men have been shot dead."

"Four men killed in your saloon?" Giorgio blanched and translated for his wife, who also blanched and wrapped her arms around their two boys and hugged them as if in fear of their being shot.

"Tell your woman there is nothing for her to fret about," Chester said. "The killer is gone, leaving us the mess to clean up."

"We will have a lot of explaining to do when the sheriff gets here," Win commented.

"I hadn't thought of that," Chester said. "He is bound to come once he hears about it."

"Him, or a deputy."

At the juncture the door to the general store opened and out lumbered the mayor's distaff half. Adolphina plowed across the street as a ship might plow through a sea, her dress billowing like a sail, her moon face set in a scowl. "What is all the ruckus?" she demanded. "I was napping and could swear I heard gunshots."

"You did, heart of my heart," Chester said. "There has been a shooting."

"What? Where?"

"Here."

"In Coffin Varnish?"

"In the saloon," Winifred clarified.

"Was anyone hurt?"

Chester enlightened her. "Four men were shot to death. Three nobodies and a newspaperman from that city south of us."

"Dear God in heaven." Adolphina barged past them to the batwings and nearly collided with Sally Worth, who was coming out. Adolphina's scowl deepened. Sniffing, she said, "Well, are you just going to stand there blocking the doorway or let a lady pass?"

"I am so sorry," Sally Worth said. "Here. Let me hold these open for you." She pushed the batwings wide. "Is that enough room or would you like me to knock out the wall?"

Adolphina hissed and stalked on in.

"You should be nicer to her," Win said to the dove.

"Why? She is never nice to me." Sally Worth was in her fifties. The wear and tear of her profession was evident in her stringy brown hair streaked with gray and her many wrinkles. Her body was still shapely, though, if a bit thick through the middle, and she still sashayed with the best of them, swinging her hips fit to throw them out with every step she took. Scratching under her armpit, she yawned and commented, "That's quite the mess you've got in there. Why didn't you give a holler? The only excitement this lice trap has ever had and I missed it."

"It happened sort of fast," Win said.

Chester avoided looking at Sally as he remarked, "It was terrible. Not fit for a woman to see."

"I am not squeamish," Sally said. "I've seen it before, more times than I can count. When you have worked in saloons all your life, you see it all."

The batwings creaked and in came Adolphina. "Who were those four men again, Chester?" She was not upset; she was not disturbed in any way.

Chester related all he knew about them, which was not much, then all he knew about their killer.

Sally Worth listened with her arms folded across her bosom, and when he was done, she said, "Jeeter Frost made his name in Texas. He was a ranch hand on the Bar T. A friend of his owned it, by the name of Tyler. A squabble started over water rights. There was a lot of shooting and burning and pretty near twenty men died. Tyler was murdered, ambushed one night by five of his enemies. Frost hunted them down and shot them dead."

"How is it you know all that?" Winifred asked her.

"I was in Texas at the time, in San Antonio. It was all anybody talked about."

Adolphina was gnawing her lower lip, a habit of hers when she was deep in thought. "So this Frost fellow is famous?"

"Not *famous* famous, like Wild Bill Hickok was, or like John Wesley Hardin," Win said. "Famous in a small way. One penny dreadful and a lot of bar talk."

"Still, people have heard of him." Adolphina's dark eyes, which were more close set than was common, bored into her husband's. "You need to call a meeting of the town council, Chester."

"I do? Why?"

"Use your head. The sheriff will come. Others, too. The curious. Maybe friends and acquaintances of the deceased."

"I hadn't thought of that," Chester said, brightening. "Why, some of them might even buy something in our store." He turned to the liverymen, who had been quietly listening. "Placido. Arturo. Would one of you Mexicans ride to Anderson's and tell the Swede I am calling an emergency meeting of the town council in an hour and he must be here?"

"Sí, senor," Placido said. He had his sombrero in his hand as a token of respect for the presence of the senoritas.

"Do you understand what has happened?" Chester struggled to think of the right word. "Do you *comprende*?"

"I speak excellent English, senor. Remember?" Placido said.

It was true, and it rankled Chester that a Mexican spoke it even better than he did. "Those priests taught you good, didn't they?"

"They taught us very well, indeed, senor," Placido said. He was always polite to everyone. Always a pleasant smile and a pleasant manner, and much more talkative than Arturo.

"Then off you go," Chester said. He noticed the Giorgios were drifting in the direction of their cottage and hollered, "Minimi, you have to be at the meeting, too."

"Me, signore? But the consiglio, it is you and Mr. Curry and Mr. Anderson. I am not a member."

"You are today," Chester said. "We have a decision to make that will affect everyone, so you might as well sit in."

"As you wish. You are the alcade," Minimi said, but he did not sound particularly happy about the invitation. His wife said something in Italian and he replied and she cast a worried look at Chester.

"What was that about, I wonder?"

Adolphina shrugged. "Who can tell with foreigners? That's the problem with our town. Too many foreigners." She lumbered from under the overhang. "I will go freshen up and sweep the place out."

Chester grunted. The council meetings were held in their store. Originally, the town council met in the saloon, which proved convenient when their throats became dry from excess talking. But when Adolphina started attending, they had to switch to somewhere respectable.

Sally Worth yawned. "Well, if all the excitement is over, I guess I will go back up and finish my nap."

"You can sleep with dead men below you?" Win asked.

"Hell, I've slept with all kinds of men under me, and over me, too." Sally grinned. "Smelly men, ugly men, stupid men, toothless men. Dead is an improvement."

"The things that come out of your mouth," Chester said.

Sally winked at him. "I never hear you object to the things that go into it. But then, you have cause not to, don't you?"

Chester glanced sharply at the retreating bulk of his wife, a red tinge creeping from his neckline to his hairline. "Keep your voice down. She might hear you."

"Not from there," Sally said. "You worry too much."

"I don't blame him," Winifred said. "If that battle-ax ever finds out, she will take a knife to his manhood, strangle you with her bare hands, and probably shoot me for letting him dally with you."

"I do as I want," Chester said curtly. "And I will thank you not to refer to my wife in that manner when I am standing right next to you."

"Men," Sally said in mild disgust, and stepped to the batwings. "But don't worry, Your Honor, sir. I am not about to give your secret away. You are one of the few paying customers I have left."

"Is that all I am to you? Money?"

Sally twisted at the hips and regarded him with amusement. "What else would you be?"

"A friend, at least. It has been a couple of years now."

"Every Wednesday evening for two years," Sally said. "Your wife permits you one hour to drink and sling the bull with Win and you spend part of that hour giving me a poke."

"We do more. We talk."

Sally tiredly brushed a stray wisp of gray-brown hair from her eyes. "You talk, I listen. You pay for that privilege." She looked at Winifred. "Explain to your friend how it is. I don't want him getting silly notions." She left them, her hips swinging.

"You shouldn't have said that to her," Win criticized. "Now she will think you care for her more than she should be cared for."

"How can you say that? She's your friend."

"She is my friend and she is a whore and I have the sense not to confuse the two. You should have the sense not to make more of her parting her legs for you than there is."

"That is harsh," Chester said softly.

"Life is harsh," Winifred Curry replied. "If you think it isn't, just ask the four bodies in my saloon."

"Adolphina could be on to something. We can benefit from their deaths."

"No good ever comes from killing," Winifred said. "Mark my words. We will live to regret it."

Chapter 5

Jeeter Frost had a crick in his neck from looking over his shoulder. He did not expect anyone to be after him, but he had not lasted as long as he had by being careless. For the first hour he used his spurs more than was his wont. The gruella, as always, did not let him down.

Jeeter was extremely fond of the mouse dun, so much so that once when a Comanche tried to steal it, Jeeter spent half a day whittling on the warrior, doing things not even Comanches did to captives.

Now and then Jeeter reached back and patted his saddlebags. He could not wait for sunset. He marked the slow crawl of the sun toward the western horizon with an impatience rare for him. He did not have many good traits, not by society's standards, at any rate, but patience had always been one. Those who knew him well, and they were few in number, sometimes commented that he was the most patient person they knew.

Jeeter had to be. He had learned early on that in order to survive on the fringe of lawlessness he must not indulge in rash decisions or rash acts. Haste led

to an early grave and Jeeter hoped to live a good
long while.

The thought made Jeeter grin. There was a time
when he did not care whether he lived, a time when
he woke up every morning certain he would not live
to admire the next sunset.

He lived by the gun, and the gun was a cruel mistress.

The gun. There were days when Jeeter wished he
had never set eye on a revolver, never held one, never
fired one. Maybe then he would never have killed anyone. Maybe then he would not be a marked man.
Maybe then no one would have heard of him. Maybe
then he would not be wandering the prairie, an outcast, with no family, no home, and no prospects other
than the surety that one day someone would prove to
be faster or cleverer.

Funny thing. Jeeter did not live in dread of that
day, as he once did. He wouldn't run from it—he
couldn't run from it—so what was the use of fretting?
He had learned a few things over the years, and one
of them was that life was too short to spend it wor-
rying about something that would happen one day
whether he worried about it or not.

For a few minutes there back in Coffin Varnish,
Jeeter thought that day had come. The Blights were
supposed to be tough, a tight-knit clan that stood up
for their own, and woe to the outsider who crossed
them. Temple Blight, especially, had made worm food
of more than a few. But the way he came walking into
that saloon, as big and confident as you please, not
bothering to draw his six-gun until he was over near
the bar—he might as well have asked Jeeter to put a
pistol to his head and shoot him.

Jeeter did not have many talents, but the one talent he did have, the one talent that separated him from the herd, was a talent for killing. As his grandmother would say, God rest her, he was a natural born killer.

That might not seem like much of a talent to some. You pointed a revolver or a rifle at someone, and you shot him. Or you stuck a knife between his ribs. Or you bashed him over the head with a rock. Or you roped him from behind so the noose settled over his neck and then you dragged him from horseback until his neck was stretched to where the head was almost off. Or you got him drunk and poured kerosene on him while he slept and set him on fire. Jeeter had done all of that and more.

The truth was, the talent did not lie in the killing. Anyone could kill. The talent showed itself in *how* the killing was done. Not in the shooting or the stabbing, but in never, ever giving the other hombre a fair break, in never, ever giving him a chance.

Take the Blights. The moment Jeeter heard them ride up, he drew his Lightning and ducked under the table. Not many would have thought of that. Some would have sat there stupidly waiting for the Blights to confront them. Some would have hid behind the bar, which was the first place Temple Blight looked. Some would have run out the back, but that would only postpone the inevitable.

No, Jeeter had done the one thing the Blights never expected. He had taken them completely by surprise. *That* was his talent. The knack for always catching the other fellow off guard. For always doing the one thing—*the one thing*—that meant he would live and the other person died. It was a knack most lacked, and it had kept him alive longer than most in his circumstances had a reasonable right to expect.

Some would say that alone made his talent worthwhile, and Jeeter would agree, to a point. Yes, he was still breathing. But there was dead and then there was a living death, a life of hand to mouth, of always looking over one's shoulders, of never being able to trust, to care, to love. A life as empty as the emptiness of the grave, only, yes, he was still breathing. But that was the only thing he had to show for his talent. The only really good thing about it.

Until now.

At length the sun rested on the rim of the world, its radiance painting the sky vivid hues of red, orange, and yellow. Jeeter came to a hollow bisected by a dry wash and rimmed with brush. He drew rein and dismounted. Stripping the gruella and gathering wood and kindling a fire and putting a pot of coffee on to brew took the better part of half an hour.

At last Jeeter could settle back against his saddle and relax. He opened his saddlebags and slid out the item he had brought with him from Coffin Varnish. In the flickering glow of the crackling flames, he admired the stalwart hero with his arm around the slender waist of a beautiful young woman as painted warriors closed in from all sides. "Jeeter Frost, the Missouri Man-Killer," he remembered the newspaperman saying. "His thrilling escapades. His narrow escapes." He ran his finger across the cover and said quietly, "I'll be damned."

A slow smile spread across Jeeter's countenance. He laughed, a genuinely heartfelt laugh such as he had not felt in a coon's age. He flipped the pages, wishing he could read the words. So many words, and all of them about him. Or some version of him that others took to be the real him. It was silly, he mused. But it was also—and here he struggled for the right way to describe it.

The moment Jeeter had set eyes on that cover, something inside him had changed. He could not say what or how or why, but he felt it. This penny dreadful, this ridiculous fluff written by someone who had never met him and knew nothing about him but had written all about him, meant there was more to his life than he ever imagined. He was not the nobody he always believed he was. He was somebody. Not somebody important. Not somebody that mattered. But somebody people would remember.

"The Missouri Man-Killer," Jeeter said again, and laughed. Hell, he hadn't been to Missouri but three or four times in his whole life.

Jeeter was born in Illinois. He lived there until he was seventeen. He got too big for his britches and took to drinking and staying out to all hours. One night he was in a knife fight. Thinking he had killed the other drunk, he fled, only to learn months later that the man recovered. By then Jeeter was in Texas, where a cowboy by the name of Weeds Graff took him under his wing. Weeds taught him to rope and to shoot and Jeeter learned the shooting so well that when they signed on with the Bar T outfit, it was his six-gun and his newfound talent for killing that held the other side at bay. For a while, anyway, until they ambushed his employer and friend.

Everyone in Texas heard about what Jeeter did next. They heard about the five men he hunted down and killed. From that day on, Jeeter became marked. He could not go a week without seeing what Jeeter liked to call *the look*. Sometimes the look was one of disgust. Sometimes it was fear. Sometimes it was a glint that warned him he must never turn his back on the person with the glint. Not that he ever turned his back to anyone if he could help it.

For years that had been the pattern of his life. Riding from town to town and settlement to settlement, seeking a place to fit in but not fitting anywhere. He was a square peg and life was a round hole.

And now along came this penny dreadful.

Jeeter sat and stared at the cover until the coffee was hot; then he poured a cup and took jerky from his saddlebags. He sat and sipped and munched and stared at that cover. He could not stop looking at it.

Toward midnight a brainstorm hit him with the force of a thunderclap. He started to laugh and could not stop. He laughed so long, and so loud, that a skulking coyote, drawn by the scents of his camp, yipped and raced away into the night.

Since Chester Luce did not own a gavel, he used a hammer, and since he did not want to mark up the counter with dents, he placed a folded blanket on top of the counter before he struck it with the hammer. "All right, everyone," he said to get their attention. "This meeting of the Coffin Varnish Town Council will officially come to order."

Winifred Curry sat next to the stove, sucking on a gumdrop. He had a sweet tooth and gumdrops were his favorite.

Minimi Giorgio sat on a stool by the dry goods section. He was nervous about being there. He gripped the edge of the stool with both hands as if afraid he would fall off.

The huge Swede, Dolph Anderson, seldom sat. He stood with his brawny arms folded across his powerful chest, his cornstalk hair and beard neatly trimmed, as always. "What be so important that you call me from my work?" His English was thickly accented, so much so that everyone else had to listen closely to tell what he said, especially Minimi, whose English was not the best.

Chester came around the counter. He did not like to stand behind it because it made him seem short, even if he was short. "You have heard about the killings?"

"Ja," the big Swede said.

"Then how can you ask a question like that? It isn't something that happens every day, and it will have an impact on our community."

"How will it impact?" Anderson asked.

Winifred stopped sucking on the gumdrop long enough to say, "Shouldn't we wait for your wife, Chester?"

Chester was about to reply that if she was late it was her own fault when steps thumped on the stairs and down she came.

Adolphina was almost as big as the Swede, and when she came and stood behind the counter, she made the counter seem small. "About ready to start, are we?"

"Yes, dearest."

"Everyone pay attention," Adolphina said. "I have been doing some thinking and—" She stopped and looked around. "Where are Placido and Arturo?"

"The Mexicans?" Chester said. "What do we need them for? They aren't on the council."

"Neither is Mr. Giorgio but you invited him," Adolphina noted. "Go get them. They should be in on this as well."

Chester's ears grew red at being ordered about in front of the other men. "Is it really necessary? What can they contribute? All they do is laze about their livery all day. They hardly ever mingle with the rest of us."

"We hardly ever mingle with them," Adolphina jousted. "No, this is business, and it will affect them, so fetch them and be quick about it. I don't have all night for this. I have sewing to do."

"Very well," Chester said, resigned to a force of nature he could never refuse. "I will be right back."

The tiny bell above the door tinkled as he went out. Winifred promptly opened the gumdrop jar and helped himself to several more, stuffing them in his shirt pocket.

"You will pay for those," Adolphina said.

"Naturally," Win responded. "Put them on my account, if you please."

Adolphina leaned on the counter. "Mr. Anderson, how is that lovely wife of yours?"

"She be fine," the Swede answered. "Filippa tell me that if I see you I am to give her regards."

"She is a daisy, that one," Adolphina said. "The only woman I ever met who works harder than I do."

Winifred almost swallowed his gumdrop. It was well known that Chester's wife spent most of her time above the store reading and eating and whatever else it was that occupied her hours. The mention of sewing had surprised him. Chester once told him that she hired her sewing out to Mrs. Giorgio.

"Filippa is a good woman, ja," Anderson said proudly. "She be fine wife. I pick well."

"She had something to do with it, too," Adolphina said. "Feminine wiles being what they are, probably more than you did."

"Feminine wiles?" Anderson repeated, saying each syllable slowly.

"It means women are smarter than men," Adolphina explained. "Always have been and always will be. Most of the great ideas men come up with they get from their women. If it weren't for us, nothing would ever get done."

The Swede's sun-bronzed brow furrowed. "That not be true, Mrs. Luce. I be good worker. I get much done."

"Yes, you do, I will admit," Adolphina conceded, and bestowed a look on him that she never bestowed on her husband. "You are one of the few men I know who are worth a damn."

Win sat up and stopped sucking. "Here, now. I don't much like being insulted."

"Then make something of yourself. You are one of the laziest creatures on God's green earth, Winifred Curry, and we both know it. You stay up half the night, you sleep half the day. You do nothing but pour drinks and precious few of them these days. If it were up to you, if you had enough money socked away, you would close the saloon and spend your days doing absolutely nothing but drinking."

Win chose not to debate her. Especially as everything she said was true.

A strained silence fell until the bell tinkled again. Chester came in and hurried to the counter.

Placido and Arturo entered but stayed well back near the door. They removed their sombreros. "You have sent for us, Senora Luce?" Placido asked.

"That I did," Adolphina confirmed, and raked everyone with an imperious glance. "A godsend has been dropped in our laps, gentlemen. I am sure some of you are familiar with what other towns have done with dead outlaws and killers, and I propose we do the same."

General puzzlement descended. Placido and Arturo and Minimi Giorgio and Dolph Anderson all looked at one another, plainly at a loss. Chester scratched his round chin and said, "I am afraid we do not follow you, my dear."

"I do," Winifred said. "My God, Adolphina, you can't be serious?"

"Why not? I figure we can milk it for a week before the bodies start to stink up the town." Adolphina grinned and enthusiastically rubbed her palms together. "Now, who here wants to make some money?"

Chapter 6

Ford County undersheriff Seamus Glickman was angry. He was angry at Edison Farnsworth and the Blight brothers for getting themselves shot and angry at Frank Lafferty for rushing to the sheriff's office to report it. But his hottest anger was reserved for Jeeter Frost. It was Frost who did the killing, and Frost who was to blame for Sheriff Hinkle having no choice but to send someone to Coffin Varnish. Coffin Varnish, for God's sake. And as luck would have it, all the deputies were busy.

If Seamus had his druthers, he would be town marshal instead of working for the county sheriff's office. It was a matter of jurisdictions. The marshal had jurisdiction over everyone and everything within the town limits; he rarely had to leave town. The sheriff, on the other hand, was responsible for the entire county. Every crime committed in Ford County had to be investigated and the guilty brought to trial. Which meant those who worked in the sheriff's office spent a lot of time traveling all over creation, or the part of creation that constituted the county.

Seamus would rather be in Dodge. He did not like to ride. He did not like horses. They were smelly and stubborn, and ever since one kicked him when he was eight and broke his leg, he had been secretly afraid of them. Not only that, but saddles chafed and hurt, and after a day in one his bottom was always so sore and stiff he could barely sit. Seamus did not like the country, either, mile after mile of wide-open space haunted by outlaws and renegades all too eager to make a ghost of a stray lawman.

Seamus much preferred town life, city life, *cultured* life. He enjoyed his creature comforts. He liked good food served in a comfortable restaurant. He liked to drink fine liquor in a plush saloon. He liked to spend his evenings at the theater and then visit one of the better brothels.

Dodge City had all those in abundance. The last time anyone counted, there were fourteen saloons, including his favorite, the Long Branch, with its billiard parlor and club room. There were half a dozen brothels, including Madame Blatsky's, who imported only the prettiest and most refined whores. As for the theater, Seamus much preferred the Comique, in large part because he owned a part interest, a fact he kept to himself since the county's more upstanding residents took a dim view of doings on Front Street and anyone who had anything to do with them.

All of which made Seamus wonder why he ever accepted the job as undersheriff. At the time it had seemed to have its merits. He was on good terms with George Hinkle, the sheriff. The job paid a hundred and forty dollars a month, plus a percentage of the taxes and fines he collected. Annually, that amounted to over twenty thousand dollars, nothing to sneeze at when the average yearly income was under a thousand.

But, God, he hated leaving Dodge! Usually Seamus avoided it by sending a deputy. But one of the deputies was returning a couple of deserters to the army, another was helping escort a federal prisoner to Kansas City, and the third went and shot his own foot while practicing with his six-shooter.

Buildings sprouted ahead and Seamus sat up straighter. He wanted to make a good impression. He took off his bowler and slapped it against his leg to shake off the dust. Before putting it back on, he took out his comb and ran it through his well-oiled black hair. He liked to slick it with Macassar oil, as much for the shine as the perfumed scent. He had a pompadour, but his hat invariably flattened it, and wide muttonchops. In his suits and polished boots, he presented a fine figure of a man, or so he often flattered himself.

As he drew closer, Seamus parted his jacket so the badge on his vest and the ivory-handled Merwin and Hulbert revolver on his left hip could be plainly seen. The pistol was another vanity. He was no kind of shot with it unless whatever he was shooting at was less than ten feet away, and even then he had to hold the revolver steady with both hands and take good aim. But then, he was not in the law business to shoot people. He was in the law business to make money. That he actually had, on occasion, to enforce the law was a nuisance he could do without.

Seamus had only ever been to Coffin Varnish once and that had been once too many. He recalled hearing that in the early days Coffin Varnish had been fit to rival Dodge as the queen of the plains, but Dodge had long since outstripped its rival in every respect. Fact is, he had forgotten Coffin Varnish even existed until Frank Lafferty came huffing and puffing into the sheriff's office. Damn him.

Nothing had changed since Seamus's last visit. The single street ran from south to north. On the right was the general store and some other buildings, four or five abandoned and in disrepair. On the left was the livery, an empty building, then the saloon, then more empty and boarded-over buildings, and finally a cottage. What in hell a cottage was doing there was anyone's guess, but Seamus remembered it from his last visit.

It was near eleven o'clock when Seamus, after a two-hour ride, drew rein at the hitch rail in front of the saloon and gratefully climbed down. As he looped the reins, he noticed a man in a rocking chair in the shade of the overhang. The man's gray hair sparked another memory. "Winifred Curry, as I recollect. You own this saloon."

"You recollect rightly, Sheriff Glickman," Win complimented him. "It has been a spell since you were here last."

"Undersheriff," Seamus corrected him. "Hinkle is the sheriff."

"Is that the same as a deputy?" Win asked.

"Higher than a deputy but lower than the sheriff," Seamus clarified, stretching.

"Then what do we call you? Is it Deputy Glickman or Undersheriff Glickman? Undersheriff is a mouthful."

"I guess calling me Sheriff Glickman won't hurt

anyone's feelings," Seamus said. Certainly not George Hinkle's, who at that time of day was usually sitting in the cushioned chair at his desk with his feet propped up, reading a newspaper and sipping coffee. Seamus was angry at him, too.

"We have been expecting someone with a badge ever since that Lafferty fellow lit out," Win informed him. "I reckon he told you about the shootings."

"I came to view the bodies and talk to any witnesses," Seamus said. "But first I can use a drink. My throat is dry from all the dust I swallowed on my way here." He started toward the batwings but abruptly stopped to avoid stepping in pig droppings. "Damn. Your street is worse than the streets in Dodge." He hated the streets in Dodge.

"Not by much." Win rose and preceded him.

The saloon smelled of stale odors and some not so stale, notably the unmistakable odor of fresh blood. Seamus knew the smell well from the short time he had spent working in a slaughterhouse when he was younger. Vile work, that, and hardly fitting for a man of his refined sensibilities. He regarded the new stains on the plank floor. "You have moved the bodies, I see."

"I didn't want folks tripping over them," Winifred said. He produced a glass and a bottle of his best Monongahela. "Want me to pour?"

"If you would." Seamus tried not to breathe too deep. Resting an elbow on the bar, he accepted the glass and let the whiskey burn a path down his throat to his stomach. "Ahhh. I'm obliged."

"It's not on the house," Win said.

Seamus fished a half eagle from a vest pocket and

flipped it to Curry, who deftly caught it. He was tempted to say Curry could keep it, just to show off, but he didn't.

"Here is your change," Win said. "You will need it."

"What is that supposed to mean?"

"I will let the mayor tell you." Win changed the subject by asking, "After you are done here, are you going after Jeeter Frost?"

"By myself?" Seamus said. "A rip-snorter like him, I would need a posse, and the county is not about to foot the bill when he is probably halfway to California by now."

"It is too bad about that gent from the *Times*," Win said. "He sort of fancied himself. Did you know him?"

"Farnsworth? Knew him well," Seamus said. Which was not entirely true. He had talked to the pompous ass every now and again, principally because Farnsworth spent a lot of his after hours at the Comique, and they shared a few drinks, but that was the extent of it.

"Being in the wrong place at the wrong time kills more men than smallpox," Winifred commented.

Seamus drained his glass and set it down. The idle chat was already wearing thin. "I reckon I should get started." The sooner he talked to everyone involved, the sooner he could head for Dodge. Maybe he could make it back by nightfall. A nice meal, his seat at the theater, and then a visit to Madame Blatsky's would set the world right again. "Suppose you tell me what you saw."

Winifred did more than that. He showed the law-

man exactly where each of the Blights had been standing when they were shot and mimicked the positions
of their bodies after they fell.

Seamus only interrupted once, to chuckle and say,
"The bastard shot them from under the table?" He
crouched and peered under the table in the corner.
"Damned sneaky, that Frost."

"You ever heard of anyone doing that before?"
Win asked.

"No, I surely haven't," Seamus said. He had heard
of men shot from behind trees and from behind boul-
ders, and he had heard of men shot from rooftops and
from horseback and from a moving stage, but he had
never heard of anyone shot from under a table.
Until now.

"It is probably just as well you are not going after
him," Winifred said. "He would only add to his tally."

"I appreciate the confidence," Seamus said dryly.
"Now why don't you show me the bodies." It was a
command, not a question.

"I would like to," Win said, "but they are over to
the livery and no one can see them without the may-
or's permission."

Seamus tapped his badge. "This tin star gives me
the right to do as I please. The county has jurisdiction,
not Coffin Varnish."

"I know, I know," Win said. "But—"

Before he could finish, a door at the back opened
and in sashayed Sally Worth. She had done herself
up, brushed her hair, and put on her best dress. It was
faded but accented the swell of her bosom and her
hips. Brazenly, she came up to Glickman, hooked her

arm in his, and curled her red lips in a seductive smile.
"I thought I heard a new voice down here." She introduced herself. "I don't believe we have ever met."

"No, we haven't," Seamus said. He never forgot a
whore. He was particular about those he slept with,
and never in a million years would he sleep with one
as old as this one. Although he had to admit she had
a nice body.

"Care to buy a working girl a drink?"

"I am on official business, Miss Worth," Seamus
said. "In fact, I am just on my way to talk to your
mayor. Luce, isn't that his name?"

"Chester Luce," Sally amended. "But he is not the
one who runs Coffin Varnish. Not really."

"Sally," Win said.

"Then who is?" Seamus asked.

"Chester's wife, Adolphina. He never does a thing
without her say-so. It was her idea to have the bodies
taken to the livery and—"

"*Sally,*" Win said sharply.

"What?"

"It will be better if Chester tells him. Let them hash
it out officially," Winifred advised.

Seamus was confused. "Hash what out? What the
hell are you talking about? I just want to get this over
with and get back to Dodge."

"Visit the general store," Win urged. "His Honor
will fill you in."

Sally touched Seamus's cheek. "And when you are
done, come on back so we can get acquainted. I will
make your ride here worthwhile."

Seamus inwardly shuddered. He would have to be
booze blind to let a dove her age lure him under the

sheets. The gray streaks in her hair, all those wrinkles, and, he noticed, a few teeth missing. "I will give it serious consideration, madam," he assured her.

"You do that." Sally beamed.

Seamus was glad to get out of there. Swirls of dust rose from under his boots as he crossed the street. Two Mexicans were in front of the livery, watching him. Two boys were out in front of the cottage, equally curious. Seamus smiled and waved. He couldn't say why, since he did not give a good damn about any of them.

The general store had not changed, either. Seamus bought tobacco on his last visit. It cost him fifty cents more than it would in Dodge. He started down an aisle, ignoring the items for sale.

The Luces were waiting for him behind the counter. Chester smiled somewhat nervously and held out his pudgy hand. "Undersheriff Glickman. It is a pleasure to see you again."

Seamus was staring at the wife. She was big enough to wrestle a bear, and win. In fact, except for her pale skin, she resembled more than anything a she-bear in a dress.

Adolphina extended her own hand. "I did not have the honor of meeting you on your last visit, but my husband told me all about you. He said you are a fine lawman, and in the next election might take Hinkle's job."

"Oh, really?" Seamus had never expressed any interest in being sheriff, and if he did, he certainly would not tell someone he hardly knew.

"We imagine you want to see the bodies?" Chester asked.

"In a bit," Seamus said. "There seems to be some confusion over who has authority over them. The saloon owner told me I had to talk to you first."

"That was nice of him," Adolphina said.

"My point is, I don't need your permission," Seamus said. "Coffin Varnish does not have a marshal. If it did, he would have jurisdiction. Since it doesn't, the sheriff enforces the law just as he does in the rest of the county outside of town and city limits."

"We could quibble the finer points of the law, but we won't," Adolphina told him.

"No?"

"Not at all. Our concern is that you intend to take the bodies with you. We would rather you didn't." Adolphina smiled sweetly. "You see, we have plans for them."

"What in God's name are you talking about?" Seamus was at a loss.

Chester and Adolphina came around the counter and Adolphina took Seamus's arm in her hands. "We would rather you see for yourself. It will save a lot of explaining."

Confused and curious, Seamus permitted them to lead him down the street to the livery. The Mexicans had disappeared and the wide double doors were closed. But on the doors, in freshly painted red letters, was the answer.

"I'll be damned," Seamus Glickman said.

Chapter 7

Frank Lafferty tried not to fidget in his chair as he waited for his editor's decision. He was dressed in his finest suit and had paid the barber a visit to give the best impression. So much was riding on the outcome that a fine sheen of sweat covered him from crown to toe. He hoped the editor would not notice.

Ezekiel Hinds, or Zeke as those at the *Times* called him, had been in the newspaper business for more years than everyone on the staff combined. A seasoned journalist who knew all there was to know and then some, he was responsible for hiring and promotions.

Lafferty desperately desired to move up. He had been at the *Times* for a year and a half, half of that as Edison Farnsworth's assistant. Farnsworth had regarded himself as God's gift to journalism and treated Lafferty as little more than his personal errand boy. He once told Lafferty, "The only way you or anyone else will ever fill my shoes is if I die."

Lafferty had resigned himself to being an assistant forever, and then Farnsworth had done something wonderful: He had gone and gotten himself killed.

Now the suspense was killing Lafferty. Hinds had

read the piece twice and was reading it a third time. Unable to keep silent any longer, Lafferty quietly asked, "Well?"

"Not bad, son." Hinds always called men younger than him "son." "Not bad at all. You stuck to the facts."

Lafferty felt the tension drain from him in a rush of release. "Thank you, sir." He beamed. He saw the job as his. He saw himself as the rising star of Dodge City journalism, and once he conquered Dodge, who knew? New York City, perhaps, or San Francisco.

"But it is not enough," Hinds said, bursting Lafferty's bubble.

Panic welled, nearly constricting Lafferty's throat, nearly making it impossible for him to squeak, "Sir?"

Hinds leaned back in his chair. He was slight of build and gray of hair. Those who did not know him would never suspect his unassuming appearance hid as keen a mind as anyone could ask for. "The facts are not always enough. Sometimes they need to be embellished. Surely you read a lot of what Farnsworth wrote?"

"He had me go over everything for spelling and grammar," Lafferty said. As much as he hated to admit it, he rarely found a mistake. Farnsworth had a swelled head, yes, but he had the talent to justify the swelling.

"Didn't you learn anything?" Hinds asked, not unkindly. He placed his forearms on his desk. "Listen, son. The newspaper business is not cut-and-dried. It is not just the facts and only the facts. Facts are dry. Facts are boring. They are the bare bones, if you will, and what our readers want is the juicy meat. Do you follow me?"

Lafferty was not quite sure what the editor was getting at, but he responded, "Of course, sir."

"Then follow his example. Take this and rewrite it. Throw in some emotion. Stir people up. Decide whether you want this Frost character to be the hero or the villain and slant your account accordingly."

"The hero or the villain?" Lafferty had always been under the impression that a journalist's first and foremost responsibility was to be objective.

"A hero. A man who shot a card cheat and then defended himself when the cheat's brothers sought revenge. A villain. A man who cowardly shot another man in the back and then murdered the brothers while hiding under a table. You decide which you want him to be."

Lafferty could not keep quiet no matter how much he wanted to. "But shouldn't that be for the readers to decide? Is it right to lead them around by the nose?"

Hinds sat back and thoughtfully tapped the edge of his desk. Finally he said, "What is the *Times*, son?"

"A newspaper."

"What else, son?" Hinds asked, and when Lafferty did not answer right away, he said, "The *Times* is a business. All newspapers are. They exist to make money. If they don't make money, they fold. Therefore it behooves them to do whatever is necessary to increase their circulations so they make as much money as they can. Follow me?"

"I never thought of it in quite that fashion," Lafferty admitted.

Hinds smiled. "That is because you are young and an idealist. I was the same at your age. Ideals are fine and dandy, but we must never let them get in the way of reality, and the reality is that people don't want just the bare bones—they want juicy meat, and the more of that meat we feed them, the more of them buy our paper. Follow me now?"

"Yes, sir."

"Then I will tell you what," Hinds said, sliding the piece across the desk. "Rewrite this. Throw in some juice. Do a good job and we will run it in the afternoon edition. Do a really good job and I will let you fill in for Farnsworth on a probationary basis."

"Probationary?"

"You must prove yourself, son. Show me you have what it takes and the job is yours. That's fair, isn't it?"

"More than fair," Lafferty said, excitement bubbling in him like bubbling water in a hot pot.

Hinds grew thoughtful again. "In fact, now that I think about it, write two pieces. One about Frost and another about Farnsworth. Make Farnsworth out to be a lion of journalism. Lament his loss to the good people of Dodge City, and to the world."

Lafferty took a risk. "I don't mention he was in love with himself and thought most people are idiots?"

Hinds laughed. "No, you do not mention he was an egotistical ass. Praise his virtues, and if you have to, make up virtues to praise. Stir the emotions of our readers. That's the juicy meat, son." When the younger man did not leap up and run off to rewrite the story, Hinds asked, "Is something else on your mind?"

"I was thinking, sir," Lafferty said. "I can turn this into a series of articles. Milk it for all it is worth." Now that he knew what was required of him, he saw all sorts of possibilities.

"That is fine but don't get ahead of yourself. Do the rewrite and we will talk some more."

Lafferty rose and offered his hand in gratitude. "Thank you, sir. I have learned more from you in the past ten minutes than I ever learned from Edison Farnsworth."

"Flattery, son, will get you everywhere."

The white one-room schoolhouse sat by itself five hundred yards beyond the town limits. That was Ernestine Prescott's doing. When she answered the appeals placed in several Eastern newspapers for a schoolmarm and came to Dodge City only to find they did not have a schoolhouse, she politely but firmly requested that it be built outside town, where her young charges could pursue their education in relative peace and solitude. Noisy streets were not conducive to study.

Dodge's civic leaders were happy to oblige. Schoolmarms were hard to come by. There were not enough of them to meet the growing demand on the frontier, and Ernestine's credentials were impressive. She had taught school for six years in Hartford, Connecticut, and for another six at a country school in the Catskills.

Ernestine was devoted to teaching and inspiring young minds. So much so, one day she realized she was pushing thirty and did not have a husband or a family or any of the trappings that went with them. That bothered her, but not nearly as much as the realization that there was a great big wide world out there she had seen precious little of. Connecticut and New York were the only places she had been.

So when by pure chance Ernestine saw in the newspaper that Dodge City was in need of a schoolmarm, she wrote them that very evening. She listed her credentials and cited her experience and threw in a comment about how much she would love to teach there, and much to her amazement, without requiring that she prove her mettle, she was accepted. Later she learned she was the first teacher to reply, and they were in such dire need, they accepted her right away. Still later she learned she was the *only* teacher who wrote them.

Now here Ernestine was, teaching school on the frontier. She had to admit Dodge was rougher than she expected it would be. She always thought the stories about frontier life were exaggerated. It could not possibly be as bad as everyone claimed or no one would live there. But Dodge was everything ever written about it, and more. A bustling hotbed of greed, lust, and violence. Oh, there were plenty of churchgoing folk, plenty of fine people who would not harm the proverbial fly, but there were also plenty who would. Plenty who liked the wild side and all its trimmings.

Ernestine stopped grading papers and put down her pencil. She was stiff from so much sitting. Rising, she moved to the small mirror above the basin where the children were required to wash their hands after playtime. Ernestine was a stickler for clean hands. Clean hands meant clean books and clean papers turned in.

Staring at her reflection, Ernestine was reminded of a remark her brother once made. *"You are a broomstick in a dress, sis."* He had not meant to be cruel. They were talking about how different they were. Her brother, Dearborn, could stand to lose a hundred pounds and that still would not be enough. She, on the other hand, truly was a broomstick. A broomstick with fine brown hair she always wore in a bun. A broomstick with a pointed chin and a beak of a nose and high cheekbones. She had a high forehead, too. Her eyes, she thought, were her best feature. A light shade of brown, almost tawny, but they alone could not redeem her. She was plain, hideously plain. No wonder she never had a beau. No wonder she would spend her days as a spinster.

Ernestine's thin lips compressed. She must stop thinking like that, she scolded herself, and attend to her responsibilities. That was the secret to happiness. Forget personal woes and focus on the job. Just the job.

Ernestine turned to go back to her desk and drew up short, dumfounded to behold a man standing in the schoolhouse doorway. She had left it open to admit the evening breeze. "My word!" she blurted. "You gave me a start!"

"I'm sorry, ma'am. I didn't mean to."

Ernestine regained her composure. Clasping her hands, she walked down the row of desks. "May I help you?"

He was standing sideways to her. With his small stature, his features made Ernestine think of a mouse. His dusty buckskins smelled of sweat and were in need of washing. "I am hoping you can, yes, ma'am," he said quietly, wringing his hat. "I wouldn't want to bother you, though."

"What is it that you want, exactly?" Ernestine politely asked. "Do you have a child you would like to enroll?"

The man turned red, bright, embarrassed red. "Good Lord, ma'am, no," he bleated. "I ain't even married."

"Am not," Ernestine said.

"Ma'am?"

"You should not use ain't. You should say, 'I am not married.' We must set an example for the children."

"But there's just you and me here, ma'am."

"Even so, we must be vigilant against bad habits, Mr.—?" Ernestine stopped and waited.

"Jeeter, ma'am. You can call me Jeeter." He held out his hand and in doing so turned to face her and the sunlight flashed on the pearl handles of a revolver at his hip.

"I trust you were not aware I do not permit guns anywhere near my school," Ernestine said sternly.

"No, ma'am, I wasn't."

"Guns are the devil's playthings. Remove it and go put it in your saddlebags and we can continue our conversation, Mr. Jeeter," Ernestine directed. "That is your horse, I take it, by the pump?"

"Yes, ma'am, it is, and no, ma'am, I can't. And Jeeter is my first name, not my last, so you don't need the Mr."

Ernestine did not know quite what to make of him.

He was polite, and had friendly eyes, but he seemed scared of her, and his English was atrocious. "I do not understand. Why can't you take off your pistol?"

The mousy man sighed and said almost sadly, "My last name is Frost, ma'am. I am Jeeter Frost."

Ernestine had the impression he thought the name should mean something to her. "Mr. Frost, then. I ask again, why can't you take off your pistol?"

"I like being alive and I have me a heap of enemies who would like me feeding worms."

"I am afraid I do not quite fathom what you are getting at, Mr. Frost," Ernestine said.

"You have never heard of me, then?"

"Should I?"

"Folks talk about me some. I guess because they have nothing better to talk about. Or maybe it's me being partway somebody. Not that I ever meant to be. Throw a little lead and suddenly you are."

"Excuse me?" Ernestine was beginning to think he was one of those eccentric characters who hung about Dodge, like the man who wore a rabbit coat and carried a carrot everywhere.

"I've dabbled in gore, ma'am. Once you do, you are branded for life. I've never hired out my trigger finger, you understand. I haven't gone that far. But I can't seem to get away from it."

"You are speaking in riddles, Mr. Frost," Ernestine chided. "Speak plainly if you want me to understand."

"I kill people, ma'am."

"You?" Ernestine smiled. The notion of this timid mouse of a man harming anyone was preposterous.

"The man-killer from Missouri, they call me, even

though I'm not from Missouri. But that's why you need to keep my visit to yourself. I killed the Blight brothers and folks are liable to make a fuss over it."

Ernestine began to think he was serious. She had not read the newspaper the day before, but she seemed to recall hearing mention of a shooting. "What does a man like you want with me?" she asked. Images washed over her, of him pulling his gun and having his way with her, and she grew uncomfortably warm.

"I want for you to teach me to read."

Chapter 8

Chester and Winifred were in their rocking chairs under the overhang in front of the saloon. They rocked and drank and gazed at the dusty haze to the south. It was the middle of the afternoon. Seamus Glickman had left the afternoon before, anxious to get back to Dodge before dark.

"So much for your brainstorm," Win said. "All that trouble you had Anderson go to building those coffins and Placido painting those signs on the livery, and for what?"

"It was Adolphina's idea, not mine," Chester responded after first glancing at the general store to ensure that she could not possibly hear him.

"They should have come by now, if they are coming at all. The story was bound to be in yesterday's newspaper."

"The shootings, yes," Chester said. "But not the rest of it. Glickman promised to spread the word, but something like that takes time. Today's paper will likely have it."

"Those bodies will start to stink by tomorrow," Win remarked.

"We can stand a few days of stink if we have to,"

Chester said. "Why do you think I had them put in the livery?"

"I wouldn't let you keep them in the saloon."

"Yes, well, the Mexicans agreed, so everything worked out as we wanted it to," Chester said.

"As your wife wanted," Win said. "And they have names, you know."

"Who?"

"Placido and Arturo."

"I know what their names are," Chester said testily. "I just can't ever seem to remember them."

"Ah," Win said.

Chester shifted in his chair. "Don't take that tone with me, Winifred Curry. I resent what you are implying. I don't think any less of them because they are Mexican than any other white man would." He grunted. "Hell, the only reason you know their names is because they come in for a tequila every now and then."

"I like them," Win said. "They mind their own business and keep to themselves, yet they were ready to help you when you asked them."

"Placido was. I'm not so sure the other one, Arturo, liked the idea."

"To keep four bodies in their stable until the bodies are ready to rot?" Win said. "I can't imagine why he had to be persuaded."

"You are much too critical today, do you know that?" Chester shifted away from him and gloomily regarded the expanse of prairie that surrounded Coffin Varnish.

"If I am," Win said, "it is only because I can't ignore the truth any longer. I have finally come to terms with it."

"With what?"

"Coffin Varnish won't last another year. You and I will be forced to close. Placido and Arturo, too. What good is a livery in the middle of nowhere? Without a store handy to meet their needs, the Giorgios will be forced to move, too. That will leave Anderson and his wife all alone. They might stay on a while, given they can live off the land. But they will be all that's left. The buildings will slowly rot away. Five years from now Coffin Varnish will be a ghost town."

"God, you are depressing."

Win stood. "My glass is empty." He started to turn but stopped, his keen eyes narrowing. "Can it be? Maybe that harebrained plan of your wife's will bring in some business, after all."

Chester shot out of his chair and moved from under the overhang. He squinted against the glare, but all he saw were heat waves. "What do you see? A rider?"

"A wagon."

Chester strained his eyes until they hurt and still did not see it. "You must be part hawk. Instead of running a whiskey mill, you should scout for the army."

"I'm allergic to arrows in my hide."

Winifred went in and Chester sat back down to await the wagon. But he was so nervous he could not sit still. A lot was riding on his wife's idea. They could hold out in Coffin Varnish longer if it worked. Or it could give them the money to buy freight wagons and move somewhere they could earn a living. So long as it was not Dodge City. He would live anywhere on earth but there.

Chester yawned. The heat and the whiskey were making him drowsy. Summers in Kansas were too hot for his liking. It had to be one hundred there in the shade. It was almost enough to make him consider filling the washtub with water and soaking in it for a while to cool down, but he had had a bath a month ago, and filling the basin was a chore.

Chester stared out over the sea of dry grass. At last he could see it, a spindly spider lumbering toward Coffin Varnish, or so it appeared thanks to the shimmering haze and the distance. How in God's name Winifred had seen it that far out, he would never know.

The spider grew and became a team pulling a carriage. A carriage, not a buckboard. Chester could not remember the last time he saw a carriage. The well-to-do owned them. City and town dwellers, as a rule. Farmers and ranchers made do with buckboards. You could haul crops and dirt and manure in a buckboard. All you could haul in a carriage was people.

Winifred emerged, his glass refilled. "They aren't here yet?" He took a sip, then asked, "Have you seen what it is?"

"I'm not blind," Chester snapped.

"Your wife says you need spectacles but you are too stubborn to get them," Win commented. Adolphina had a list of complaints about Chester as long as Win's arm. Why Chester stayed married to her, Win never could figure out.

"My eyes are fine, I tell you," Chester said, galled that Adolphina had trampled on his trust.

"Maybe it is the mayor of Dodge, come to pay his respects," Win teased.

"Go to hell."

"What was it you called him the last time you and him locked horns?" Win snapped his fingers. "Now I remember. You accused him of stealing the railroad out from under you. Which was some feat, seeing as how the railroad never showed any interest in laying tracks here."

Chester swore. He knew that. Knew damn well that the Atchison, Topeka, and Santa Fe railroad had been laying track in a beeline for Fort Dodge, and the post commander, the post quartermaster, and the post sutler pooled their finances and bought a plot of land directly in the track's path. Two saloons and a general store were up and ready to cater to the work crews when the tracks got there. Dodge City was born, spelling Coffin Varnish's eventual doom. "Do me a favor and quit bringing up old history."

Win did not help Chester's mood by chuckling.

Fortunately, the carriage arrived in a cloud of dust and the thud of hooves. The driver was a black man in expensive livery. He expertly brought the team to a halt and quickly climbed down to open the near door, announcing, "We have arrived, sir."

From the carriage stepped a man of middle years dressed in a sartorial splendor that put Chester, and most everyone else in Kansas, to shame. His tailored jacket, vest, and pants were a light shade of gray, his bowler slightly darker. He carried a cane with the gold likeness of a hound for a knob, and his boots practically gleamed. He looked about him with an air of amusement and spotted Chester and Win.

"Might I impose on you gentlemen for information?"

"Only after you introduce yourself," Chester said. "This may not be Dodge, but we have manners here."

"My apologies, sir. I daresay that was remiss of me. I am Charles Nelek. Perhaps you have heard of me? I own several establishments in Dodge."

Win's interest perked up. "I have heard of you. You own the Kitten Club, among others." He had long wanted to pay the establishment a visit, but it would cost more than he earned in a year. Hell, two years. "Your girls are supposed to be the loveliest in Dodge."

"I thank you, sir. They thank you, too. Those I brought with me, at any rate."

From within the carriage came giggles and titters.

Chester came out of his chair. He, too, had heard all about the Kitten Club. The women were exquisite, the food excellent. An experience to remember forever, as one friend put it. "Permit me to formally welcome you, sir. I am the mayor of Coffin Varnish, Chester Luce."

"You don't say?" Charles Nelek said while turning to the carriage. "You may come out now, ladies. Watch your step. And be advised the sun is a furnace."

Out they came, three of them, a blonde, a redhead, and a black-haired beauty, all three perfection, from their pale complexions to their china-smooth skin to their ample busts and pencil-thin waists. Their dresses were marvels of color and fit. Each wore a style of hat currently fashionable back East, with flared brims and a lot of lace. They also had parasols, which they immediately opened to protect their face and neck.

"Oh my," Winifred breathed.

"May I introduce Sugarplum, Sasha, and Leah?" Charles Nelek said, with dips of his chin. "Ladies, we have the honor of addressing the mayor, so be on your best behavior."

Chester sensed that Nelek was poking fun at him, but he didn't care. Doffing his hat, he went up to the ladies to shake their hands. "Pleased as can be to make your acquaintance, ladies. Anything you want during your visit, anything at all, you need only say the word."

Win was a step behind him. "That's right. We may not have as much to offer as Dodge, but whatever we have is yours."

"Such gracious hospitality," Nelek said. "What we would like most is to get in out of this sun and have something to drink."

Win gestured at the batwings. "After you, then."

Sugarplum twirled her red parasol, her golden hair shimmering under the lace. "Is it possible to get some ice cream anywhere?"

Chester and Win shared pained glances and Chester said, "I am afraid not, young lady. There is no ice to be had anywhere in Coffin Varnish."

"How do people survive in this awful heat?" Sasha asked.

Nelek wrapped his arms around her and Sugarplum. "Ladies, we must remember we are roughing it. Dodge is an oasis of luxury compared to the rest of this godforsaken territory."

Chester could not let the slur go unchallenged. "I wouldn't know as I would go that far."

"Oh, really?" Nelek said. "Tell us. Can Coffin Varnish boast of a water closet anywhere in its limits?"

"A what?" Win asked.

Nelek smiled smugly and gave the women on his arms a playful squeeze. "See what I mean, my dears? But don't be disheartened. On the contrary. It will make the story of our adventure all the more entertaining."

They repaired to the saloon and Win offered them his best whiskey. It earned a quirk of the lips from Charles Nelek. The ladies, Win noted, drained their glasses in a gulp.

"Now that we have wet our parched throats," Nelek said, "we would very much like to view the display Undersheriff Glickman told me about."

"Oh *yes!*" Sugarplum squealed. "The dead people!"

"You will be the first to see them," Win mentioned.

Leah giggled and squirmed in her chair. "We will? Did you hear that, girls? We will be the envy of everyone."

"I can't wait to tell Claudia," Sasha said. "Her and her two-headed snake she saw once."

Chester had been so entranced by the three visions that he was slow to rouse and say, "I trust that Undersheriff Glickman also mentioned it is a dollar a person for the privilege?"

"Yes, he did," Nekel replied. "A bit exorbitant, wouldn't you say?"

"Not at all," Chester said. "These aren't ordinary dead people. They are the handiwork of a notorious desperado. A killer who has his own penny dreadful. Jeeter Frost is halfway to famous."

"Or will be after this," Win said.

"Still, a whole dollar . . . ," Nelek quibbled.

Sugarplum showed her less than sugary side by snapping, "Damn it, just pay the man, Charley. We didn't come all this way to listen to you haggle. And it's not as if you haven't hoarded every cent you ever earned."

"That tart tongue of yours will get you in trouble one day," Nelek warned.

"Oh, please. All I have to do is cross my legs and you will come begging for it," Sugarplum said. "If you want to act all tough and important, be my guest. But don't threaten me or I will be on the next stage for San Francisco. McCabe has been after me to come to his place."

"Now, now," Nelek quickly said. "Let's not talk rashly, shall we? Did I say I wouldn't pay this gentleman? Do you think I would bring you all this way and then not view the deceased?"

Chester accepted the money with the air of a man accepting the Holy Grail. He ushered them outside and down the street to the livery, the ladies chattering like chipmunks the whole while about the perfectly vile heat and the hideous dust everywhere and the awful smells, and wasn't it all just grand fun?

Win accompanied them, and at a nod from Chester, helped open the double doors.

"Oh my!" Sugarplum exclaimed.

The four bodies had been propped upright in coffins built by Dolph Anderson. Each bore a crudely scrawled sign with the name of the victim. The three Blights had their arms folded across their chests. But it was Edison Farnsworth who drew the ladies like buzzing flies.

"He is blown all apart!" Leah squealed in delight. "Oh, it is hideous! You can see his organs and bones and everything!"

"Wait until we get back and tell everyone!" Sasha gushed.

Charles Nelek did not realize it, but he made Chester and Win extremely happy when he remarked, "Gentlemen, I do believe you have a gold mine on your hands."

Chapter 9

"Letters have always been chicken scratches to me," Jeeter Frost said as he stared hard at the *McGuffey's Reader*. "You say this one is an *e*?"

"That it is, Mr. Frost," Ernestine Prescott said. Her students had long since been dismissed for the day. Outside the schoolhouse, the gray shroud of descending twilight blanketed the prairie. "It is the fifth letter of the alphabet, after *d*, which you have already learned, and before *f*."

"Sort of looks like a tadpole, don't it?" Jeeter asked with a grin.

"Doesn't it," Ernestine corrected, and allowed herself a grin of her own. "Yes, it does, somewhat."

Jeeter looked up from his desk. He was small enough that he fit, but it was a tight squeeze. "I can't thank you enough, ma'am, for helping me."

"Nonsense, Mr. Frost," Ernestine said. She had on the prettiest of the three dresses she owned, and had washed her hair. "I am an educator. It is my duty to enlighten the ignorant."

"That's sure enough me, ma'am," Jeeter said, nodding. "Ignorant as sin. I don't know much about anything except Colts. That's all I am. An ignorant man, good with a Colt."

"You are too hard on yourself," Ernestine said. She stood beside her desk, a ramrod, her hands primly folded. "In the first place, we are all of us ignorant to some degree. In the second place, I can't believe the only skill you have is killing."

"It's more of a talent, ma'am," Jeeter said. "Like the talent you have for teaching. You are awful good at it."

"Why, thank you," Ernestine said, unfolding her hands and then folding them again. "You deserve some of the credit. You are an excellent student."

"Me, ma'am?" Jeeter said, and laughed.

"You also have excellent manners," Ernestine remarked, "which I must admit I did not expect."

Jeeter self-consciously ran a hand over his oily hair. His hat was on a peg by the door and he cast a yearning glance in its direction before saying, "My folks take the credit there. I can be almost a gentleman when I put my mind to it."

"You have impressed me," Ernestine said. Suddenly coughing, she said, "Suppose we get back to your studies. Practice writing the *e*, oh, twenty times."

"Yes, ma'am." Jeeter picked up his pencil. He hesitated, the tip of his tongue sticking from the corner of his mouth, then painstakingly imitated the *e* in the *McGuffey's Reader*. When he was done, he held the paper so she could see. "Look! I done it!"

"You did it," Ernestine corrected. "Now write it nineteen more times." As he bent to the task she turned and walked to the window. It would take him a while. He did his best, but he was as slow as a turtle. The sprinkling of lights in Dodge reminded her night had fallen. She should tell him to leave. She had her reputation to think of. A schoolmarm must be above reproach, and here she was, alone with a man. She walked back to her desk and sat in her chair. She did not tell him to leave.

"I really am doing good, ma'am?"

His question surprised her. Not that he asked it, but his sincerity. Ernestine had never met anyone who yearned to learn as keenly as he did. "It has only been three days and already you are up to e. Yes, I would say you are doing quite well, Mr. Frost."

Jeeter bent to the sheet of paper again. "You can call me Jeeter if you want, ma'am. It's just the two of us here."

Ernestine glanced up sharply. But there had been no hint of impropriety in his tone. "And you may call me Ernestine if you so desire."

"You are sure I won't get you into trouble, coming here as I do?"

"That is the fifth time you have asked, and no, you will not," Ernestine assured him. "Who I teach on my own time is none of anyone's affair." She laughed lightly. "Besides, Dodge has another matter to keep tongues wagging. From what I hear, there has been a steady stream of otherwise sensible citizens traveling to Coffin Varnish to admire your handiwork."

Jeeter looked up, the tip of his tongue sticking out. "How's that again, ma'am?"

"Haven't you heard? The four men you killed are on display. They are quite the attraction. At a dollar a head, someone is making a lot of money."

"Are you joshing me, ma'am?" Jeeter was astounded. He had been avoiding human contact, except for coming to the schoolhouse for his lessons, and spent his nights camped out on the plain.

"Why, no, Mr. Frost, I am not," Ernestine said. "You sound upset."

"Wouldn't you be, ma'am?" Jeeter came out of the desk, or tried to. He had to wriggle some to unfurl to his full height. "I reckon as how I better pay Coffin Varnish a visit."

"Not right this minute, surely?" Ernestine said. "You have only been here half an hour and we agreed on an hour's lesson each day."

"Yes, ma'am, but—"

"But nothing, Mr. Frost." Ernestine got up and came over and put her hand on his arm. "Kindly retake your seat."

Jeeter could not remember the last time a woman touched him. A woman he had not paid to touch him, that is. He quickly sat and picked up the pencil. "Whatever you say, ma'am."

Ernestine returned to her desk. Her hand was hot where she had placed it on his arm, and she rubbed it against her hip. But it only became hotter. "Why would you want to go there, if you do not mind my asking?"

"I shot those men," Jeeter said. "I should have a say in what's done with them. And I say the decent thing to do is to bury them."

Clasping her hands behind her, Ernestine composed herself. He was constantly saying things that surprised her, and this was one of them. "That is quite noble of you, Mr. Frost."

"Shucks, ma'am, I wouldn't know noble from buffalo chips," Jeeter told her. "I just know I don't want nobody I shot made a spectacle of."

"Anyone you shot," Ernestine said. "Or perhaps someone, depending on whether you intended the singular or the plural."

Jeeter set down the pencil. "When you talk like that, Ernestine, my brain goes numb."

Ernestine smiled. It was the first time he had called her by her first name. "What will you do if you go to Coffin Varnish?"

"Ask them, polite-like, to bury the bodies," Jeeter said. "And if they refuse, I'll ask again, only not so polite."

"I imagine the whole issue will soon be moot," Ernestine commented.

"What do cows have to do with it?" Jeeter asked.

"Cows?" Ernestine repeated, and giggled. She covered her mouth with her hand but could not stop.

"What is so all-fired hilarious?"

With an effort Ernestine smothered another giggle, and replied, "Moot is not the sound cows make. In the sense I used it, I simply indicated that going to Coffin Varnish would be pointless." His confusion was so apparent that she added, "The deceased have become rather ripe. So much so, yesterday's newspaper mentioned that the bodies were to be buried sometime today."

"Oh." Jeeter still felt an urge to ride to Coffin Varnish and give them a piece of his mind. "Then I reckon we might as well keep on with my lessons. If you want to, that is."

"Mr. Frost, if I were not teaching you I would be grading papers, and I consider teaching you the more pleasant of the two." Ernestine felt herself blush. That had not come out precisely as she intended, although, God help her, it was the truth.

Jeeter was so flabbergasted that for a few seconds he could not get his vocal cords to work. Finally he said, "That's awful nice of you. I'll try to make you proud of me."

"Let us take a look at *f*," Ernestine said.

Chester Luce rapped his hammer on the blanket on the counter and announced, "This meeting of the Coffin Varnish Town Council is hereby called to order."

Present in the general store were Chester and his wife, Win, Placido and Arturo, Dolph Anderson, and Minimi Giorgio.

"Two in one week," Winifred Curry said from a chair near the pickle barrel. "The world is liable to come to an end."

"You will treat these proceedings with the dignity they deserve," Chester said, and tried to square his round shoulders. "Now then, the purpose of this meeting is to discuss those corpses."

"There's dignity for you."

Adolphina came around the counter and loomed over Win. "That will be enough out of you. This is serious business."

"We buried them an hour ago, thank God," Win said. "What is there left to talk about?"

Chester answered, "The money we made." He pulled a leather poke from an inner pocket and opened it. "All told, it comes to three hundred and forty-seven dollars."

Silence fell, until Dolph Anderson recovered enough to ask in barely understandable English, "How much that be again, Mr. Luce?"

"Three hundred and forty-seven dollars. It is not as much as I hoped, but it is nothing to sneeze at."

"You wanted more?" Win marveled.

"A lot more," Chester said. "Last I heard, Dodge has grown to about seven hundred people. Not even half paid us a visit, since some of the three hundred and forty-seven came from folks who came here twice."

"Even so," Win said, and whistled.

Chester began counting money out on the counter, making piles. "Let's see. As we agreed, here is fifty dollars for you, Win, and fifty for the missus and me, and fifty for Dolph, and fifty more for Minimi, and fifty for Placido and Arturo—"

"Fifty each," Winifred said.

"I don't recall agreeing to that."

Win smacked the pickle barrel. "Damn it, Chester. They kept those bodies in their livery longer than they should have, just to please you. Now their stable stinks to high heaven."

"If I give each of them fifty, that will only leave forty-seven for the town treasury," Chester protested.

"Which is forty-seven more than it's had in a month of Sundays," Winifred argued. "Fair is fair. Placido and Arturo both earned equal shares."

"My wife doesn't get an equal share and it was her idea," Chester reminded him.

"Give it to them," Adolphina said.

"Pardon me?"

"You heard me. Win is right. If anyone earned full shares, they did. Fifty to each and it is a shame we can't give them more."

"If you truly want me to," Chester said.

"Do it."

Reluctantly, Chester counted out another pile. The rest went into a tin on a shelf behind the counter.

Minimi hugged his share to him, saying, *"Grazie, signore. Grazie. Lei e molto gentile."*

"Speak English, you silly Italian," Chester said. "You are in America now."

"I thank you, sir," Minimi said, correcting his oversight. "You are very kind. I wish it was more."

"Don't we all," Chester said.

Placido and Arturo came forward to accept their shares. "I, too, would like to thank you, Mayor Luce," the former remarked. "It will take us a month to air out the stable, but it was worth it."

"If not for the smell, we could have had those four on display until they rotted away," Chester said.

"Smell and rot sort of go hand in hand," Winifred commented.

Jokingly, Chester declared, "It is too bad we don't know where Jeeter Frost got to or we could invite him back to kill someone else."

Adolphina was thoughtfully fingering the tin. At her husband's comment, she swiveled around and said, "That is an idea worth pursuing."

"I was kidding, dearest."

"I wasn't."

Winifred and the rest all looked at Chester, who shrugged and shook his head.

"The first time was a fluke. We can't have people shot down on a regular basis," he said.

"Why not?" Adolphina demanded. "Think of how much money we could make. People would come from all over the territory, not just Dodge. We could make five hundred dollars a month. Maybe a thousand."

"Have you been drinking?" Win asked.

"This be joke, ja?" Dolph said.

Adolphina ignored them. "I have given it a lot of thought. The possibilities are appealing."

Placido had removed his sombrero when he entered the store. Now he wagged it at her, saying, "What do you propose, senorita?"

"That we place notices in as many newspapers as we can with the money we have left," Adolphina said. "We will invite every badman, curly wolf, and gun shark who is so inclined to come to Coffin Varnish and settle their differences."

"That is insane," Win said. "We wouldn't be able to step outside for all the lead flying around."

Adolphina enlightened him. "Not if we arrange it so they only shoot each other at specific times of the day. We will charge for the privilege, then charge for people to view the losers. That way we make money at both ends. Lots and lots of money."

"My God. You *are* serious!"

"Never more so," Adolphina said. "It is high time Coffin Varnish lived up to its name. If, in the process, we make a lot of money, where is the harm?

"You can't spend money if you are dead," Winifred said. "No one has ever done anything as harebrained as this. Forget it, for all our sakes, or calamity will come calling."

Adolphina smiled. "Let us place the notice in the newspaper and find out."

Chapter 10

Undersheriff Seamus Glickman was good and mad. He had not minded—at least not that much—being forced to leave Dodge the first time. Shooting affrays happened all the time in Ford County. They were to be taken as a matter of course. But *this*! He got so mad thinking about it that he swore at his horse for no reason. Then his head snapped up.

Coffin Varnish had appeared up ahead.

Seamus glumly wished the earth would open up and swallow the whole damn town. He parted his jacket and patted the ivory handles of his Merwin and Hulbert revolver. For two bits he would shoot the whole bunch of them. Idiots, he fumed, the whole kit and caboodle.

Mad as he was, Seamus made for the saloon rather than the general store. As usual, Win Curry sat in the shade of the overhang, and greeted him with a smile.

"Good morning, Sheriff Glickman. How do you do this fine day?"

"Don't how do you do me," Seamus snapped, dismounting. "What in hell has gotten into you people? Did the whole population get drunk on your red-eye?"

"Uh-oh," Win said.

Seamus opened his saddlebags and took out the latest edition of the *Dodge City Times*. He walked under the overhang and shook the folded newspaper practically in the saloon owner's face. "Was this your idea or some other lunatic's?"

"I warned them it would not go over well," Win said. "But they never listen to me."

"They being the good mayor and his wife?" Seamus guessed.

"You are a genius or as close to one as I will ever meet."

"Save your humor for someone who will appreciate it." Seamus spun and stalked toward the general store. "They might not have listened to you, but they will by God listen to me. I am here to put a stop to this nonsense."

Win was out of his chair and caught up within a few strides. "Mind if I tag along? Coffin Varnish is mighty short on entertainment and this promises to be a humdinger."

Seamus spied the two Mexicans over by the livery. The polite one, Placido, smiled and touched the brim of his sombrero, but Seamus did not return the gesture. For all he knew, those two were in on it. Hadn't they displayed the original bodies in their livery?

"You have met Adolphina, haven't you?" Win asked, knowing full well that Glickman had.

"What does that have to do with anything?" Seamus growled.

"I want you to be prepared. I am on your side."

Seamus stopped and faced him. "Why? You live here. I should think you would be all for it."

"I am all for breathing," Win said. "Let me put it another way. If the wolves in the area go rabid, you don't invite them to your house for supper or you will be the main course."

"I could not have said it better myself," Seamus admitted. He shook the newspaper again. "Didn't you try to reason with them? Didn't you impress on them the sheer folly of their enterprise?"

"At the town council meeting I talked until I was blue in the face," Win informed him.

"And? What effect did you have?"

"The same effect as talking to trees."

Seamus moved on. "I, by God, will have an effect. The sheriff is fit to burst a vein. Other newspapers will pick up on it. Before long Coffin Varnish will be the laughingstock of the state." He was almost to the general store when the door opened and a smiling Chester Luce filled the doorway.

"Sheriff Glickman! How wonderful to see you again."

Thrusting the newspaper at him, Seamus snapped, "How would you like this shoved up your backside?"

"I take it this is not a social call?" Chester said. He had seen Glickman enter town and could tell how furious he was. The newspaper hinted why. But Chester refused to be intimidated. He thought of Adolphina, and the money they would make. All that wonderful money.

"Don't play the innocent with me," Seamus said. "You will explain yourself, and it had better be good."

"Wouldn't you care to come in and discuss this over refreshments rather than stand out here in the hot sun?" Chester asked.

"The sun be damned. Explain. Explain right now."

Chester continued to think of the money, only the money. It gave him the fortitude to say, "Perhaps you would be so kind as to make clear exactly why you are upset?"

By now Seamus was so mad he came close to punching Coffin Varnish's mayor in the nose. Containing his anger, he unfolded the newspaper and opened it to the advertisements. He cleared his throat. "Public Notice," he read, louder than he needed to. "The town of Coffin Varnish hereby serves notice that as of this date, anyone with a grudge is invited to come to Coffin Varnish and settle their differences howsoever they may choose. Shootings will be allowed under town sanction at specified times of the day, provided a permit is obtained. A burial fee is also required, should it prove necessary." Seamus stopped and glared at the mayor.

"Is there a problem?" Chester asked.

"I'm not done." Seamus read the last line, his voice a snarl. "All badmen, curly wolves, leather slappers, pistoleros, feudists, and shootists are cordially invited to Coffin Varnish to hash out their differences." He crumpled the newspaper and shook it. "Have you gone out of your mind?"

"Are you sure I can't interest you in something to drink?"

That did it. Seamus grabbed hold of the front of the mayor's shirt and nearly yanked him off his feet. "I should pistol-whip you."

"Really, now," Chester said, prying at the other's fingers. "Is this manhandling necessary?"

A choice selection of cusswords was on the tip of

Seamus's tongue when a large bulk loomed behind the mayor and a hand bigger than his shot out and seized his wrist.

"Release my husband this instant," Adolphina Luce demanded.

Taken aback by the strength in her grip, as well as her gender, Seamus let go and she let go of him. "Mrs. Luce. Are you aware of what your husband has done?"

"More than aware since it was my idea," Adolphina said. She resorted to her most disarming smile. "Is there a problem?"

"You can't invite killers into your town."

"Who says we can't?" Adolphina retorted. "There is no law against it that we know of."

"There is a law against murder," Seamus said, "and soliciting for murder."

"But we are not soliciting anything," Adolphina remarked. "We merely extended an invitation."

"A quibble, at best, and a distinction a judge is not likely to agree with," Seamus said. He and the sheriff had talked it out before he left Dodge, and he had a mental list of criticisms, legal and otherwise.

"Are you here to arrest us?" Adolphina asked.

"If I could, I would," Seamus said. Once again he shook the newspaper. "I am here to put a stop to this madness. You will place a notice in tomorrow's *Times* stating that your previous notice was in error."

"We will do no such thing."

Seamus never hit women but he dearly yearned to make an exception. "Damn it, woman. Listen to reason. The county is prepared to take whatever steps are necessary to stop you."

"By the county you mean the sheriff," Adolphina divined. "But since you had already admitted you do not have grounds to arrest us, what is left? Take us to court?"

"If the county has to, it will."

"Legal proceedings cost a lot of money," Adolphina said. "They also take a lot of time. There are appeals and more appeals. It could be years before the legal aspects are resolved."

"Don't do this," Seamus said.

"The case might go all the way to the Supreme Court."

"Don't do this, Mrs. Luce."

Adolphina placed her hand on Chester's shoulder and smiled. "I am afraid you have ridden here for nothing, Undersheriff Glickman. Go back and tell Sheriff Hinkle and whoever else is opposed to our idea that we stand firm in our commitment."

Seamus ground his teeth in exasperation. He looked at her husband and then at Win Curry. "Don't either of you have anything to say? Why is she doing all the talking when she is not an elected official?"

"My wife speaks on my behalf," Chester said, "and on behalf of the good people of Coffin Varnish."

"Good people!" Seamus snorted. "Idiots is more like it. Jackasses who will find themselves six feet under if they are not careful."

"Watch your language in the presence of a lady," Adolphina said.

In disgust, Seamus threw the newspaper in the dust. "Fine. It is on your heads. I will talk to the sheriff and he will send word to the governor. After that, it is out of our hands." Wheeling, he strode toward his mount.

Winifred hurried after him. "Don't go away mad. Would you care for a drink before you leave?"

"I would like a club to beat some sense into those simpletons." Seamus did not stop. He unwrapped the reins, hooked his foot in the stirrup, and swung up.

"It was not my doing," Win stressed.

Seamus lifted the reins and scowled. "You live here. Whether you agreed or not, you will suffer the consequences. What do they hope to get out of it, anyhow?"

"More bodies to display at a dollar a view."

"Money? They are doing this for the money?" Seamus shook his head. "They invite killers to come to town, invite killers to kill one another, and then your friends will put the dead killers on display for a measly dollar?"

"Not so measly," Win said. "But maybe nothing will come of it. Maybe no curly wolves will show."

"You better hope they don't. When you have a wolf by the tail, it can turn on you." With that bit of wisdom, Seamus clucked to his buttermilk and reined to the south. The Luces were staring at him. He smiled at them, a cold, bitter smile, and focusing on the woman, raised a hand in farewell. "I won't shed a tear at your funerals."

"I get the impression he does not like us," Chester commented as the lawman reached the end of the street and spurred the buttermilk into a trot.

"Him and his expensive clothes and his ivory-handled pistol," Adolphina said. "He is a fine one to criticize us for trying to make a little money." She squinted at the bright sun. "I can use a nap. I will be upstairs if you need me."

"Yes, dear." Chester closed the door and crossed the street. "That was interesting, wouldn't you say?"

Win was in his rocking chair under the overhang, slowly rocking. "I wish I could sell out and leave."

"What? Where would you go?"

"Somewhere. Anywhere. Hell, I don't know. But I don't want to be here when the pistoleros and badmen start drifting in. It won't be healthy."

Chester settled into the chair he customarily claimed. "That is panic talking. You are letting Glickman spook you."

"Listen to yourself," Winifred said. "How can I have known you so long yet know you so little?"

Just then Sally Worth came out of the saloon. She wore a new dress cut low at the bosom to accent her charms. Stretching, she arched her back, then scratched herself. "I swear. I sleep in much too late. Half the day is gone and I am just waking up."

"That is some dress," Chester said, praising her.

Sally's eyes twinkled. She turned in a circle while running a hand down her body. "You really like it? I bought it with my earnings from the three days we had those bodies on display."

"Glickman was just here," Win let her know. "He asked our illustrious mayor to change his mind about our invite to the lobos of this world."

Sally put a hand to her throat. "You didn't give in, I hope?" she asked Luce.

"I did not," Chester said proudly.

"Not with his wife supplying the backbone he needed," Win said.

Grinning, Sally bent toward Chester and winked. "You see, Your Lordship? Your missus is good for something, after all."

Chester turned red. "I have never made any statements to the contrary, and I will brand as a liar anyone who says I did."

Sally Worth laughed, and after a bit, so did Chester.

"At long last I understand," Win said.

Both Chester and Sally looked at him and Chester asked suspiciously, "Understand what, might I ask?"

"When I was a sprout my ma used to read to us. She liked books about those old-time Greeks and Romans."

"Yes. So," Chester goaded when Winifred did not continue.

"One time she read about how Rome was set on fire, and while the city burned, their mayor or whatever he was played a fiddle and admired the flames." Winifred sniffed. "I never savvied how anyone could do that until just this minute."

"I thought we were friends. I take that as a slur on my office," Chester said indignantly.

"Take it however you like," Winifred responded. "Because there you two were, laughing, knowing full well we have unleashed the whirlwind."

"You worry a thing to death," Sally said.

"And you don't worry enough." Winifred resumed rocking. "But have it your way. All that is left now is for us to sit back and wait for the killing to commence."

Chapter 11

Ernestine Prescott was a hundred yards from the schoolhouse when the brazenness of what she was doing brought her up short in breathless wonder. Stars sprinkled the heavens. Behind her, artificial stars twinkled the length and breadth of Dodge City.

Not ten minutes ago, Ernestine had snuck out of the boardinghouse where she was staying. She had been scared she would bump into one of the other boarders and they would ask where she was off to. Not that nine o'clock was all that late. But for a single woman to be abroad at that hour was most unseemly. For that single woman to be the schoolmarm was a notch below scandalous.

Thankfully, Ernestine had made it out the back and down the alley. To avoid Front Street she had gone half a dozen blocks out of her way. Now here she was, about to commit the ultimate folly. If she was caught, if any parents or civic or church leaders happened by and saw a light and came to investigate, she might well be summarily dismissed.

But Ernestine was determined to see it through. Personally, she did not think she was doing anything wrong. Not really. It was not as if she was a dove working the other side of the tracks. She was a teacher, meeting a student. That the student was a grown man with whom she had spent a lot of time—alone—the past week was not a reflection on her moral fiber. Truly it wasn't. She was willing to swear on a stack of Bibles.

Ernestine hurried on. She wanted to have the door unlocked and the lamp lit when he arrived. She was so intent in groping in her bag for the key that she did not notice the gruella until it nickered. Startled, she glanced up, blurting, "Who's there?" A silly thing to say, she told herself.

A shadow came from the corner of the schoolhouse. "It's me, Jeeter. Sorry if I spooked you, ma'am."

"Not you, your horse," Ernestine said nervously. She found the key and stepped quickly to the door.

"I want to thank you again for doing this," Jeeter Frost said. "It is awful sweet of you."

Her cheeks burning, Ernestine replied, "I would do the same for any of my students."

"Maybe so," Jeeter said. "But it means a lot to me, you taking extra time like this so I can learn to read that much sooner."

"You are making fine progress, Mr. Frost." Ernestine twisted the key and entered. The inside was black as pitch. She moved along an aisle between rows of desks with the ease of long familiarity. It took a minute for her to light the lamp. She adjusted the wick and turned, nearly bumping into Jeeter Frost. "My word! You shouldn't sneak up on a person like that."

"Sorry, ma'am," Jeeter said. "Old habits, and all." He took off his hat and claimed his usual desk. "What letter are we up to again? I keep forgetting."

"You are up to *v*. All that is left is *w, x, y,* and *z*," Ernestine revealed. "Another two days, I should warrant, and you will have learned the entire alphabet."

"I'll be switched," Jeeter said with distinct pride. "Had I known learning it would be so much fun, I'd have done it years ago."

Ernestine grinned. "Few of my young charges regard schooling as fun. To them it is more akin to torture." She opened a drawer and took out the *McGuffey's Reader* Frost had been using. As she handed it to him, their fingers brushed.

"What first?" Jeeter asked. "Want me to write a *v* twenty or thirty times?"

"Actually," Ernestine said, leaning back against the desk, "before we commence your studies I was hoping you would tell me the rest of your story about that incident in Newton you were involved in."

Jeeter chuckled. "It beats me all hollow why you let me prattle on about my past. I have told you more about myself than I have ever told anyone."

"You honor me with your confidence," Ernestine said. She did not mention how illuminating the revelations had been. She felt she knew him better than she knew anyone except herself, and the knowledge she gleaned had cast this supposedly notorious killer in a whole new light.

"As for Newton, there wasn't much to it," Jeeter said. "Back in seventy-one, it was, before Dodge City came to be. Then Newton was the wildest and woolliest of the cow towns. The dance halls and saloons were open twenty-four hours of the day. A man could do anything, buy anything."

"As you can in Dodge now, south of the tracks," Ernestine commented.

"Oh, Newton was wilder, ma'am. It was about the toughest, roughest place I've ever been, and that's saying something. I spent a lot of time gambling in those days, usually at Tuttle's. One night I was there when some cowhands came up the trail from Texas."

Ernestine listened in rapt attention, her eyes shining with more than reflected lantern light.

"It was the end of the drive and they naturally decided to tear up the town. All the outfits did in those days. They would clean up and get liquored up and make the rounds of all the saloons. Six of them came into Tuttle's, and that's when the trouble began." Jeeter stopped, reliving it again in his mind's eye.

"You were playing cards, you say?" Ernestine goaded when he did not go on.

"Yes, ma'am. I had just been dealt a flush, the best hand I had all night. I bet all I had. If I had won the pot, I'd have been a couple of hundred dollars richer. In those days that was a lot."

"It still is," Ernestine felt compelled to say.

"I reckon. Anyway, along about then, some drunk punchers got into an argument with some other fellas. There was a lot of name calling and pushing and shoving, and a cowboy came stumbling out of nowhere and fell on our table and upended it. Down went the money, our cards, everything."

"That made you mad?"

"It sure as blazes did!" Jeeter exclaimed. "The cards were all mixed up on the floor. We couldn't end the hand. Everyone was given their money back, so I suppose I should have been grateful. But when I saw the cowboy who did it standing there smiling like it was a big joke, I lost my temper. I drew my revolver and pistol-whipped the bas—" Jeeter caught himself. "Sorry, ma'am. I tend to forget myself sometimes."

"That's all right. Go on," Ernestine urged.

"Well, his pards did not take kindly to me breaking his nose and a few of his teeth, so the next thing I knew, lead started to fly. Two of them were down when a slug caught me in the shoulder. It didn't break the bone but it sure hurt, and to make my predicament worse, my arm went numb."

"Oh my. What did you do?"

"The only thing I could. I border-shifted and cut loose with the Colt in my left hand. I'm not as good with my left as my right, but I ain't no slouch, neither. Two more kissed the sawdust. By then Tuttle had grabbed the scattergun he kept under the bar and roared that the next hombre who threw lead would be blowed to kingdom come."

"Blown," Ernestine said.

"What? Oh. Sorry. But that stopped the fight. Lucky for me the Newton sawbones was there and patched me up on the spot. He patched up three of the four cowboys I shot, too. The fourth was beyond patching."

"To think how close you came to meeting your maker," Ernestine said softly.

"I've come close more times than you have fingers and toes," Jeeter told her. "But I never thought much of it. It's just how things are."

"I am glad you have survived as long as you have," Ernestine said. "Otherwise we would never have met, and I would rate that a severe loss."

"Shucks, ma'am. No need to flatter me so. I know I am imposing on your goodwill and good graces."

"Mr. Frost, I say in all sincerity that I have enjoyed our sessions more than I have ever enjoyed just about anything."

Jeeter Frost did not know what to say to that. It sounded to him as if she was saying she liked him, liked him a lot, but that was ridiculous. He was a killer; she was a schoolmarm. He was the dregs of the earth; she was the salt. He was an outcast, shunned by decent folk everywhere; she was all that was pure and virtuous in the world. Finally, when he could not take the strained silence any longer, he forced out, "That was sweet of you to say, ma'am, but you don't need to pretend on my account."

"That is the first unkind thing you have said to me," Ernestine quietly responded.

At that Jeeter felt his skin grow warm, as his skin was wont to do in her company. "I would never, ever be unkind to you, ma'am. You are the kindest gal I have ever met. There is no one I hold in higher regard."

"I trust you will not consider it too bold of me if I say I hold you in high regard as well."

"I don't see how that's possible, ma'am. I shoot people, remember?"

"Please call me Ernestine. Yes, you have been quick on the trigger, but in every instance you were provoked or acting in self-defense."

Jeeter tried to wrap his mind around the incredible wonder of what she was implying. "Are you saying— surely not—that you condone the deeds I've done, ma'am?"

"My name is Ernestine. No, I do not entirely approve, but neither do I condemn you. The Good Book says to judge not, lest we be judged."

"Well," Jeeter said, at a loss as to what else to reply.

"Am I making you uncomfortable?"

"I am a mite confused, ma'am," Jeeter said. "Does this mean you think of me as a friend, sort of?"

Ernestine hesitated. Now that she had broached the subject of her feelings, she was deathly afraid of revealing more than she should. "I hold you in high regard, Mr. Frost. And again, call me Ernestine."

"This beats all." Jeeter smiled warmly. "A lady like you, saying all these nice things about me."

"You are too hard on yourself, Mr. Frost."

"No harder than everyone else is," Jeeter observed. "Most folks treat me like I have some disease, like one of those, what do you call them, lepers?"

"Society does not always heed the Good Book," Ernestine said. She realized her palms had grown sweaty and was so astounded, she lost her trail of thought.

"Ain't that the truth?" Jeeter said. "When I was little I never could savvy why everyone couldn't be nice and get along. Now I'm a lot older and I can't say I savvy it any better."

"You have a gentle soul, Mr. Frost," Ernestine remarked.

"Me, ma'am? Gentle?" Jeeter started to laugh but stopped. It would be rude, he decided. "If you say so. But I doubt there's another person anywhere in Kansas who would agree."

"Perhaps that is because they do not know you as well as I do. You have not bared your soul to them as you have to me."

Her mention of "bare" made Jeeter fidget. He suddenly felt awkward and foolish crammed into that desk, and shoving to his feet, he moved toward the window.

"Is something wrong?" Ernestine asked.

"No, ma'am. Yes, ma'am. Hell, ma'am, I am so confused, I am not sure whether I am awake or dreaming." Jeeter pressed his forehead to the pane and closed his eyes. He felt queasy, as if he was going to be sick, and strangely light-headed. Under his breath he said, "What is happening to me?"

Ernestine came up behind him. She knew full well she should not do what she was about to do, but she did it anyway. She put her hand on his shoulder. "Would you care for a glass of water? I have a pitcher."

Jeeter could not focus for the life of him. He felt her hand, and that was all. Her hand. On him. "Water would be wonderful, ma'am," he said, his throat as dry as a desert. He was almost glad when she removed her hand and stepped back to her desk. Almost. He waited, afraid to say anything. Her next question compounded his confusion.

"How old are you, Mr. Frost?" Ernestine asked as she poured.

"Thirty-one, ma'am. I am no spring chicken."

"I am thirty. We are almost the same age. I find that quite interesting. Don't you find it interesting?"

"If you say it is, then it must be," Jeeter said, uncertain how that was a factor in anything.

Ernestine brought the glass to him. "Here you go."

Their fingers touched, and Jeeter's heart skipped a couple of beats. He gratefully gulped the water and wiped his mouth with his sleeve. "Thank you, ma'am."

He hoped they would go back to his lessons so he could feel comfortable again, but it was not to be.

Gazing past him out the window at the dark prairie, Ernestine said softly, "Do you know what they call a single woman my age? A spinster. A woman who will never marry. A woman with no prospects."

"That's not true, ma'am," Jeeter said, coming to her defense. "You are as pretty as can be. There ain't a man anywhere who wouldn't be honored to come courting."

"Isn't a man anywhere," Ernestine corrected. "You flatter me, but the truth is, I am too plain and prim. In my more honest moments, I can admit my flaws and foresee the consequences."

"Flaws, ma'am?" Jeeter said. "I don't see any."

"Would you like to know the truth, Mr. Frost? I do not like being a spinster. I do not want to end my days alone."

"Ma'am?" Jeeter was ready to bolt. They were treading on territory where he would rather not tread.

"Do you really find me pretty?"

Jeeter saw where she was leading and a thunderclap filled his ears and seared his body.

"You are shocked, aren't you?" Ernestine said. "I have overstepped the boundaries. I have shamed myself and you think less of me as a woman. But you see, that is what I am, a woman. I have a woman's feelings and a woman's yearnings. Everyone else places me on a pedestal, but I tread the same earth they do."

To shut her up Jeeter did the only thing he could think of, the thing he most wanted to do. His blood roaring in his veins, he enfolded the schoolmarm in his arms and kissed her.

Chapter 12

Sheriff Hinkle had his feet propped on his desk and was reading the *National Police Gazette* when Seamus Glickman walked into the sheriff's office and over to his own desk. Without looking up Hinkle asked, "What did you find out?"

"It has been two weeks now and there has not been a lick of trouble in Coffin Varnish," Seamus reported. "The *Times* sent one of their reporters up there yesterday, and that piglet of a mayor, Chester Luce, was crying in his cups about how no curly wolves have come calling."

"I told you not to worry," Hinkle said. "I told you nothing would come of it."

"I'm still not persuaded," Seamus said. "It takes time for word to spread. We might still have a batch of murders on our hands."

"You need to learn to relax. You are too tense and high-strung." Hinkle placed the *Gazette* on his desk and leaned back with his fingers laced behind his head. "A few more weeks and everyone will have forgotten about it. Life will go on as usual."

"Damn it, George," Seamus said. "You don't take things seriously enough."

"Why get all bothered over things you can't control?" Hinkle rubbed his chin and then his stomach. "What time is it?"

"Ten o'clock."

"That's all? I'm famished. I didn't eat enough breakfast."

Seamus plopped into his chair and picked up a copy of the publication he liked best, the *Illustrated Police News.* He preferred it over the *Gazette* because the *Police News* ran more stories dealing with crimes that had to do with the ravishing of women, and he was hugely fond of ravishing women. "I hope you don't have much for me to do today. I'd like to stick around the office and take it easy."

"What kind of attitude is that for the undersheriff to have?"

"It is the same attitude the sheriff has, and I never hear him complain."

George Hinkle chortled. "And therein is the secret of a long and contented life. Never do today what you can put off until tomorrow. And never, ever get all worked up over trifles."

"Coffin Varnish isn't a trifle."

The sheriff sighed and bent to his reading. "There is a task I would like you to do some night soon."

"Oh?"

"We have had a report that a strange man has been seen hanging around the schoolhouse. A couple of parents saw him. I want you to go over there and keep a watch."

"On the schoolmarm?" Seamus laughed. "Have you ever seen a more homely female in all your born days?"

"She isn't a beauty, I will grant you that," Hinkle said. "But she *is* our schoolmarm, and if some shenanigans are going on, we need to know about it before it becomes common knowledge."

"Wonderful," Seamus said. "When do you want me to spy on her?"

"Some night soon."

"I will get around to it," Seamus said. "But what man would take up with her when there are so many prettier to be had? You couldn't pay me to ask her out."

"Now, now," Sheriff Hinkle said. "She might be a peach of a girl for all you know."

"Have you seen her? Have you talked to her? It wouldn't surprise me if she wears a chastity belt."

Hinkle laughed. "Yes, I have talked to her, and yes, she strikes me as the sort of woman who would rather be burned alive than let a man touch her. But stranger things have happened than her having a beau, and if she has found one I would like to know about it so I can smooth ruffled feathers. Again, it is not urgent. Get back to me if you learn anything."

"Yes, sir."

"Look at the bright side. At least I am not asking you to ride to Coffin Varnish again."

"The next time you should go. Maybe you will have more influence with them than I did. But watch out for the mayor's wife. She is the power behind the throne, and big enough to break you over her knee."

"Why, Seamus. Did she intimidate you?"

"Intimidate, nothing. If she were a man I would not have let her talk to me the way she did. She is one of those women who wears the britches and flaunts it."

"Well, soon you can forget about her and Coffin Varnish and their crazy scheme."

"That suits me just fine."

The sun was at its zenith when the card game got under way at the Long Branch. Aces Weaver took part, but then Aces was always at the Long Branch. His friends liked to joke that the tall drink of water lived there. Aces was a gambler but not a very good one, which was why he plied his trade in a cow town like Dodge and not on a riverboat plying the mighty Mississippi.

The second player was Joe Gentile. He worked as a clerk at Wright, Beverly and Company, the premier general store in all of Dodge. It was his day off and he had a few extra dollars, so he elected to sit in, in the hope of acquiring a few more.

On Gentile's left sat Paunch Stevens. He dabbled in real estate. To look at him, with his big belly and bald pate, he would not be deemed of any account. But Paunch also had a temper, and a Smith & Wesson he was not shy about producing when his temper was aroused. When he sat down at the table, Aces and Joe Gentile glanced at one another but did not say anything.

The last player to take a chair was William Everett Caine. He owned a freighting company and possessed more money than sense. His nickname was Club. He had a clubfoot, and limped, and was sensitive about having it brought to his attention, which was why he wore a Webley revolver in a holster next to his belt buckle for a cross draw. The Webley was an English model with a bird's-beak butt and walnut grips. It was not as common as Colts and Remingtons and Smith & Wessons, and many thought it looked downright strange. But no one mentioned that to Club Caine. He was English, and sensitive about that, too.

The game had been under way about an hour when the trouble started. Paunch Stevens slapped his cards down on the table and growled, "You win again, you damn Brit."

"I will thank you not to take that tone with me," Club said.

"What does that make now?" Paunch grumbled. "Five hands in a row? Hell, if I had your luck, I would give up selling property and gamble for a living, like Aces, here."

"In some games luck is better than others," Club said.

Paunch made a sound reminiscent of the snort of an agitated bull, then declared, "Especially when a player improves his luck any way he can. Watch how you deal the next time it is your turn."

The other players froze.

"Are you implying I cheat?" Club Caine asked in a deceptively mild manner.

Aces Weaver forced a laugh. "He's not saying any such thing, Club. The cards won't come his way, is all, and he's fit to be tied. We've all had days like that."

"Just so he is not implying I cheat," Club replied. "I will not have my reputation tarnished by the likes of him or anyone else."

"What do you mean by the likes of me?" Paunch Stevens asked. "I take that as a slur."

"Take it however you like so long as you make it clear you were not suggesting I cheat."

Paunch Stevens had been drinking since the game

began, drinking heavily. He tilted the glass to his thick lips to drain it, let out a sigh, and then said so politely and matter-of-factly that it was a full ten seconds before the import sank in, "I will do and say as I damn well please, you lime-sucking son of a bitch."

Aces Weaver saw Club Caine redden and sought to avert a catastrophe by exclaiming, "Don't take him serious, Club! He has been sucking a bottle down since he came in."

Paunch did not help any by immediately saying, "I am nowhere near drunk, thank you very much."

"You bloody bastard," Club said.

Joe Gentile thrust both hands out, blurting, "Gentlemen! Gentlemen! Let's not forget this is a friendly game. No slinging insults, if you please."

"Tell that to him," Club said stiffly.

"I will insult who I want," Paunch asserted.

Aces Weaver was sweating profusely. He had been in too many saloons when revolvers were resorted to, and he had witnessed too many bystanders take stray lead due to escalating wars of words. Again he tried to defuse the situation by turning to Paunch. "What's gotten into you? You have never acted this way before."

"Maybe I don't like Brits. Did you ever think of that?"

"Tell him the truth," Club Caine said.

"What truth?" From Joe Gentile.

"This isn't about cards. This isn't about where I am from," Club said. "It is about Harriet Fly."

"Oh Lord," Aces said.

Joe Gentile pushed his bowler back on his thatch of curly brown hair. "Who?"

Aces answered him. "Harriet Fly. She works over to the Birdcage. The tall redhead with hair down to her knees."

"The one who was on Bat Masterson's arm for a while?" Joe Gentile said. "And took up with Six-Toed Pete after Masterson moved on to greener pastures?"

"That's the one," Aces said.

"What does she have to do with our card game?"

Club Caine placed his hand on the edge of the table close to the Webley revolver in the holster next to his belt buckle. "I can tell you. You see, the popsie in question gave Pete the brush-off. Paunch tried to move in, but Harriet did not want anything to do with him. He was most persistent. It got so bad, she told him to sod off or she would go to the marshal."

"May you rot in hell," Paunch Stevens growled.

"I still don't get what she has to do with our card game," Joe Gentile admitted.

Club Caine's ruggedly handsome face split in a triumphant grin. "It is simple, young man. Harriet Fly has had me around to her apartment every night for the past week, and Paunch can't stand the thought of her favoring me over him."

"Is this true?" Joe asked Stevens.

Paunch Stevens's jaw twitched and his hands opened and closed. "Harriet Fly would have been mine if this randy goat had not come along and begged her to be his."

"I have never had to beg a woman in my life," Club Caine said, and smiled. "I can't help it if she thinks I have more to offer her than you do. In every respect," he stressed.

Pushing his chair back, Paunch rose. "Enough. Let us settle this like men should." He swept his jacket aside to reveal his Smith & Wesson. "That is, if you have the sand."

"I have more sand than you do," Club Caine said. "More sense, too. Whoever prevails is bound to wind up behind bars. The marshal has been making a point of late of cracking down on malefactors."

"On who?" Aces Weaver asked.

"Lawbreakers," Club said, enlightening him. "Especially those who break the ordinance about not wearing firearms in the city limits."

"Which no one abides by," Joe Gentile mentioned.

Paunch Stevens sneered at Caine. "Your excuse won't wash. If you were half the man Harriet thinks you are, you would go for your gun, ordinance or no ordinance."

"Not when there is a better way," Club said. "A way to satisfy our honor and not be arrested afterward."

"I am listening."

"Coffin Varnish," the Brit said.

"I saw the newspaper, the same as everyone else," Paunch responded. "It's a lot of bother to go to when we could walk out into the alley and get it over with here and now."

"Coffin Varnish," Caine repeated. "We might as well do it legally. Unless it is you who does not have a spine."

"Oh, I have backbone," Paunch spat. "More than you will ever have." He motioned. "Let's go. We can be there by dark if we hurry."

"Tomorrow morning. Will ten do?"

"What is wrong with right this minute?" Paunch Stevens asked. "I will never be more ready."

Club Caine stood and grinned. "I want to spend the night with Harriet." He gathered up his chips. "You would do well to find someone you care for to keep you company, Yank, for tomorrow you breathe your last."

"I care about me," Paunch said.

Joe Gentile was a study in anxiety. "I wish you two would reconsider. An insult is not worth dying over. Nor is a woman."

"What is, in your estimation?" Paunch demanded, and did not wait for an answer. "You are, what, twenty? That's the problem with the young today. You are not willing to die for anything." He turned and tromped off, saying over a shoulder, "See you in Coffin Varnish, Brit. I will be there promptly at ten. Don't keep me waiting."

"I can stop this, you know," Aces Weaver said. "I bet if I go to the sheriff he will send deputies to arrest the two of you."

"You do that," Club Caine said, "and the first thing I will do when I am released on bail is come looking for you, and it won't be to shake your hand."

Aces Weaver gestured in resignation. "You try to help some people and that is the thanks you get."

Chapter 13

For Coffin Varnish the day started like any other.

Out at the Anderson farm, Dolph was up before sunrise to trudge to the barn to milk the cows. Filippa was dressed by first light and went out to the chicken coop to gather eggs. She had breakfast ready when Dolph finished milking and let the cows out to pasture. After breakfast he always hitched up the wagon and took their surplus milk and eggs into town to sell to Chester Luce.

In the Giorgio household, Gemma was a firm believer in early to bed and early to rise. She always roused Minimi and their sons out of bed as dawn broke and insisted they wash up and dress before sitting at her table. Their breakfasts were small, as was the Italian custom. Coffee for her husband, milk for her sons, and eggs and a roll for everyone. The milk and eggs she bought each day at the general store.

Placido and Arturo were seldom out and about before ten. Arturo always swept out the stable while Placido fed and watered the horses. They owned three, which they rented out on those rare occasions when someone wandered in wanting to rent one.

At the general store, the mornings started punctually

at seven whether Chester wanted them to or not. Adolphina was always first up but not for long. She would wake him and, after he dressed, send him to the kitchen to make breakfast. It was a secret only they shared, since the woman was expected to do the cooking, but Adolphina hated to cook. By eight breakfast was done, Adolphina usually went back to bed, and Chester hung the OPEN sign in the front window. Usually Dolph arrived to sell his eggs and milk by eight thirty.

Winifred Curry did not stick to a routine. He got up when he felt like it, usually between eight and ten, and opened the saloon. Then he treated himself to his first drink of the day and ate if he was hungry.

Sally Worth slept in as long as she wanted. Some mornings she was up early; other times she did not appear until early afternoon. Whether she had plied her trade the night before had a lot to do with when she stirred.

On this particular morning Sally couldn't sleep, so she was up and dressed by nine. She had Win pour her a drink and went out and sat in one of the rocking chairs to enjoy the relative coolness while it still lasted. She was peacefully rocking and sipping when a rider came up the street from the south and drew rein at the hitch rail. He had a big belly and wore nice clothes, which told Sally he made a decent living at whatever he did, which piqued her interest. "Good morning, there, handsome."

Paunch Stevens smiled. "I have been called a lot of things, lady, but that is not one of them." He stiffly dismounted and swore. "Why can't someone invent a comfortable saddle? My backside is killing me."

"Would you like it massaged?"

Paunch blinked, and regarded her with renewed interest. "A fallen dove, here? You must be rich and do it for the fun."

Sally laughed. "I wish. I scrape by, barely, and only by the good graces of the gent who owns this saloon."

"Ah. He is your man," Paunch said.

"Not how you mean, no. He is a friend, a good friend. Him and me go a long ways back."

"You don't say." Paunch came under the overhang and swatted dust from his suit. "Perhaps after I conclude my business here today, you and I can get together. I will be in a mood to celebrate."

Sally came out of the rocking chair as if she had been shoved. Beaming, she hooked her arm in his. "Mister, I am all yours."

"Not until I conclude my business."

"What would that be, if you don't mind my asking?"

"I am here to shoot someone," Paunch informed her, and headed into the saloon. He wanted to fortify himself before Caine arrived. His anger of the day before had faded and been replaced by a cold dash of reality. "I understand it is legal in this town."

"Oh my," Sally said. "I was beginning to think the mayor wasted money on that notice in the newspaper."

"How is that again?" Paunch asked as he steered her toward the bar.

"You are the first person to come here to kill, mister. Congratulations, I guess."

Win was wiping the counter. He greeted Paunch Stevens, poured him a rye, and listened to him explain why he was there. "So it has come to pass. You better go fetch the mayor, Sally."

Grumbling, Sally went out.

Chester Luce was rearranging the dry goods when the bell over the door tinkled. He liked to rearrange. When business was slow, which was practically always, he sometimes spent entire days moving items from one shelf to another and back again. Turning, he hid his surprise at seeing Sally. She rarely came into the store, in large part because Adolphina made no secret of her disdain for loose women. "Miss Worth. What can I do for you?"

"I have brought news, Mayor," Sally said, casting a worried glance at the door to the Luce living quarters.

"Is that ornery pig making a nuisance of himself again?" Chester asked. "I keep telling those Mexicans to keep it penned up."

"It is not the pig," Sally said. "It is your wish come true. There is a man over to the saloon who has come here to kill somebody."

"Really and truly?" Chester said, excitement coursing through him like rapids through a chasm. "I had about given up hope."

"Better hurry on over there before he changes his mind," Sally Worth suggested.

"I take it you do not approve?"

"Not of killing, I don't. I have seen my share, heard about a lot more, and if there is one thing I have learned, it is that no good ever comes of taking a human life."

"Oh, come now," Chester said. "No good comes from taking the life of outlaws? No good comes from taking the lives of marauding Indians? Your argument is specious."

"I don't even know what that means," Sally said.

"And I'm not arguing, Your Honor. I am telling you God's gospel truth."

"With all due respect, Miss Worth, what do you know of the Almighty? You, a blatant sinner."

Sally Worth appraised him critically, then said, "Well, now. I always thought you were different from your wife, but I was wrong. Yes, I am a sinner, but who among us isn't? Just because I part my legs for money does not mean I don't know the difference between what is right and what is wrong, and what you have done is wrong."

"I didn't hear you object when all those people came to town to view the bodies," Chester noted. "You about wore yourself out those three days, which is quite a feat considering you were flat on your back. How much did you earn?"

"That was low, Chester," Sally said.

"It was God's gospel truth, to quote you. So do not presume to take on airs with me. You stand to benefit as much as the rest of us off the killing you so despise."

"At my age I can't afford not to," Sally said. "But that does not mean I have to like it."

"Whether you do or you don't is of no consequence," Chester said flatly. "And for your information, you and I are in the same boat as everyone else in Coffin Varnish. Our town is in desperate need of an influx of money or it will wither and die. If it helps, think of the killing as a civic necessity."

"You have air between your ears," Sally said.

Chester walked toward the pegs on which his jacket and hat were hung. "I thank you for coming to tell me. You may go now." He did not turn around until the bell tinkled and the door closed. Before leaving he went to the full-length mirror and checked that his suit was dust-free. In politics, impressions were everything.

The sun's glare made Chester squint. He hurried across the street, noticed a sorrel at the hitch rail with a fairly expensive saddle. Its owner was at the bar, drinking. Win was behind the bar. There was no sign of Sally Worth, which suited Chester just fine. He liked her but she had a tendency to forget her station in the scheme of things.

Introductions were made.

Paunch Stevens got right to the point. "In a little while a gent by the name of Club Caine will show up. He and I are at odds. We have agreed to shoot it out and came to your town to do the deed."

"I commend you on your decision," Chester said. "You will find that we bend over backwards to make this as easy as we can."

"What is the first step?" Paunch asked.

"Maybe it would be best to address both of you at the same time," Chester said. "So I do not need to repeat myself."

"I suppose that makes sense." Paunch emptied his glass and asked Win Curry to refill it.

"Haven't you had enough?"

"I will decide whether I have or I haven't," Paunch said. He smacked the glass down on the counter.

Win shrugged and poured. Long ago he had learned not to argue with belligerent drunks.

Chester asked for a whiskey, then went out and sat in a rocking chair. No sooner was he comfortable than a rider appeared. He guessed who it was. With growing excitement he waited for the next participant to arrive, and when the rider finally drew rein, Chester studied him with interest. He noticed how the man limped when he turned from the hitch rail, and noticed, too, the unusual revolver the man wore. "You would be the other duelist."

"The what?" Club Caine said. "Oh. Yes. I guess I am, at that, although I do not regard this as a duel in the strict sense of the term." He nodded at the other horse at the hitch rail. "Paunch Stevens is already here, I gather?"

"He showed up about an hour ago," Chester said. Rising, he extended his hand and revealed who he was. "Now that you are here, I can explain to both of you exactly how this works."

Club Caine flexed his bad leg a few times. "There is really only one thing I want to know. Who sees to the burying, afterward? I will be damned if I lift a finger in his behalf."

Chester stepped to the batwings and called out for Paunch Stevens to join them.

Paunch took his time. He had heard the horse ride up. He finished his drink, paid, and strolled out, not at all concerned that the liquor had him feeling as if he could walk on clouds. "So you actually came?"

"Did you hope I wouldn't so you could go around telling everyone I am afraid of you?"

Chester moved between them. "Gentlemen, if you please. Save the barbs for later. We have business to discuss. How about if we repair to the bar as this might take a while?"

"I wouldn't mind another drink," Paunch Stevens said.

"None for me," Caine declared.

Paunch snickered. "Any man who can't hold liquor usually can't shoot worth a damn, either."

"You will find out just how well I shoot soon enough."

Chester waved his hands. "Enough of this bickering. Mr. Stevens, you go first. I will follow with Mr. Caine."

"Make sure he doesn't shoot me in the back," Paunch said. "That would be his style."

"You despicable pig," Club said.

Paunch Stevens laughed.

To Winifred Curry, the advent of the three into his saloon was immediate cause for worry. "No shooting in here! It took me half a day to clean up the blood from the last mess."

Chester puffed out his chest and grandly sauntered to the bar. "The shooting will take place in the street. We must first discuss the preliminaries."

"The what?" Paunch Stevens said.

"The permit fee, the burial costs," Chester recited. "All those must be dealt with before you can draw your guns."

"The hell you say?"

"Didn't you read our notice in the *Times*? Mention was made of all of it," Chester said.

Club Caine nodded. "I read the notice."

"Good. Then as soon as you each have paid the fee and signed the form our lawyer drew up, I will set a time for the killing to commence."

"Hold on," Paunch said. "What is this fee you keep mentioning? And why in hell do we have to sign something?"

"The form releases Coffin Varnish of all liability,"

Chester explained. "Our lawyer thought it prudent. After all, we do not want you to blame our town if all you do is cripple one another."

"You have thought of everything," Club Caine said.

"I've tried," Chester said. "Although, the truth be told, it was my wife who insisted we talk to a lawyer and have papers drawn up."

"You still haven't said how much the fee will be," Paunch noted. "No one mentioned anything about any damn fee."

"Surely you did not think you could kill for free?" Chester replied. "Each of you must obtain a permit."

The door at the back opened and in came Sally Worth. She had brushed her hair and changed into her best dress. "How do I look now?" she asked Paunch Stevens, but he did not answer.

"How much do these permits cost?"

"One hundred dollars."

"Each?" Paunch said in amazement.

"Each," Chester said. "Then there is the burial cost. Another fifty from each of you, to be used only if you are killed and returned to you if you are not."

"Let me get this straight," Paunch said. "You expect us to give you one hundred and fifty dollars before we can squeeze a trigger?"

"That is correct," Chester confirmed.

"Why, that is nothing but out and out robbery," Paunch complained, "and I, for one, will not stand for it. I came here to kill this English son of a bitch and that is exactly what I aim to do." With that, Paunch stabbed a hand for his Smith & Wesson.

Chapter 14

Seamus Glickman was the only one in the sheriff's office when Aces Weaver hurried in. Seamus looked up from the *Illustrated Police News* and nodded in friendly greeting. He had played cards with Weaver a few times. Then Seamus saw the expression on the gambler's face. "If it is trouble I do not want to hear about it."

"It could be trouble," Aces Weaver said.

"I do not want to hear it." Seamus resumed reading and did his best to ignore the man standing barely three feet from his desk. But he could not ignore Weaver's feet. They poked into the edge of his vision like unwanted intruders. "Why haven't you left yet?"

"I need to talk to someone," Aces said. "If not you, then Sheriff Hinkle."

"He is in court, giving testimony," Seamus revealed. "He will not be in until later today, if then."

"One of the deputies, then?" Aces hopefully asked.

"All performing official duties," Seamus said. "I have been left to hold down the fort."

"Who is upholding the law?"

"Very funny," Seamus said, but he was not amused, not in the least. Irritated, he tried to concentrate on the lurid account of a buxom young woman from Philadelphia who fell into the clutches of opium fiends. The drawings that accompanied the story were enough to make a prostitute blush.

"I will wait for a deputy, then," Aces said.

"Like hell you will. I do not intend to sit here all day being assaulted by your feet."

"My what?"

"I know I will regret asking," Seamus said, "but what is so all-fired important that it can't wait?"

"It is about Coffin Varnish."

"Why did I ask?" Seamus spread the newspaper on his desk and leaned on his elbows to read it. "I guess you haven't heard. There is to be no mention of that wretched excuse for a town in my presence."

"What do you have against Coffin Varnish?"

"What don't I?" Seamus retorted. "The mayor's backbone is in his wife's body. The saloon owner is drinking his own saloon dry. The town whore is old enough to have been around before the Flood. And the entire population consists of two bean-eaters, a family of pope lovers, and a Swede with less brains than my little toe. Shall I go on?"

"You didn't mention the notice in the newspaper," Aces Weaver said. "Inviting folks to go there and kill each other."

"You had to remind me of that, didn't you?"

"It is why I am here."

Resigned to the fact that the gambler was not going to leave unless shooed away, Seamus reluctantly stopped reading about the buxom young woman and sat back. "All right. Since you persist in being a pest, I will listen to what you have to say. Then you will leave and never grace our doorstep again for as long as you live."

"You are joshing me, right?"

"Of course," Seamus said. "Now out with it. The Arabs have just got their hands on Pearl Trueblood and I am anxious to learn her fate."

"Arabs?" Aces said. "Here in Dodge?"

Seamus tapped the *Police News*. "Get to the point of your visit. You are sorely trying my patience."

"Do you know Club Caine?"

"He owns a freight line."

"And Paunch Stevens?"

"He owns half of Front Street. Two of our city's more prominent citizens, I would say."

"They won't be prominent much longer. They left this morning for Coffin Varnish to kill each other."

Seamus stiffened in alarm. This was serious business. Caine was a close personal friend of people high in state government, and Stevens had strong political ties to a senator. "Please tell me it is you who is joshing me?"

"I would like to but I can't."

"What put them at odds?"

"I believe her name is Harriet Fly. I have not met the lady myself, but I understand she boasts the biggest melons this side of the Mississippi."

"Caine and Stevens left earlier, you say?" Seamus asked, rising.

"I don't know exactly when. To be honest, I didn't expect them to go through with it. But Joe Gentile told me he saw Caine ride out a couple of hours ago, heading north."

"A couple of hours?" Seamus consulted the clock

on the wall. "Damn. They are probably there by now."

"Most likely," Aces agreed. "About all you can do is pick up the pieces."

Seamus gave the artistic rendering of Pearl Trueblood a last longing gaze, then made for the door. "At least I will have tried."

Ernestine Prescott found it hard to concentrate on the American Revolution when all she could think of was Jeeter Frost. She could still feel his lips on hers even though he had slipped away from the schoolhouse well before dawn so as to avoid being spotted by early risers.

Ernestine nearly giggled. Her behavior had become downright wicked. If the parents of her charges learned what she was doing, they would dismiss her without hesitation. A schoolmarm was expected to be the living embodiment of moral and ethical virtue. Much to her surprise, and great delight, she had discovered she was, after all, as human as the next woman.

Ernestine had never met a man like Jeeter. He wasn't cultured or educated. He wasn't rich. But there was something about him, some quality she could not define, that made him irresistible. When she was around him, all she wanted to do was touch him. Her, of all people. She had never been with a man in her life, and only ever kissed one once, and here she was, behaving like a hussy and jeopardizing her teaching career.

Suddenly Ernestine became aware that her charges were staring at her. "Who can tell me why the minutemen were called that?" She scanned the rows and pointed at her brightest student. "How about you, Sarah?"

Instead of answering, Sarah raised her hand and pointed at the window. That was when it dawned on Ernestine that her class was not staring at her; they were staring at something behind her. She turned, half fearing Jeeter had broken his promise to stay away during school hours, and felt her stomach tighten at the sight of a middle-aged couple, the parents of Billy Doughty, the class troublemaker. She smiled at them but they did not return the smile. Puzzled, she motioned for them to come around to the front of the schoolhouse.

"Why are your parents here, Billy?" Ernestine asked as she went past his desk. She had talked to them a month ago when Billy saw fit to bring a garter snake into class to try and scare the girls.

"I don't know, Miss Prescott," the boy dutifully answered, but something in his eyes alerted her that he did in fact know but was not saying.

Her mouth went dry. "Continue reading your history book, everyone," Ernestine directed as she opened the door and stepped out into the bright sunlight.

The Doughtys were coming around the corner. Mrs. Doughty, always a severe woman, looked more severe than usual. She had her thin hands clasped in front of her and wore a drab gray dress and gray bonnet. "Miss Prescott, we need to have a word with you."

"Certainly," Ernestine said. "But your boy has been behaving himself of late."

"It is not William we are here to discuss," Mrs. Doughty said. "It is you."

Panic welled up in Ernestine, but she smiled and said calmly, "Me? In what regard, Mrs. Doughty?"

"You know very well."

Mr. Doughty shot his wife a look of disapproval, but only Ernestine noticed. "I am sure I have no idea."

"Very well. I will speak plainly." Mrs. Doughty paused. "A man was seen leaving your schoolhouse at an hour most folks consider ungodly."

Ernestine grew so light-headed she thought she would swoon, but she did not let on. "Who saw this man leave?"

"I am not at liberty to say."

"What hour was it?"

"Before dawn, I was told," Mrs. Doughty said, and sniffed. "Heaven knows what he was doing here."

Mr. Doughty frowned. "Be civil, Abigail."

"I have the children to think of," Mrs. Doughty said. "A thing like this must be addressed."

"What thing?" Ernestine went on the offensive. "For the life of me, I do not see what this has to do with me. In the first place, as you both well know, I seldom stay past dark. In the second place, did this informant of yours actually see this man leave by the door?" She had them there. Jeeter always snuck out by the window.

"Well, no," Mrs. Doughty said. "But he was seen very near the schoolhouse."

"So he could have just been passing by?" Ernestine pressed her.

With great reluctance Mrs. Doughty said, "I suppose."

"Was this man seen in my company at any time?"

"Not to my knowledge, no."

"Then what are you suggesting?" Ernestine asked. "You know me, Abigail. Are you implying I am a loose woman?"

Mrs. Doughty became flustered. "No, no, I would never do that. I was merely bringing it to your attention."

"For which I thank you. Hopefully, no one has spread this behind my back. A lady has her reputation to think of."

"Indeed," Mr. Doughty said. "Come along, Abigail. We have imposed on her enough."

"I appreciate your coming to me," Ernestine said, relieved she had nipped the rumor in the bud.

"I thought you should know," Mrs. Doughty said. "Especially with the sheriff involved."

Ernestine's world spun and nearly crashed. "What was that?"

"The sheriff," Mrs. Doughty said. "The person who told me also reported it to Sheriff Hinkle. No one from his office has been around?"

"No," Ernestine said, struggling to come to grips with the implications of the stunning revelation. "Evidently the sheriff has more faith in my virtue than the person who is spreading loose tales about me."

"I told you," Mr. Doughty said sternly to his wife. "We should not have come here. Now I feel the fool."

"It had to be done."

They walked off arguing.

Ernestine gripped the doorjamb to keep from collapsing. Her legs had gone weak and her knees were threatening to buckle. She was deathly afraid, but not for herself. She could deal with the gossip. No, she was afraid for Jeeter. If the sheriff or a deputy caught him leaving the schoolhouse, there would be Hades to pay.

Ernestine needed to think. She needed to be alone. But the school day was hardly half over. Composing herself, she closed the door and returned to her desk. She picked up a pencil and, without seeing them, stared at a sheath of papers that needed to be graded.

Another dimension to her dilemma occurred to her. If she told Jeeter, he might take it into his head to make himself scarce. He would not tangle with the law if he could avoid it. He had told her once that one of the reasons he had lasted so long was that he never shot a lawman and in fact went out of his way to avoid them.

He might leave.

The thought seared Ernestine like a flaming sword. Her heart hammered in her chest and she had to take deep breaths. That must not happen. Jeeter meant a great deal to her, more than anyone, ever. She did not want to lose him.

Ernestine wavered. Maybe she should keep it to herself for the time being. Since the sheriff had not been around, odds were, she reasoned, that Jeeter and she could go on as they were doing.

Her eyes moistened at the injustice of it all. Life was so unfair. Here, she had finally found a man she cared for, and circumstances over which she had no control were conspiring to tear him away from her. She refused to let that happen. She would stand firm and do whatever was necessary to ensure that Jeeter and she enjoyed the happiness to which they were entitled.

Her decision made, Ernestine busied herself with

her duties. But keeping silent did not sit well with her. It was the coward's way out, and Ernestine was a firm believer in confronting problems head-on.

She was in the middle of the daily spelling lesson when a solution to her crisis hit her with the force of a thunderclap. She had just asked a student to spell the word *myopic*. He did, but she stood there, too overcome to tell him he had spelled it properly and could sit back down.

Did she dare? Ernestine wondered. The step was so bold, so brazen, as to dazzle her with her own shamelessness. Or was it shameless if the two people truly cared for one another?

The question sparked another: Did Jeeter Frost care for her as much as she cared for him?

Ernestine realized he had never once said how he felt. He had never once given voice to his feelings. For all she knew—she nearly gasped at the notion— she was a mere dalliance, a woman he kept coming to visit because she let him do things women should not let men do.

"Oh my!" Ernestine blurted.

"Miss Prescott? Are you all right?"

With a start, Ernestine saw that every child in the room was staring fixedly at her with concern writ on their youthful faces. "I fear I have a bit of a headache today, Sarah, but thank you for asking. Horace, you did fine. That is how you spell myopic."

Myopic, Ernestine thought. How fitting, and how ironic. She must find out how Jeeter felt about her, and if she was a dalliance—if that was all she was to him—she would buy a knife or a straight razor and slit her wrists.

Chapter 15

Chester Luce had talked it over with Adolphina and they had decided that all the pistol duels would take place in the street. Safer for Coffin Varnish's citizens, however few there were. They had also decided the duels would take place one hour after the permits were paid for, to have ample time to notify everyone.

"If we do this right," Adolphina had said, "if we take sufficient precautions, the killings will go off without a hitch. The leather slappers will be happy with how smoothly everything goes. We will be happy with the money we are making. All will be well."

But all was decidedly *not* well.

Chester was appalled when Paunch Stevens tried to jerk his six-shooter. "No, by God!" he bawled, and lunged at Stevens, grabbing his wrist.

"Not in here!" Win Curry yelled, whipping a shotgun from under the bar. "I will blow you in half!"

Sally Worth, incredibly enough, laughed.

Only Club Caine was calm and silent. He made no attempt to draw his Webley, although when Stevens went for his hardware, Caine swooped his hand to the Webley.

Paunch Stevens was furious. "Let go of me, damn you! You could have gotten me killed!"

"You, sir, are in violation of town ordinance," Chester countered, even though, the truth be told, there was no town ordinance covering a situation like this. Chester was making it up as he went along.

"To say nothing of being a cheap bastard," Sally Worth threw in.

Paunch fixed his glare on her. "How is that again?"

"You want to have it out with this other gent," Sally said, "but you don't want to pay for the permit and the burial. I call that cheap. So will most everyone else who hears about it."

To Chester's immense relief, her comment caused Paunch Stevens to deflate like a punctured water skin.

Stevens took his hand off the Smith & Wesson. "I suppose I was being a bit rash. But a hundred and fifty dollars seems outrageous."

Chester released Stevens's wrist but was ready to grab it again if need be. "Outrageous? For the privilege of killing a man? Where else in Kansas, where else *anywhere,* can you do what we are giving you the opportunity to do?"

"That is true, but—" Paunch Stevens began.

Now that the scare was over, Chester was mad—good and mad. He poked Stevens in the chest. "No buts about it! If you think we are only in this for the money, you are wrong." Actually, they were, but Chester had never been one to let the truth stand in the way of a good lie. "If that were the case, we would demand a lot more than a hundred dollars. For the service we are offering, a thousand would be more than fair."

Sally Worth cackled. She had poured herself a drink

and was nursing it at the end of the bar, her elbows under her. "If you charged that much, no one could afford it."

"When I want comments from you I will ask for them."

Sally arched an eyebrow. "Don't take that high and mighty tone with me, mister."

"Hush," Chester said.

"Like hell I will!" Sally declared. "I know you, Chester. You and that wife of yours, lording it over the rest of us."

Winifred said, "Sally, please."

"Oh, you are no better than he is," Sally snapped. "Why you went along with this harebrained notion, I will never know. Or is money all you care about, too?"

"That is unfair," Win said, "and untrue. I have never been all that interested in being rich. Hell, if I was, do you think I'd have stayed in this godforsaken excuse for a town as long as I have?"

Sally had no answer for that.

"I stay because I like the pace of life," Win said. "I like things slow and easy. I like not having to shave if I don't want to, or having a boss breathe over my shoulder."

Club Caine thumped the bar to get their attention. "I did not ride all this way to listen to you people bandy your petty problems about. Let's get this over with. That is, if Mr. Stevens is still eager for this to be his last day on earth."

Paunch Stevens bristled and started to reach for his revolver but stopped and snarled, "The sooner I can empty my pistol into you, the better I will feel."

Apparently everything was striking Sally as hilarious because she laughed anew, then said, "Grown men acting like ten-year-olds. There are times I am mighty glad I am a woman, and this is one of them."

"What are you on about?" Club Caine asked her.

"Men," Sally said. "How silly they are. You don't see grown women waving revolvers at each other, do you?"

"You are threepence short of a shilling yourself," Club Caine said.

Sally tilted her head. "What did you just say?"

"That you are a bit dotty," Club answered. "It must be because you have about gone by."

"You are English, aren't you? With that accent and all."

"I was born and raised in a city called Liverpool, yes," Club revealed. "Why do you ask?"

"It explains why you talk so strange," Sally said. "You being a foreigner and all."

Paunch Stevens snorted. "You tell him, lady."

"Sod off, the both of you," Club rejoined, then turned to Chester Luce. "I have had all the silliness I can take for one day. Where are the permits? Is there a form for us to sign?"

Chester was momentarily at a loss. It was Adolphina who had come up with the idea of requiring permits, and he had thought it delightful once she explained about the fees he should collect. But it had never occurred to him to go have the permits printed, or even to draw them up himself.

"Well?" Club Caine asked. "Is there a problem?"

"There is nothing to sign," Chester said. "You pay the fee, I make out the form and keep it on file."

"One form for both of us or one form for each of us?"

Chester almost said, "What the hell difference does it make?" He could not understand why the Englishman was making such a fuss. "One form for each of you. I will need you to write down your names, where you live, next of kin, that sort of thing."

"What are we to write with?"

Chester's irritation mounted. He had not thought to bring ink, pen, and paper. "To make things easier, just tell me what I need to know and I will write it down later. I have a good memory."

"Rather a shoddy way of doing things," Club Caine said. "Wouldn't it make more sense for us to write it on the actual permit? Why do I have the impression you do not have this whole thing worked out yet?"

"Nonsense," Chester said. To agree was to suggest he did not know what he was doing. He turned to the bar. "Win, can I borrow paper and something to write with?"

Winifred came back with "How do you borrow paper? Once you use it, it is of no use to me."

"Quit quibbling and help out," Chester chided.

"I would like to oblige you but I can't. The only paper in this whole place are the labels on the bottles."

"Organized as hell," Club Caine muttered. "Bloody Yanks."

"I have plenty of paper in my store," Chester said. "If you two gentlemen would be so kind as to follow me, we will soon have the preliminaries out of the way and you can get down to the killing."

"That suits me just fine," Paunch Stevens said. He

had refilled his glass and took a healthy swig. "All this jabbering made me thirsty."

"I am surrounded by idiots," Club Caine said. "But very well. Let us repair to your establishment." He started toward the batwings.

Chester turned to follow, promising, "The delay will be short, I can assure you."

"Jabber, jabber, jabber," Paunch Stevens said. He set down his empty glass and winked at Winifred Curry. As he winked he drew the Smith & Wesson. Win opened his mouth to shout, but Paunch pointed the gun at him, put a finger to his lips, and shook his head. Then, grinning, he extended the revolver in the direction of Club Caine. "It is a good thing you are so short, Mr. Mayor."

"What did you say?" Chester had not been paying attention. He glanced over his shoulder and very nearly screamed. The Smith & Wesson's muzzle seemed to be pointed right at him. "No!" he bleated.

"Don't mind if I do," Paunch Stevens said.

Thunder boomed, and a leaden bee buzzed past Chester's ear. In pure reflex he fell to the floor, squawking in terror.

Club Caine was knocked violently forward. He stumbled, recovered, and sank to one knee. Unlimbering the Webley, he pivoted, a look of intense concentration on his face.

Paunch Stevens laughed. "That will teach you to steal my woman." He took a step, swaying slightly, and sighted down the barrel. Again his revolver spewed smoke and lead.

The slug missed.

Club Caine gripped the Webley with both hands

and was taking deliberate aim. Beads of sweat had broken out on his face. "Back shooter!" he rasped.

"Tea drinker." Paunch fired a third time and a corner of the left batwing exploded in a shower of wood slivers. "Damn." He stared at his revolver in disbelief. "How do I miss at this range?"

"I won't," Club Caine said. The Webley cracked and Stevens's hat went flying. "Bollocks!"

"Stop shooting!" Chester shouted, waving an arm. "You haven't paid for your permits yet!"

Paunch took an unsteady step. "Forget your stupid permit. In another couple of seconds this will all be over."

"That it will!" Club Caine cried, and banged off his second shot. He winced as he fired, and his whole body twitched.

"Ha!" Paunch Stevens bellowed. "You couldn't hit the broad side of a barn if you were standing next to it." His Smith & Wesson bucked. "Take that, woman stealer!"

Club Caine looked down at himself. "Bloody hell," he said. "You missed again. Drink more whiskey, why don't you?" Suddenly rising, he lurched toward his enemy. "I will do this right even if you can't."

"Can't I?" Paunch angrily countered. "This time for sure."

"Enough!" Win Curry had his shotgun. But he could not decide which one to point it at, so he was not pointing it at either of them when Caine and Stevens pointed their revolvers at him. Win ducked, not a heartbeat too soon, and the mirror behind the bar, the mirror he had sent all the way to St. Louis for, dissolved in a shower of broken bits.

Paunch Stevens laughed and swung back toward Club Caine. "That will teach the meddler!"

"That it will!" Caine continued limping toward him. "Out of my way!" he commanded the quaking figure at his feet.

Chester Luce was happy to oblige. He was awhirl with fear. Everything had gotten out of control. He would be lucky now if *he* was not killed! Staying on the floor, he scrambled under a table and threw his arms over his head.

"Lily-livers," Paunch spat. He was trying to aim at Caine. Then Caine's Webley went off and he was punched in his big belly by an invisible fist. There wasn't much pain, certainly not enough to prevent him from squeezing off another shot of his own. "I will do you in if it is the last thing I do."

Club Caine only had a few feet to go. "Boasts and hot air!" he cried. "Hot air and boasts!"

Paunch Stevens was trying to remember if he had fired four shots or five. If he only had one shot left, he must be sure not to miss. "How many shots do I have left? I have lost count."

"Count this," Club Caine said. By then he was close enough to press the Webley against Stevens's ribs and fire.

"Damn you," Paunch Stevens said. He looked down at the bright scarlet stain spreading across his belly. "That one hurt." His legs trembled and he staggered. Thrusting out his other arm, he braced himself against the bar to keep from falling. "You better not have hit my vitals."

"Bloody hell. Why aren't you dead yet?" Club

Caine stepped back and sought to steady his Webley in both hands.

It was then that Sally Worth did something she should not have done, something people commented on for months afterward whenever the affray was talked about. Sally laughed and merrily exclaimed, "You two are pitiful! My grandmother can shoot straighter than you and she has never shot a gun in her life."

"Think so, do you?" Paunch Stevens said. Rankled by her insult, he snapped off a shot in Sally's general direction. He did not aim. He was just so mad, he wanted to shut her up.

Everyone saw the result. Paunch, Club Caine, who glanced at her when the Smith & Wesson went off, Win, who had poked his head up from behind the bar, and Chester, peeking from under the table. They all saw a hole appear in the center of Sally's forehead even as the rear of her cranium erupted in a shower of brains and gray and brown hair. Under different circumstances her look of amazement would have been comical. As it was, she collapsed without a sound, pinkish fluid seeping from the new hole.

"I'll be damned!" Paunch exclaimed in delight. "I hit something."

"You are an inspiration," Club Caine said. Lunging, he jammed the Webley's muzzle against Stevens's forehead and emptied the Webley into the man's skull. He had to step aside to avoid being bowled over as the heavy bulk fell.

Then he was the one gripping the bar for support, and smiling. "All's well that ends well, eh?"

Chapter 16

Seamus Glickman was a quarter of a mile out of Coffin Varnish when an inner sense that he was being followed prompted him to glance over his shoulder. Despite his feeling he did not really expect to see anyone, so he was mildly taken aback to behold a rider seeking to overtake him. The man was riding like a madman, at a full gallop, arms and legs flapping as if he were an ungainly goose trying to take wing. When Seamus recognized the flapper, his surprise changed to anger, and he drew rein.

The other was not long in coming up beside him. The man's mount was lathered with sweat and winded.

"Trying to ride that poor beast into the ground, are you?" Seamus asked.

"I would ride ten into the ground to get a good story," Frank Lafferty answered. He, too, was slick with sweat. "And a shooting is always news."

"Let me guess," Seamus said. "Aces Weaver told you?"

"It might turn out to be the best dollar for a tip I ever spent," Lafferty said enthusiastically. "Think of it. Two of Dodge City's leading citizens swapping lead over a woman!"

"Nine times out of ten, there is a woman involved

somewhere," Seamus mentioned. The tenth time was either a long-standing grudge or resentment over a slur.

"Harriet Fly, no less," Lafferty said. "A cow in a dress. How any man would take to fighting over her is beyond me."

"There is no accounting for taste, boy," Seamus said. He clucked to his mount and the young journalist did the same. "I don't suppose if I ask you to turn around and go back to Dodge that you would?"

"You must be joking," Lafferty rejoined in disbelief.

"Some stories are better not written."

"But if there has been a shooting—" Lafferty started to argue.

"All the more reason," Seamus said, raising his voice over the drum of hooves. "Listen. So long as no one took the idiots in Coffin Varnish up on their addlepated notion, the sheriff did not mind their lunacy. But if Caine and Stevens have swapped lead, they have opened the floodgates. A thing like this could catch on and bring no end of trouble."

"Aren't you making more out of it than there might be?"

"No, boy, I am not. Sheriff Hinkle does his best to make the Jeeter Frosts of this world unwelcome in Ford County. Now, thanks to the jackasses in Coffin Varnish, we are extending an invite to every curly wolf from here to California and back again to come and kill. Can't you see the problems that will cause?"

"All the more reason for me to write about it," Lafferty said. "So I can present your side of the issue. So the people can be informed."

Seamus had not thought of that. Public outrage was a powerful force—force politicians were more apt to respond to than anything else. "It has to be done right."

"Never fear. I won't glorify it if blood has indeed been spilled," Lafferty said. "Maybe nothing has come of it, though. Maybe they came to their senses and called it off."

Seamus was not optimistic. Paunch Stevens had a notorious temper, and Club Caine was not to be trifled with.

A commotion at the saloon did not bode well. The Mexicans were there, standing in the hot sun in their sombreros. The Italian family was under the overhang, the boys trying to peer in the window, the mother not letting them. No one said a word as Seamus strode inside. He stopped at the sight of two bodies and a god-awful amount of blood. "Son of a bitch," he snapped.

"I will thank you to keep a civil tongue in your head," Adolphina Luce said. She was bent over Club Caine, who was in a chair, stripped to the waist. "There is a lady present."

Seamus almost asked, "Where?" but bit it off. He stared at the dead dove, then at what was left of Paunch Stevens, then at Win Curry, who had his lips glued to a bottle and was as pale as a sheet. Chester Luce was watching his wife tend Club Caine's wound. Seamus went over. "How bad is he?"

"I can answer for myself," Club said. "The cur nicked me in the shoulder. In a month I will be as good as new." He smiled broadly. "As you can see, he got the worst of our exchange."

"I want details," Seamus said. "You might be charged with murder."

"Not bloody likely seeing as he shot first."

"That's true, Sheriff," Chester Luce said, his voice squeaking more than normal. "If there was ever an instance of self-defense, this was it."

"You and your damned stupid idea," Seamus said.

Adolphina looked up, her washcloth poised. "I will not remind you again, Sheriff Glickman. I will be treated with respect whether you want to treat me with respect or not."

Seamus, angry as hell, said to Caine, "How could you? I can understand Paunch. He never could think straight when his dander was up. But you I credited with more sense."

"Thank you," Club said. "But some things just need to be done. He was talking about me behind my back and insulting a lady of my acquaintance."

"Hardly cause to kill a man."

"Do you suffer insults?" Club asked. "From what I have heard, no, you do not. You are a fine one to cast stones."

"Oh, hell," Seamus said, and turned. Lafferty was hunkered by Paunch Stevens and furiously scribbling notes. "What are you writing?"

"Descriptions, while they are fresh and vivid. Half his head is missing! It is gloriously hideous."

"The whole world has gone insane," Seamus opined, and moved to the bar. "Give me a drink. I don't care what so long as it is not water."

Winifred Curry's eyes were moist. "I liked her," he said hoarsely as he slid a bottle across. "Liked her a lot. She and I were friends for years."

"The whore?" Seamus said without thinking.

"Who else?" Win chugged more bug juice. "I swear, I am going to get so booze blind, I can't stand up."

"Before that happens, suppose I start with you. Tell me everything you saw, everything you heard. Leave nothing out."

It took half an hour for Seamus to get the statements. When he was done he went out for a breath of air. The Mexicans and the Italian family were still there, and so were the Swedish farmer and his wife. "I trust you are all proud of yourselves," Seamus said bitterly.

"I not approve," Dolph Anderson said somberly. "To kill be very bad. My wife, she agree."

"As do I," Placido said.

"Then why didn't you speak up when your idiot mayor came up with the idea?" Seamus asked.

"He is mayor," Anderson said simply.

"Sí, senor," Placido echoed. "He decides what the town does. I feed and rent horses and shovel their manure."

In disgust, Seamus snapped, "Fools, the whole bunch of you. Because none of you have a backbone, one of your own has died."

"I will miss Sally Worth," Placido said. "She was always nice to Arturo and me. She had lived so much of life, she understood."

"She won't be doing any more living," Seamus said, rubbing it in. He heard the batwings creak.

Frank Lafferty hurried to the hitch rail. He was grinning as might a kid who had just been given a long-sought present.

"You are lighting a shuck already?"

"If I want to make the next edition." Lafferty swung up with all the grace of a lump of clay. He had to try twice to slide his other foot into the stirrup. "The paper will sell out."

"It is nice to see you so broken up that two people have been killed," Seamus said.

"Spare me your sarcasm, if you please," the journalist replied. "I merely report events."

"Report them? Or revel in them?" was Seamus's rejoinder.

Lafferty was in too good a mood to let the criticism affect him. He hauled on the reins and slapped his legs and headed south in a swirl of dust.

"There are days I hate this world and everyone in it," Seamus remarked. Suddenly he wanted out of there. He wanted to shed the whole sick, twisted affair. But he was not quite done. He went back in.

Club Caine was gingerly sliding into his shirt, with Adolphina's help. The bandage she had applied bulged white against Club's skin. "Still wearing that sour face, I see?"

"You would wear one too if you were in my boots," Seamus said. "You don't realize what you have done."

"I have defended my honor and I feel wonderful," Club declared.

"An innocent woman died, or doesn't she count?"

"Since when do you care so much about worn-out hags? She was not much to look at, you must admit."

"Club, I have always liked you," Seamus said. "But that was cruel." The devil of it was, though, Seamus knew the man was right. He never much cared what happened to others, and he did not much care about the whore. What he did care about, what bothered him most, was the fact that his tidy, orderly life had been disrupted, with the very real possibility of a lot worse to come.

"Suit yourself, Yank," Club said. "Me, I am riding back to Dodge to find Harriet so we can celebrate."

"The sheriff will want to talk to you. You might be called before a grand jury."

"Whatever is required. No charges will be filed. Not under the circumstances." Club rose and turned to Chester and Adolphina. "I believe I owe you some money."

"Blood money," Seamus remarked.

"Coffin Varnish officially thanks you," Chester said as he accepted. Adolphina immediately took it from him.

"Who is going to pay for Sally's burial?" Winifred asked. "I wouldn't mind, her being my friend and all, but I wasn't the one who shot her."

"Already taken care of, my friend," Chester said, and winked. "I went through the pockets of the deceased. He had more than enough."

Seamus could not stop himself. "You people sicken me." He walked out and forked leather and rode off without a backward glance. If he never saw Coffin Varnish again, it would be too soon, but he doubted he would be so lucky.

He was in no hurry to reach Dodge City. Hinkle would be furious, and he couldn't blame him. A whirlwind had been unleashed, a tornado that could sweep all of them up in a vortex of unending violence. No, he told himself, not unending. There had to be a way to put a stop to it, to nip the stupidity in the bud. The county commissioners could weigh in. The governor should be notified. Before another month went by, a political deluge would rain on Coffin Varnish, rain on the heads of that butterball of a mayor and his bull of a wife.

Seamus couldn't wait.

It was everything Lafferty hoped it would be.

The shooting was the talk of the town. The *Times* did indeed sell out, and the owner decided to print a second edition. The staff was astounded when that sold out as well. They debated a third and decided not to.

Lafferty's boss was immensely pleased. "Keep this up and you will be the next Edison Farnsworth."

That was fine, but Lafferty had higher aspirations. He was thinking of London, or maybe Paris.

The world was Lafferty's journalistic oyster, provided Coffin Varnish went on inviting would-be killers to buck each other out in gore. The way Lafferty saw it, his career and Coffin Varnish's notoriety were inextricably linked. With that in mind, he did not slant the story as he had told Glickman he would; he did not heap scorn and ridicule on Coffin Varnish. Instead, he discreetly implied that maybe, just maybe, Coffin Varnish was doing Ford County, and Kansas, a favor by offering itself as a killing ground. Lafferty wrote in his concluding paragraph:

> After all, the more badmen and shootists who flock to Coffin Varnish, the fewer shootings Dodge and other cities and towns must contend with. Brave Coffin Varnish is doing the rest of us a favor by drawing to herself all those who make our streets unsafe. Instead of condemning her, might it not be better to praise her civic

leaders for having the courage to do what no
one else ever has? Instead of demanding they
cease and desist, might it not be wiser to let them
continue in their admittedly bizarre but nonethe-
less beneficial practice? Wise or folly, my fellow
citizens, which is it?

Lafferty thought that last a nice touch.

His newfound fame was a tonic he could not get
enough of. Strangers bought him drinks and plied him
with questions. He had been there. He had seen the
aftermath with his own eyes. He basked in his fledg-
ling fame, intoxicated by the attention paid to him, by
the praise.

Lafferty did not mind that another celebrity was
created. Club Caine was treated with respect border-
ing on awe. When Club entered the Long Branch, a
hush fell. Whispers broke out. Fingers pointed. Lafferty went over and offered to buy Club a drink.
Within moments they were surrounded by men anxious to bask in the glow of greatness.

Lafferty ate it up.

The only sour note came later that night as Lafferty
was strolling down Front Street.

"I hope you are proud of yourself." Seamus Glickman stepped out of the shadows, a folded newspaper
in his hand. He threw it in the dirt at Lafferty's feet.
"Take that to the outhouse. It is all it is good for."

"You sound mad," Lafferty said.

"You have no idea what you have done."

"I am making the most of it, I admit," Lafferty said.
"But your worries are unfounded. The situation is

temporary. Someone will put a stop to it before too long. Sheriff Hinkle, if no one else."

"You better hope someone does," Seamus said. "Or I will drag you to Coffin Varnish, pay their fee, and see if you can shoot as well as you write."

"Your joke is in poor taste," Lafferty said.

Seamus bent toward him and poked him in the chest. "Who said I was joking?" he grimly growled. Then, pivoting on a boot heel, he stalked off.

Chapter 17

Jeeter Frost was happy. He could not remember the last time he was happy. Truly, really, feel-it-in-his-heart happy. He kept wanting to pinch himself to see if he was awake.

Amazing, the difference a woman made, Jeeter mused. He breathed deep of the dry earthy smell of the prairie. In the gathering twilight he and the gruella were moving shadows. He rose in the stirrups but could not see the schoolhouse. Soon, he told himself. Be patient.

But it was hard to be patient when Jeeter spent every minute away from Ernestine thinking about her, missing her, wishing he was with her. He had never felt this way about anyone except maybe his mother when he was small, and that had not been the same.

There was a word for how Jeeter felt. A word he never expected to apply to him. A word others experienced but never him. Until now.

Jeeter was in *love*. There. He admitted it. But admitting it did not make him feel any more comfortable about it. He was happy, yes, but he was uneasy as well. Because when you cared for someone, when you wanted them as much as he wanted Ernestine, you put yourself at risk. The risk it might not last. The risk that you might lose them.

Never in his life had Jeeter been so scared of anything as he was of losing Ernestine. Part of his fear stemmed from his astonishment that a fine lady like her cared for a worthless husk like him. Another part stemmed from the fact that she had not made her own feelings plain. All the hours they had been together, all the intimate moments they shared, and not once had she come right out and revealed her feelings. He took it for granted she liked him as much as he liked her, but what if he was wrong? he asked himself. What if it was one-sided?

Jeeter decided enough was enough. Tonight he would ask her. Tonight he would find out the truth. It made him nervous. It could be he would spoil everything. It could be she was not ready to commit herself.

"God, why is life so mixed up sometimes?" Jeeter asked the gruella. He spied a white shape in the distance, and a swarm of butterflies took wing in his stomach.

The lamp was in the window, her signal it was safe.

Jeeter came to the back of the schoolhouse and reined up. He let the reins dangle, not the least worried about the gruella wandering off. It never did. That horse was the one constant in his life, the only thing besides himself that he had depended on all these years.

At Jeeter's light knock Ernestine opened the door. Where previous nights she had drawn him into her arms and warmly kissed him, tonight she stepped to one side and said formally, "Welcome, Mr. Frost. Come in and have a seat, won't you?"

The swarm multiplied into a legion. Jeeter's legs felt rubbery as he moved past her, his spurs jingling. "Is something the matter, ma'am?"

"What could be the matter?" Ernestine rejoined. "I just want to talk."

Jeeter went all the way to her desk, faced her, and leaned against it with his arms across his chest. He should say something but his tongue was glued to the roof of his mouth.

Her hands clasped in front of her, Ernestine came slowly down the aisle. "I have been doing some thinking," she said softly. "Some serious thinking about you and me."

Oh no, Jeeter thought.

"I feel I have been remiss in a certain respect," Ernestine said. "I have let things get out of hand."

Jeeter found his voice although it did not sound like him. "In what way?"

Ernestine stopped, her head bowed. "I have let you take liberties. Liberties no one has ever taken with me."

"Do you regret those liberties?" Jeeter asked, his voice much calmer than he felt. His happiness, his future, rested on her answer.

"I do."

The room spun, and Jeeter reached behind him to brace himself. His throat had become so dry he had to swallow several times before he could say, "I am right sorry to hear that, Ernestine."

"You can't blame me. A woman has her reputation to think of. If our trysts were to become common knowledge, I would lose my job. The stigma would follow me wherever I went."

"I am a stigma now?" Jeeter was not sure what that meant, but it did not sound flattering.

"You can't help it," Ernestine said. "Your past has caught up with you."

"Oh," was all Jeeter could think of to say.

"Please understand. A woman in my position must stay above reproach. The slightest suggestion of impropriety and my life is in shambles. I do not want that. I do not want that at all."

"I wouldn't want that for you, either," Jeeter admitted. Invisible hands had hold of his chest and were squeezing, and the cozy schoolhouse with its comfortable glow had become cold and sterile.

"You can see what I am leading up to, can't you?" Ernestine asked.

"Yes, ma'am," Jeeter said, devastated. He had to get out of there before he made a spectacle of himself.

"Haven't you something you would like to say?"

Jeeter had never suspected she could be so heartless. To cast him aside, and then want him to speak. She might as well bury a knife in him and be done with it. "Not especially, ma'am, no."

"Nothing at all?"

"What is there to talk about?" Jeeter asked. "You have made up your mind. I don't agree but I respect you too much to argue."

Ernestine's right hand rose to her throat. "This is not what I expected. This is not what I expected at all."

"You and me both, ma'am." Jeeter was fit to burst. "I reckon I'll be going. Don't fret none. I won't grace your doorstep ever again."

"Oh, Mr. Frost."

Forcing his legs to work, Jeeter touched his hat brim. "I apologize for any inconvenience I caused you."

"Inconvenience?" Ernestine repeated, and uttered a strange little laugh. "I would not have traded places with any woman in the world."

Jeeter was only half listening. He moved past her, saying to himself, "I ain't never been in love before." A hand caught his sleeve, bringing him to a stop, and he was acutely conscious of the warmth she gave off as she stepped up close to him.

"What did you just stay?"

"I would rather not repeat it, Ernestine. It hurts too much."

"No. Please. I am not sure I heard you correctly. What did you say?"

Jeeter could not look her in the eyes. His own were misting and he had to restrain himself from tearing them out of their sockets. "I said I ain't never been in love before. That's not good grammar, but since you are tossing me out I reckon grammar don't mean much to me anymore."

"Oh God," Ernestine said.

"If there is one he is laughing himself silly at my expense for thinking a beautiful lady like you could care for me."

"Oh, Jeeter."

"That's all right, ma'am. I made a fool of myself. I accept the blame. Just let me go now so I can suffer in peace."

"You truly love me?"

Jeeter halfheartedly sought to tug his arm loose, but

she would not let go. "It is cruel to rub it in like that. Laugh when I am gone."

Suddenly Ernestine's arms were around him and she was pressing a wet cheek to his. "Oh, you magnificent, wonderful fool, you."

"Was that a compliment or an insult? It sort of sounded like both." Jeeter was more confused than he could ever recall being. "And why are you crying, Ernestine? I am doing what you want. Let me reach the door and you will be shed of me."

"But I do not want to be shed of you," Ernestine said huskily. "I love you."

Jeeter needed a pinch more than ever. Either that, or a kick to the head. "I don't savvy any of this. A minute ago you were kicking me out. Now you are in love with me? I know females are supposed to be fickle, but you take it too far."

"Oh, Jeeter, Jeeter, Jeeter," Ernestine said, and pressing her face to his neck, she began to cry.

"Dear God. Not tears, too." When she did not respond, Jeeter stood and let her weep herself dry. He had heard somewhere that was the best thing to do. She was a good while stopping, though.

Then Ernestine drew back, sniffled, and said, "Excuse me." She went to her desk, opened the top drawer, and took out a handkerchief. Turning her back to him, she dabbed at her eyes and blew her nose. "Sorry," she said when she eventually turned around.

"Do I go or do I stay?" Jeeter asked.

"You stay if you want to and—"

"I want to more than anything," Jeeter interrupted.

"You did not let me finish," Ernestine said, but not unkindly. "You can stay if you want to and if you were telling the truth about being in love with me."

"Do you want the plain of it, Ernestine?"

"I would like that very much."

"I have never been in love before, so maybe I don't rightly know exactly how a body should feel when he is. But if love is wanting someone more than you have ever wanted anything, if love is hurting inside when you are away from them, if love is wishing you could spend every minute of the day with them instead of only a few hours at night, if love is being confused all the time and not quite knowing why you are confused, then, by God, I am in love."

"My sweet Jeeter."

"If you don't feel the same, tell me now and I will go," Jeeter said. "I would never inflict myself on you, not in a million years. You are the nicest, kindest, prettiest gal in all creation, and the last thing I ever want to do, the very last thing, is to hurt you."

Ernestine came down the aisle and embraced him. "We have been at cross-purposes."

"If you say so. All I know is that I about passed out when I thought you did not want to see me anymore."

"We can't have that," Ernestine said quietly, and giggled. "You are a fine man, Jeeter Frost."

"That is the first time anyone has ever said anything like that to me," Jeeter informed her.

"Get used to it," Ernestine said. "I will compliment you often, for you have many fine qualities, whether you admit them or not."

"A lot of folks would disagree."

"I am not them." Ernestine raised her head and

looked him in the eyes. "I am the one person in this world who loves you with all her heart and will stand by you forever if you will stand by her."

"Does this mean what I think it do?"

"What you think it does," Ernestine corrected him. "Yes, I guess so. I have just asked you to marry me."

Jeeter had not meant that. He had not meant that at all. He was just getting this love business worked out in his head and now she sprang marriage on him. He was so stunned, he could not think of any words to say.

"Cat have your tongue?"

"More like a grizzly," Jeeter said. "We need to back up."

"We do?"

"You just asked me to marry you?"

"Yes."

"That's not right. I may not never been married, but I know the man is supposed to do the asking."

"Who says? There is no law dictating that the man must always broach the subject. A woman is entitled, if she desires. And you, dear man, have a knack for tying your tongue in knots."

"You noticed?" Jeeter sheepishly smiled. "All right. Let's say I let it pass so long as you never tell anyone it was you who asked me and not me who asked you. Do you have any notion what you are letting yourself in for?"

"I believe I do, yes, but you may clarify it for me."

"You saw the penny dreadful. Everyone considers me a killer. Not fit for polite company. If you marry me, they will think you ain't fit for polite company, neither."

"Either," Ernestine corrected. "And what have I told you about using ain't?"

"Sorry. My mouth keeps forgetting what my head has learned."

Ernestine clasped his hands in hers. "Jeeter, I do not care what others think. That is bold, yes, but love is bold. The fault is theirs. Judge not, the Good Book says, yet they have judged you, and wrongly, at that."

Jeeter encompassed the schoolhouse with a sweep of his chin. "But what about your job? Some folks are bound to raise a fuss and say it's not right, you teaching children when you have taken up with the likes of me."

Ernestine hesitated. "I have an idea, Jeeter. I do not know if you will like it, but here goes." She took a deep breath. "What do you say to getting married before the hour is up? To finding the justice of the peace and saying our vows? Then in the morning we will head wherever you want, somewhere new, somewhere we can both star over fresh."

"Do you have a place in mind?"

"I have been thinking California would be nice," Ernestine said. "It is far enough from your usual haunts that you can change your name and no one will ever know you. And they are in need of teachers."

"California?" Jeeter had been thinking maybe Topeka.

"Is there a problem?"

"No, no, not at all," Jeeter said. "California is a far piece, but if that is how far we have to go to live our lives in peace and quiet, then California it is."

"In that case, let us find the justice of the peace."

A flash of fear spiked through Jeeter, and he froze.

"What is it?" Ernestine asked.

"Are you sure about this? I don't want to ruin your life."

Ernestine laughed and drew him to her. "Silly man. I am as certain as I have ever been about anything. Now kiss me, and then we will begin our marvelous future together."

"Together," Jeeter Frost breathed in awe.

Chapter 18

The collection of shacks and soddies had no name. Not officially. Everyone called it Crooked Creek because it was on the north bank of Crooked Creek. Who first gave it a name no one knew, although Crooked Creek Sam, as he was called, who owned the saloon, liked to claim credit. No one argued with him because Sam Hoyt could become downright mean when his dander was up.

Sam's customers knew that if they caused trouble in his place, he was liable to whip a revolver from under the bar and cut loose at the offenders without a by-your-leave. So everyone behaved.

Still, Sam did not like it when, along about ten that night, the four Haslett brothers came into his place and moved to the far end of the bar. They were always quarrelsome, and were constantly spitting tobacco. It wasn't the spitting he minded; it was the fact that they never used the spittoon.

Sam liked it even less when fifteen minutes later four more men entered and came to the near end of the bar. The short hairs at the nape of his neck prickled. Trouble was brewing, and he might be caught in the middle.

The newcomers were the Larn brothers. They, like the Hasletts, were from the South. They, like the Hasletts, were cantankerous. But the worst of it was, the Larns and the Hasletts hated one another.

Sam decided to show them he would not abide any foolishness by taking his old Colt Dragoon from under the bar and setting it down on the counter loud enough to draw their attention. "I will not abide any shenanigans."

Abe Haslett, who resembled a beanpole with limbs and a large Adam's apple, stared at the Dragoon, then said, "No need for threats. We are not here to spill blood. You have my word."

"And mine," declared Stern Larn, the oldest of the Larn brood. "We came to palaver about the big shoot."

"The what?" Sam asked.

Happy Larn, the second oldest, chuckled and said, "We want to end the feud once and for all."

Crooked Creek Sam was a Northerner. He was the first to admit he found Southerners and Southern ways peculiar. For instance, the Larns were all named after emotions. There was Stern Larn, then Happy Larn, then Cordial, and finally the youngest, Verve Larn. Who in their right mind gave their kids names like that? South Carolinians, apparently.

"That's right," Abe said. "Back to home the Hasletts and the Larns have been feudin' for nigh on a hundred years. Now we aim to settle it."

Sam regarded the Haslett faction. In addition to Abe, there was Jefferson, Quince, and Josephus. Josephus, not Joseph. All four were string beans. All four had Adam's apples a turkey buzzard would envy. All four wore shabby homespun and stank to high heaven. And all four could drink everyone else in Kansas under the table. "Explain something to me, if you don't mind. Why come here to settle your feud? Why not settle it back home?"

Abe Haslett answered, "We left Spiny Ridge pretty near two months ago. Heard about all the money to be made out West. Never figured on meetin' up with no Larns."

"We never reckoned on meetin' up with any Hasletts when we took it into our heads to see some of the country," Stern Larn said.

"God works in mysterious ways," Happy Larn said, and laughed.

Crooked Creek Sam had first heard of the brothers when they swapped lead in Dodge City. The marshal had arrested them. Since no one was hurt, and it was their first offense, the judge fined them and let them go. By some quirk of fate, they had drifted to Crooked Creek and taken to frequenting his saloon. Now this. "How do you aim to end the feud?"

"Coffin Varnish," Abe Haslett said.

"I gave you a bottle but you have barely touched it," Crooked Creek Sam noted.

"No, not coffin varnish the drink," Abe said. "Coffin Varnish the town."

Understanding dawned, and Sam said, "That notice in the *Dodge City Times*?"

All the Larns and all the Hasletts nodded.

"We read about those other fellers," Verve Larn said. He had the habit of never being still. He was always twitching, shifting, scratching, rubbing his nose. "That Caine and the one who got his brains blowed out." He stopped. "Well, Stern read it to us, since he's the only one of us can read."

"We figure if they can blow out their brains, we can blow out ours," Stern Larn said.

Sam needed a drink. After he had poured and his throat was on fire, he coughed and said, "You realize all of you could end up dead?"

The eight looked at him as if he were a few bales short of a wagonload.

"That's what feudin' is all about," Abe Haslett said.

"It's another word for killin'," Stern Larn said.

"You can't talk it out?"

Stern and Abe both started to talk at once; then Abe stopped and gestured at Stern. "After you."

"Our clans have been feudin' since Hector was a pup. With all the blood that's been spilled, talkin' it out would be an insult to those who have gone to their reward."

"That it would," Abe agreed. "Why, our ma would horsewhip us if we dishonored our kin that way."

Sam gave thanks he had been born in Ohio. "What started this feud of yours?"

"A Larn shot a Haslett over a pig," Abe said.

Stern shook his head. "No, it was a Haslett shot a Larn, and it was over a chicken."

"It was a pig."

"It was a chicken."

"Pig."

"Chicken, damn you."

The Larns glared at the Hasletts and the Hasletts glowered at the Larns. Verve started to sidle his hand toward his hip.

"None of that!" Sam bellowed. "You are here to

talk, remember? If you want to wipe each other out, fine and dandy, but you will not do it in my saloon."

"A truce, remember?" Abe Haslett said.

"A truce, brothers," Stern stressed for the benefit of his siblings.

Several on both sides echoed, "A truce."

Sam refilled his glass. He had built his saloon on Crooked Creek instead of in Dodge because he did not like towns and cities with their hustle and bustle. He liked a slow pace of life—the slower the better. He was not all that fond of people, either, Southerners in particular. He had lost an uncle and several cousins in the War between the States, and he had never forgiven the South for fighting a war over something as stupid as states' rights and slavery, but that was neither here nor there. "Get this talk over with. You are commencing to aggravate me."

"I don't like your tone," Stern Larn said.

"Me neither," Abe Haslett said.

Sam picked up his revolver. "I don't give a good damn what you do and do not like. This is my place and I can say and do as I please."

"Yankees," Abe spat.

"They are the same everywhere we go," Stern mentioned.

"Get your talk over with," Sam repeated. He wished other customers were there. The hicks were less apt to act up if there were other customers.

"Always lookin' down their noses at us," Jefferson Haslett said.

"I don't look down my nose at anyone," Sam lied. "Haven't I treated you decent, the times you have been in here?" He was always agreeable, even when he did not want to be. It was good business.

"That you have," Stern Larn allowed.

"You never insulted the South," Abe Haslett said.

"There you have it," Crooked Creek Sam said. "So we'll have no more talk of Yankees and noses and such. You can't blame me for wanting you to control your tempers while you are under my roof."

"I reckon not," Cordial Larn said. Where the rest of the Larn brothers had hair as black as a raven's wings, Cordial's was the same tawny hue as the pelt of a mountain lion. His eyes were different from theirs, too, blue where theirs were brown.

"Good. Now that that's settled, let me ask you. When do you propose to hold your lead-fest?"

"Our what?" Quince Haslett asked. He had the dubious distinction of having not only a big Adam's apple, but a big nose as well, so big that his face was more nose than anything else.

"Your lead chucking," Sam said. "Or are you aiming to fight it out in Coffin Varnish with knives?"

"Knives are too messy," Abe said. "You get blood all over the place. Plus, you can't always be sure. You stick a man in the gizzard and expect him to fall, but he keeps on fightin'."

"I never have put my trust in knives," Stern Larn said.

"Pistols will suit us." From Jefferson Haslett. He sported a bushy mane of hair and a jaw like an anvil.

"When?" Crooked Creek Sam said.

"We haven't gotten around to that yet," Cordial Larn said. "We have to work out the details."

Happy Larn laughed. "Our kin back home will be powerful upset they missed the frolic."

"Are there many in your family?" Sam asked.

"About one hundred and eighty, give or take a few," Stern Larn said.

"Two hundred and forty on our side," Abe Haslett revealed, and grinned. "We are better at breedin' than they are."

"There have always been more of you Hasletts," Stern Larn said.

"We are rabbits and you are gophers," Josephus Haslett boasted. He was the shortest of the brood, which was not saying much since it was only by a few inches.

Happy Larn lost some of his happiness. "I do not like being called a gopher. You will take that back."

"I will not," Josephus said.

"You will take that back or else," Happy said.

Crooked Creek Sam swore. "Here we go again. If you can't flap your gums without arguing, maybe none of you should talk except for Abe and Stern."

"I will talk when I please," Happy informed him.

"Me too," Josephus said.

That was when Sam made his mistake. It slipped out of his mouth as smoothly as a slick grape and had the same effect as waving a rattler under someone's nose. "Stupid Southerners. How many times must I tell you before you will listen?"

Silence fell, except for the ticking of the clock on a shelf. No one moved except for Verve Larn, who never could stand still for more than two seconds.

"What did you call us?" Abe Haslett broke the quiet.

"Not a thing," Sam said. He was aware he had blundered, but he was confident he could soothe any hard feelings.

"Like hell," Stern Larn said. "I heard you, too, as clear as day. You called us stupid Southerners."

"Not *you*," Crooked Creek Sam said, smiling. "Not any of you."

"Then who?" Cordial Larn asked.

Sam made his second mistake. He answered without thinking. "I meant Southerners in general."

Another silence, but shorter than before.

"Anyone born south of the Mason-Dixon Line is naturally stupid, is that how it goes?" Jefferson Haslett asked.

"Don't be putting words in my mouth," Crooked Creek Sam said. He was beginning to lose his temper.

"It was your word," Jefferson said. "Stupid."

"Look," Sam reasoned. "You take things much too serious. I could just as well have said stupid Northerners."

"It was stupid Southerners," Verve Larn said. "My ears hear just fine."

Abe Haslett nodded. "Could be you are one of them who looks down their nose at us. Could be we don't take kindly to that. We don't take kindly at all."

Crooked Creek Sam placed a hand on his Colt Dragoon. "Don't threaten me. You have treed a cougar when you threaten me."

"I ain't seen one of those percussion Colts in a coon's age," Abe Haslett commented. "They were prone to misfire."

"Not mine," Sam said.

"Big and heavy, those old models," Stern Larn said.

"Even us stupid Southerners know enough not to rely on one."

"Takes a real gun shark to handle one halfway decent," Jefferson Haslett said.

"And you don't strike us as a gun shark," Happy Larn threw in.

Crooked Creek Sam broke out in a cold sweat. He recognized the signs: the hard stares, the pinched mouths, the tense bodies. "Now, you just hold on! Every last one of you, hold on!"

"He sounds scared to me," Stern Larn said.

"To me too," Abe Haslett agreed. "Usually when someone is scared they have done something they shouldn't."

"He shouldn't ought to call people stupid," Cordial Larn said.

Sam had put up with all he was going to. "I want you out of my saloon! Every last one of you coon-eating sons of bitches!"

The next moment Abe and Stern and Cordial had their six-shooters out, and the others were unlimbering theirs.

"Didn't you hear me?" Crooked Creek Sam screeched.

"What do you say?" Abe Haslett asked. It was hard to tell who he was asking since he was staring at the Dragoon.

"I say the North has insulted us enough," Stern Larn said. "I say for once the Larns and the Hasletts have common cause."

"Twice," Abe said. "We wore the gray together."

"It is a shame we are enemies," Stern said. Then, to Sam, "Any last words, you stinkin' Yankee?"

Crooked Creek Sam could not believe what was happening. "I will give you more than a word, you lousy Reb." He started to level the Dragoon but could not make up his mind who to point it at. The moment's indecision was costly. The last sound he heard was the crashing boom of revolvers. The last sight was a roiling cloud of gun smoke.

The shooting went on and on. It stopped only when every cylinder was empty.

"We done shot him to pieces," Verve Larn said, grinning.

"It is too bad we have to do the same to us," Abe Haslett said. "Coffin Varnish, here we come."

Chapter 19

It was a warm night. The breeze that had picked up from out of the northwest did little to alleviate the heat of the day. The sky was clear, the stars a sparkling host shining benignly down on Kansas.

"It is a night made for romance," Adolphina Luce remarked.

Chester Luce was so shocked he nearly tripped over his own feet. They were taking a rare stroll down Coffin Varnish's dusty street. He had been watching out for horse, pig, and chicken droppings, and glanced up in bewilderment. "Did I hear you right, my dear?" He could not remember the last time his wife had been in a romantic mood. There had been their wedding night, of course, and five or six times after that. It got so that he wearied of waiting for her to say yes, and stopped hinting.

"Romance," Adolphina confirmed, her usual hard tones softened. "A girl thinks of romance when she is happy."

The shocks kept coming. Chester never thought of her as a girl. Not as old and as big as she was. A woman, yes, a bear, often, but she had given up any pretense at girlish ways long before she met him. And to hear her say she was happy was enough to convince him he must be dreaming. But no, a pile of horse droppings made his nose want to curl in on itself, and no dream ever did that. "I am glad you are happy," he said. "Was it Gemma's meal?" They had been invited to supper at the Giorgios', another first. Gemma had cooked traditional Italian fare, with lots of pasta and thick sauce and meat rolled into balls, and it had been delicious. Much more so than anything his wife ever cooked. Her food tended to be bland and unappetizing. Some nights, he had to force himself to have three helpings.

"No, it is not that. Who can stand all that garlic she uses? And those brats of her always underfoot. If I were her, I would take a board to their backsides. That would cure them."

Chester had considered the boys well behaved. Although the oldest, Matteo, had made an unfortunate remark to the effect that Adolphina was the first woman he ever met with a mustache.

"Things are going nice for once. A girl is happy when things go nice. When they go the way she wants them to go."

"We sure had a lot of people come to view Paunch Stevens," Chester said. "We made more money off him than we did off that first bunch."

"There will be more," Adolphina said. "A lot more. I can feel it in my bones. I feel something else, too." She squeezed his arm.

It had never occurred to Chester that money made women romantic. The revelation put his brain in a whirl.

"That newspaperman promised to give us copies of

the next edition of the *Times*," Adolphina mentioned. "The edition in which he is writing about us."

"I just hope the article is favorable," Chester said. In politics, press that praised was everything.

"He promised it would be. He said not to worry, that he is on our side, that he will write about us so people are on our side, too."

"When did he say that?" Chester asked. "He did not say it to me."

"To me," Adolphina said. "When I had him up for coffee. You were busy showing the body and giving a speech at the livery."

Chester was not so sure he liked the idea of his wife and the journalist alone in their parlor. Then he looked at her and his jealously evaporated. "It is obliging of him."

"Oh, he is thinking of himself, make no mistake," Adolphina said. "Newspapers all over have been picking up his reports on Coffin Varnish. He says we are the talk of the country. Can you imagine?"

"It is the killing, not us."

"No. It is us, letting folks kill, that has everyone astir. We are doing something no one has ever done before. A few more shootings and we will be famous."

"Sure we will," Chester said, and laughed.

Adolphina stopped and turned him so he faced her. "You begin to worry me. Can it be you do not see the opportunity being handed to us? I would hate to think I married a dunce."

Worried her romantic mood was waning, Chester said, "Have I ever let you down?"

"More times than I can count," Adolphina said. "But that is neither here nor there. What matters now is that you seize the moment and use this new fame of ours to good advantage."

"We will have more money than we have had in years," Chester predicted, and was horrified when she gave him her look that could wilt a rock.

"Oh, Chester. How you do disappoint. I am not talking about the money, although, yes, the money is considerable. I am talking about long term. I am talking about you rising in the world. I am proud of you being mayor, but mayor is not all there is."

"You are?" Chester was under the impression she had been distinctly underwhelmed by his being elected.

"You have served Coffin Varnish long and well, or as well as you are able," Adolphina said. "But there are bigger political arenas. There is state government, there is the federal government."

"You can't mean—"

"Think, Chester, think. Fame is money in the bank to politicians. It is votes on election day. Why be a big fish in a little pond when you can be a big fish in a big pond? When you can parley the fame from these killings into state or national office?"

"You are serious, by God."

"Never more so. If that newspaperman does as he promised, everyone in Kansas will hear about you. You could run for state senator. Later, you can run for U.S. senator."

A keg of powder went off in Chester's head. She was right, as usual. The possibilities were spectacularly grand. "Or I could run for Congress."

"No, no, forget the House. They are a nest of chipmunks. They chatter a lot but never do much. The Senate is where the power is, the power and the money. Become a United States senator and your future, and our fortune, is assured."

A rare warmth spread through Chester. "You care about my career?"

"Of course, stupid. The higher you rise, the better for both of us. For you, power and prestige. For me, power and a mansion and a carriage and servants to do the cooking and the mending."

"Servants cost money," Chester carped.

"A United States senator can afford them. A senator can afford anything." Adolphina smiled wistfully. "We can dine out every night. We can travel. Senator Chester Luce. How does that sound?"

Chester was intoxicated by her brilliance. "Oh, Fina," he said, using his pet name for her. She had warned him never to do it in public or she would slap him, but she didn't slap him.

"I might be getting ahead of myself, but in time, who knows? You could go beyond senator."

"What is there beyond?" Chester asked. The answer struck him with the force of a hammer blow. "Oh, you can't mean *that*."

"Why can't I? If Grant can get voted in, why not you? You aren't much shorter and fatter. Sure, he won the Civil War, and that made him famous, but what else had he done? Fame is the key. Fame is how you rise above the common herd to lord it over them."

Chester's head filled with visions of the White House, of him addressing a joint session of Congress, of him picking a bevy of pretty secretaries. "Adolphina, I am impressed. I never knew you were such a deep thinker."

"One of us has to be."

* * *

Miles to the south another couple strolled arm in arm under the twinkling stars.

Ernestine Prescott was giddy with glee. She felt young again. The years had been stripped away and she was no longer a spinster teacher. She was a girl in love, ablaze with life and vitality. Then Jeeter Frost threw a bucket of water on her inner fire.

"I don't feel right about this."

"About us?" Inwardly Ernestine trembled, afraid he had changed his mind about loving her.

"About us going off together."

Ernestine stopped. "Oh."

Jeeter was trying hard to be sensitive to her feelings. He did not want to upset her again. Their misunderstanding in the schoolhouse had taught him that she was not always thinking what he thought she was thinking. "I don't feel right about you giving up your job."

"Oh!" Ernestine said again, brightening. "I can always find another. There are not enough teachers to fill the need."

"I still feel guilty," Jeeter said. Here he was, taking her away from everything she knew, from the security and comfort that came of being a highly respected member of the community.

"If I don't, you shouldn't." Ernestine touched his cheek. His stubble tickled her fingertips. "I am doing this of my own free will. You must remember that."

"It don't help much."

"Doesn't," Ernestine corrected, and smoothed her dress. "Now then. Our first order of business is the justice of the peace. I happen to know that Mr. Dundleman, on Fifth Street, is a justice. His grandson attends my school. He is a widower and he lives alone, so we can slip in and out without disturbing anyone else. Then we will go to my boardinghouse and you can help me pack. By midnight we can be on our way."

"That's not right," Jeeter said.

"What isn't? Disturbing Mr. Dundleman so late?"

"No, riding off across the prairie in the middle of the night," Jeeter said. "We should wait until morning."

"Wait where? At the boardinghouse? I daresay my landlady would be scandalized. At a hotel? The marshal and the sheriff might want words with you, and it is best we avoid them." Ernestine shook her head. "No, if we leave by midnight, we should reach Coffin Varnish about the middle of the night."

"Coffin Varnish?"

"They don't have a lawman. They know you there, and according to the newspaper, you did them a favor killing those Blights."

"There is nothing in that fly speck but a saloon, a livery, and a store," Jeeter recalled. "No place for us to stay."

"Wrong," Ernestine said. "Today's newspaper mentioned that they cleaned out an empty building so people who came to view Paunch Stevens could spend the night if they wanted."

"And you want us to spend the night there?"

"Why not?" Ernestine rejoined. "We will sleep in late, then head west. In a month we can be in California."

"You have it all worked out," Jeeter marveled. It unnerved him a little, her being so smart, and all.

"I like to work things out before I take the first step," Ernestine mentioned. "I am a teacher, after all, and teachers, by their nature, are thinkers."

"I have a puny thinker, myself," Jeeter said. "It never has done me much good."

"Education and discipline, my husband to be," Ernestine said gaily. "They are the keys to a happy life." Clamping his arm in hers, she wheeled and strode briskly toward the lights and noise of Dodge.

Uneasiness crept over Jeeter. Although the newspaper made the shootings in Coffin Varnish out to be self-defense, the law wanted to question him. The sheriff had been quoted as saying he did not approve of leather slappers riding into his county and shooting folks. "We have to watch out for tin stars."

"Avoiding them should not be difficult. At this time of night they are on Front Street, visiting saloons and bawdy houses under the pretext of doing their job."

Jeeter chuckled. "Pretext, huh? We might need to find me a dictionary if I am to savvy half of what you say."

Ernestine grinned and replied, "As it happens I own several. You may use them whenever you want. Once we say our vows, what is mine is yours and what is yours is mine."

"I don't have a whole lot," Jeeter told her. "My revolver, my horse, the clothes on my back, that is about it."

"I do not own a great deal, either. My clothes, my books, a few pots and pans. I never bothered to buy furniture since my room at the boardinghouse came furnished."

"How many books and pots, exactly?" Jeeter envisioned the need for a pack animal.

"Oh, I should say no more than sixty volumes and half a dozen cooking utensils."

"Sixty!" Jeeter exclaimed. "You have your own library." Some might weigh a pound or more. It definitely called for a packhorse.

"Many are reference works I use when I teach," Ernestine revealed. "Some are novels I am fond of. Mary Shelley, for instance. I just love *Frankenstein*. Harriet Beecher Stowe, and *Uncle Tom's Cabin*, is another of my favorites. Hawthorne, and his *The Scarlet Letter* and *The House of Seven Gables*. Goodness, how that man can write. And let us not forget Poe and Dickens and Charlotte Brontë and her *Jane Eyre*."

"Jane who?" Jeeter had never heard of any of them. Suddenly the gulf between his world and hers filled him with dread. "All I know are pistols and horses," he said glumly.

"About which I know next to nothing," Ernestine said. "You will teach me about them and I will teach you about books."

"I am getting the better of the deal."

"Say that again after we have lived together a while."

They were almost to a side street that would take them into Dodge when a rider came out of it and spurred his mount in their direction.

In the pale starlight the badge on his vest was plainly visible.

Chapter 20

Seamus Glickman had forgotten all about the sheriff wanting him to pay a visit to the schoolmarm. The shenanigans in Coffin Varnish were to blame. He was reminded when Sheriff Hinkle came up to him in Tulley's and said, "I just had another report of a strange gent hanging around the schoolhouse. What did you find out when you went out there?"

Seamus was tempted to lie but didn't. "I never got around to it," he admitted.

George Hinkle frowned. "I am not a stickler for orders and the like, but when I ask to have something done, I expect it done. Ride out there right now and talk to the schoolmarm."

"This late?"

"I have seen the light on out there even later some nights. Miss Prescott is dedicated to her work."

Seamus thought of the spindly, almost severe figure he had glimpsed on a few occasions. "Do you really think she keeps a man under those petticoats?"

"No, I do not. But some of the parents are talking and won't stop wagging their tongues until they hear from us that the schoolmarm is not making a mockery of public morals."

"And I thought having to shoot stray dogs wasn't fit work for a lawman," Seamus observed. "Now we are virtue inspectors."

Sheriff Hinkle laughed. "That is what I like most about this job. One minute we are arresting a cowboy for disturbing the peace, and the next we are shooing pigs off the street."

"You can have the pigs, and you can have our schoolmarm."

"Be nice to her. Your visit is official."

"You know me, George," Seamus said. "I smile and am polite even when the person I am being polite to is a jackass. Or, in her case, a broomstick no man with any appreciation for womanhood would care to fondle."

"I will be in the office," Sheriff Hinkle said. "Report to me as soon as you get back."

"Yes, sir."

Now here Seamus was, riding out of Dodge City by a side street to go question the schoolmarm. He had half a mind not to do it and say he had. As far as he was concerned, the law had no business meddling in the private lives of people. What Ernestine Prescott did in the privacy of her bedroom was her affair and no one else's. That a few busybodies had complained only showed that some folks were too damn willing to impose their notion of what was right on others.

His horse nickered, and Seamus looked up. A man and a woman were approaching on foot. Just as he set eyes on them, the woman pulled the man to her and turned so her back was to the road. They did not look around as he came up to them.

Seamus drew rein. A dove and a cowboy, he assumed, and said gruffly, "Enough of that. You know better. In a saloon, yes. In a hotel, yes. But not out here where everyone can see."

"Sorry," the woman said, still embracing the man. "We were carried away."

"Get carried away in private," Seamus said, and clucked to his mount. Light glowed in the schoolhouse window, so Hinkle had been right about the schoolmarm. Dismounting, he walked up to the door and knocked. When there was no response, he knocked louder, and when that failed to bring her to the door, he worked the latch and poked his head inside.

"Miss Prescott? Sorry to disturb you."

Seamus sighed. She wasn't there. The schoolhouse was empty. That she had gone off and left the lamp on suggested she would return. He was about to go in and wait for her when his sorrel whinnied and was answered by another horse from somewhere behind the schoolhouse.

Puzzled, Seamus took a few steps back. "Miss Prescott?" he called out. His reply was another whinny.

Suddenly Seamus thought he understood. The schoolmarm's gentleman caller was there, out back with the schoolmarm. For once the gossip had been true. Grinning, he hastened around the corner. The man might ride off, and Seamus wanted to see who it was. He hoped the man was married. Wouldn't that be something? He chuckled to himself. The scandal would be sensational.

But all Seamus found was a horse. A gruella, its reins dangling. He scanned the prairie, then cupped a hand to his mouth. "Miss Prescott? Are you here?" Apparently not, since there was no answer. Seamus started to head for the front of school, then stopped and stared at the mouse dun.

A gruella. A vague sense that the horse was somehow important came over him. Something pricked at his mind, a memory, words someone had said, something that had stuck with him.

"A gruella," Seamus said aloud. He tried and tried but could not remember. Shrugging, he was almost to the side of the schoolhouse when it came to him in a rush of vivid memory. Coffin Varnish. The shootings of the Blights and Edison Farnsworth. Seamus had asked everyone what they saw and heard, and the saloon owner, Win Curry, offhandedly mentioned that he had been in front of the saloon when Jeeter Frost rode up on—

"A gruella!" Seamus exclaimed. He closed his fingers around the ivory handles of his Merwin and Hulbert revolver and again scanned the plain. "It can't be," he said. "It just can't be."

The schoolmarm and Jeeter Frost? The notion was so ridiculous that Seamus laughed. But the laugh died in his throat. He recalled that Sheriff Hinkle had brought up the rumors about the schoolmarm about the same time as those first killings in Coffin Varnish. Everyone had assumed Jeeter Frost was just passing through and happened to run into the Blights. But what if everyone was wrong? Seamus reflected. What if Frost had a reason for visiting? What if that reason, incredible as it seemed, was the schoolmarm?

Seamus abruptly remembered the man and woman he had passed on the way there. He remembered how neither had looked at him, remembered, now that he thought about it, that the woman had been thin and wore a dress no self-respecting dove would be caught dead in. The man had been short, and Jeeter Frost was supposed to be short, and might have been wearing buckskins.

"Son of a bitch!" Seamus cursed his stupidity, and ran. He practically vaulted into the saddle and applied his spurs. His sorrel, unaccustomed to such rough treatment, shot toward Dodge as if fired from a cannon. But he only went a short way when he reined up.

"What am I doing?" Seamus leaned on the saddle horn to contemplate. So far as he knew, Jeeter Frost was not wanted by the law. Frost killed the Blights, but by all accounts he shot them in self-defense. Sheriff Hinkle would like to question Frost, but that was all. So why go barreling into town after the killer and the schoolmarm when Jeeter Frost might take exception and decide the county could do without an undersheriff?

Seamus was under no delusions about his ability with a six-gun. He was fair. Only fair. Whereas Frost had to be a wizard, given the number of hombres he had reportedly slain. Even allowing for exaggeration, Frost was still as deadly a customer as Seamus ever came across. Who in their right mind would make a man like that mad?

Not Seamus. He had survived as long as he had by sticking to what he jokingly liked to call his golden rules: Never poke a rattler, never get in the path of stampeding animals, and never, ever prod a man liable to exact payment for the affront in lead.

His mind made up, Seamus gigged his horse into a different street than the one he left Dodge by. He couldn't wait to see the look on Sheriff Hinkle's face when he told him. The schoolmarm and the worst short-trigger man in three states. Hinkle would find it as hilarious as he did.

Horace Dundleman had been a justice of the peace since Dodge City was founded, and before that, in St. Louis a good many years. He liked the job. He met a lot of interesting people, and Horace liked people. He also liked that it was not physically demanding because at his age, seventy-one, he was not as spry as he used to be. His joints ached and creaked, and his vision was so bad he needed spectacles.

Those spectacles delayed Horace when someone began pounding on his door. He groped for them on the nightstand and accidentally knocked them onto the floor. The knocks grew louder and more insistent as Horace groped about near the bed until he found them. Finally perching the spectacles on his nose, he went to the closet, opened it, and took his heavy robe from a peg.

"Hold your horses! I'm coming!" Horace hollered as he shuffled down the hall past the parlor that served as his office. He threw the bolt that would admit his visitors. "It is awful late."

Ernestine Prescott glanced nervously behind her before slipping inside. She had her arm wrapped around Jeeter Frost's and had no intention of letting go. "I am sorry but it could not be helped."

Behind the thick lenses of his spectacles, Horace's owl eyes blinked. "Miss Prescott? What are you doing out and about at this hour?" He did not come out and say that schoolmarms should be discreet in their behavior, but he was thinking it.

"You perform weddings, do you not, Mr. Dundleman?"

Horace could not have been more stunned if she pulled out a gun and shot him. He blinked anew, then focused on her companion. The man reminded him of a ferret, and was obviously on edge from the way he fidgeted and was sweating. "I perform civil ceremonies, yes," Horace said guardedly, thinking to himself that surely the schoolmarm was not thinking of doing what her question suggested.

Ernestine smiled. "Then I would like very much for you to perform one for us, here and now."

"At this hour?"

Jeeter Frost did not like how the old man looked at him. He did not like that a lawman had seen them on their way there. He could use a drink, could use a drink badly. To his annoyance, he was sweating like a stuck pig, and worried he was about to make the worst mistake of his life. He cared for Ernestine so much, he was afraid of shackling her with himself. But if it was what she wanted, then by God he would go through with it. "You heard the lady," he growled. "What difference does the hour make?"

"None, really," Horace admitted. "But this is sort of sudden, is it not?" He addressed the schoolmarm.

"Yes, it is," Ernestine said. "So please. Can we get on with it?"

Horace adjusted his spectacles and then his robe. He was stalling. "There are formalities to observe, you know. A form to fill out. A fee to pay. Usually people fill out the form and come back in a few days."

"We don't have a few days," Jeeter said. "Just get on with whatever you have to do."

"No need to be cross with me, mister," Horace said. He was old but he would not kowtow to anyone, particularly runts with an attitude.

"Don't rile me, old man," Jeeter warned.

Ernestine gave his hand a hard squeeze. "None of that kind of talk, if you please. This is a special occasion. I want to have fond memories of it."

Horace sensed fear in her tone. Something was going on here, something out of the normal. He looked at her more closely and saw that she was nervous, too, which was not like her at all. The few times he had spoken to her, she had been a portrait of calm and serenity. "Is everything all right, Miss Prescott?"

"Of course, Mr. Dundleman," Ernestine said. "But it is not every day a woman is wed."

"No, it is not," Horace agreed. "All the more reason for the woman to be positive she wants to say I do."

"I am positive."

But she did not sound positive to Horace, and as he led them into the parlor he racked his mind for a way to delay joining them as husband and wife. Only for a day or so. He fumbled with the lamp, got it lit, and turned it up so the parlor flooded with bright light. Only then did he see the Colt Lightning on the groom's hip. Only then did he get a good look at the groom's features.

"Something wrong?" Jeeter Frost demanded. The old geezer was staring at him as if he had risen from a grave.

"No, no, nothing at all," Horace said. "It is just unusual, is all, for a man to drag a woman in here in the middle of the night to get hitched."

"It's hardly the middle of the night," Jeeter said. He was losing his patience with the old man. "And as for the dragging, I do as I damn well please, or as she damn well pleases."

Ernestine pouted. "I won't ask you again. Be polite, for my sake if for no other reason."

"Just so the old buzzard gets it over with," Jeeter said.

Horace stepped to his desk and opened the top drawer. The forms were in a neat pile on the right. "You must fill one of these out. It asks your name, your age, a few other things."

"You are a nosy old coot," Jeeter said. The form intimidated him. He had learned the alphabet, but he wrote letters as slow as molasses.

"Not me, mister," Horace said. "It is for the government, for their records, so everything is nice and official."

"Official be hanged," Jeeter groused.

Ernestine sighed. "You will not desist, will you? You push and push when there is no cause. I am here with you, aren't I? You need not be so forceful."

Horace wondered what she meant by that. He sat in his chair and fiddled with his robe. "I don't suppose you would let me go get dressed?"

"No," Jeeter said.

"I will fill in the form," Ernestine offered. She took pride in her precise handwriting. When she was done she slid the form toward Dundleman. "We do not have a ring. Is that all right?"

"It is not essential," Horace said, running his gaze down the paper. He read the groom's name. He read it twice, and a lightning bolt seared him from head to toe. Struggling to keep his voice level, he said, "So you are to become Mrs. Jeeter Frost?"

"Do you have a problem with that?" Jeeter demanded.

"No, sir," Horace lied. "There is no problem at all."

Chapter 21

Seamus Glickman took his time returning to the sheriff's office. He stopped at the Long Branch for a drink.

Front Street was bedlam, as always at that hour. People, horses, wagons, buckboards, carriages, dogs and pigs and poultry, mingled and mixed in a perpetual whirl. Animals were not supposed to run loose, but hardly anyone kept theirs leashed or penned. The town council had imposed fines, but people still couldn't be bothered. They saw it as their God-given right to let their pigs do their business in the middle of the street.

Seamus bellied up to the bar and smacked the counter to get the bartender's attention. He sipped the whiskey brought to him and let the sights and sounds of the saloon wash over him. The games of chance, poker and faro and roulette, the babble of voices and laughter, the thick cigar smoke, and the perfume of the doves—this was his element.

When George Hinkle's term of office was up, Seamus planned to turn in his badge. He would devote himself to acquiring a saloon of his own. That, and his partial interest in the Comique, would ensure a comfortable income, enough to spoil himself with the creature comforts he was so fond of.

Seamus thought it a shame he had not been born into money. Wealth would become him. The best clothes, the best liquor, the best food, the best women, they were the nectar that sweetened the tedium of life. He became so absorbed in his musing that he was on his third glass before he realized it. A glance at the clock told him he should be on his way. Hinkle had said to report to him as soon as he got back.

Seamus was in good spirits as he reined to the rail in front of the sheriff's office. The door was open, which puzzled him, and deputies and other men were coming and going in a hurry, which added to his puzzlement. Climbing down, he encountered Deputy French, who was coming out.

"Glickman! Where have you been? The sheriff has had us looking all over for you."

"He has?"

"You better get in there. I have to go to the stable for the packhorse we will need to bring the body back. Although why we don't bury him there is beyond me."

"Body?" Seamus said, but Deputy French had already hurried on down the street. Squaring his shoulders, Seamus entered, and nearly collided with an elderly man he recognized as the justice of the peace, who was just leaving.

"Watch where you are going, sonny."

Seamus opened his mouth to tell the old man where he could go. But George Hinkle stepped between them.

"Finally! Where the hell have you bent? I sent you to do a simple job and all hell has busted loose."

"I did as you wanted," Seamus said. "I went to the schoolhouse but the schoolmarm wasn't there." He started to smile, to tell the sheriff about the schoolmarm and the shootist.

"She wasn't there because she was at the justice of the peace, being forced to wed against her will."

"What?"

"That was Horace Dundleman. He says Jeeter Frost dragged Miss Prescott to his place and made him marry them."

"What?"

"Dundleman says there was nothing he could do to stop it. Frost was wearing that fancy Colt of his and was in a foul temper. Dundleman says he was lucky Frost didn't shoot him."

"What?"

George Hinkle studied Seamus. "Why do you keep saying that? Where have you been, anyhow? I expected you back long ago."

It took some doing but Seamus collected his wits. "I was patrolling Front Street."

"You should have come straight back, like I told you to," Hinkle said. "All hell has broken loose. In addition to Frost stealing our schoolmarm, there has been another killing. Out-and-out murder this time, no self-defense."

"Coffin Varnish?" Seamus naturally assumed.

"Crooked Creek," Sheriff Hinkle said. "Sam Hoyt has been shot. No word on who is to blame, but whoever it is did a thorough job. Sam has twenty to thirty bullet holes in him."

"What?"

"There you go again," Sheriff Hinkle said. He

moved to the gun cabinet, opened it, and took out a Winchester. "We have a murder and a kidnapping on our hands. I will investigate the murder. You will lead a posse and go after Jeeter Frost and Miss Prescott."

Seamus needed to sit down. He could use another drink, too. "A posse?"

The sheriff glanced sharply around. "You begin to worry me. Yes, a posse. What else did you expect? That we would let a killer waltz in and steal the flower of our womanhood without lifting a finger to stop him?"

"You are sure about the marrying?"

Hinkle helped himself to a box of cartridges. "You saw Dundleman with your own eyes."

"No, I meant are you sure she was forced?" Seamus could not shake the image of the woman and the man by the side of the road, and how it was the woman who pulled the man close and kissed him.

"Are you suggesting that our schoolmarm, a model of decorum for the whole community, would want to wed a man like Jeeter Frost?"

"We shouldn't jump to conclusions," Seamus said.

"Where is the jump? Our schoolmarm disappears. She shows up at the justice of the peace with a notorious gun shark who insists the justice of the peace marry them then and there." Hinkle began feeding cartridges into the Winchester. "The whole town will be out to stretch Jeeter Frost's neck, and I can't say as I blame them."

"I better organize that posse," Seamus said despondently. Once again circumstances conspired to force him to leave Dodge.

"Being tended to as we speak," Sheriff Hinkle said. "I told Deputy Powell to round up twenty sober men who can ride."

"Do we have any idea which direction they went?" Seamus had no desire to spend hours riding in circles.

"No, we do not."

"Has anyone checked the schoolhouse? Or wherever the schoolmarm is staying?"

"No one is at the schoolhouse. I had Powell check," Sheriff Hinkle said. He sat on the edge of his desk and pursed his lips. "That is a good idea about the other. I seem to recollect she is at the boardinghouse over on Third. Head on over there and talk to the landlady. Have her let you into the schoolmarm's room and see if Miss Frost has taken any of her personal effects."

So much for a quiet, relaxing night, Seamus reflected. "I will come straight back this time."

"You better."

Seamus was as certain as he could be that things were not as Hinkle thought they were. The schoolmarm had not been abducted. She was with Frost because she wanted to be. But Seamus was not about to try and convince George Hinkle or anyone else. They would laugh him to scorn. Worse, Hinkle might accuse him of making it up to try and get out of leading the posse.

Seamus bent brisk steps toward the boardinghouse. It was a frame dwelling, larger than most, with extra rooms at the back for boarders. He had been there once before. The windows were dark save for one at the rear. He drifted around to the alley that bordered it and was almost to a gate in a picket fence when a large shape moved out of the shadows and stared at him with its ears pricked.

Seamus stifled an oath. It was the gruella! Beyond it were two other horses, one with a saddle, the other laden with packs.

Suddenly the lit window took on new significance. Drawing his Merwin and Hulbert revolver, Seamus opened the gate. He winced when a hinge creaked. Leaving the gate open, he crept to the back door. It was ajar. He quietly opened it and sidled along the wall to the first door on the right. It, too, was ajar. He heard rustling and a female voice.

Seamus smiled. He was about to impress the hell out of Sheriff Hinkle by rescuing the schoolmarm and taking Jeeter Frost into custody. He carefully placed his other hand on the door and slowly pushed. Luck was with him. The door did not creak.

Ernestine Prescott was taking folded clothes out of a dresser and placing them on the bed next to an open carpetbag. She was humming to herself.

Seamus took a couple of steps and leveled his revolver. It might scare her, but it served her right for all the bother she was putting people to. "Going somewhere, lady?"

Whirling, Ernestine put a hand to her throat. "Oh my! You quite startled me!"

"You have startled quite a few folks, yourself," Seamus informed her. "I am taking you to the sheriff."

"No, you are not," declared a harsh voice, and a hard object was gouged into his lower back. "Toss your hardware on the bed, law dog, or I will blow you in half."

Seamus's skin prickled. He had blundered by not looking behind the door when he entered. "I am not here to hurt anyone," he said.

"Then you shouldn't sneak into rooms with your pistol out. Now do as I said with your six-shooter. I am not a patient man."

"Jeeter Frost, I presume?" Seamus said as he flipped his revolver onto the quilt.

"My, don't you talk nice?" Jeeter Frost came around to one side, the Colt Lightning rock steady in his hands, his eyes glittering like those of a wolverine about to pounce. "You would be Glickman."

"You know me?"

"I know of you. I make it a point to ask about the local law when I mosey into a town. Fancy pants, was how you were described to me, and it fits. You are almost as pretty as my new wife."

Ernestine came and stood next to Jeeter. "That will be enough of that. You are married now. You must be civil."

"Hell," Jeeter Frost said, but he smiled as he said it.

Seamus looked from one to the other. "I was right. You weren't forced to take a vow against your will."

"Excuse me?" Ernestine said.

Briefly, keenly aware every moment of the muzzle pointed at his chest, and the fact that the man pointing it had killed more men than he had fingers and toes, Seamus explained about the justice of the peace, and the posse being assembled. "Once word spreads, the whole town will be out for your husband's hide, lady."

"I don't know as I like that," Jeeter Frost said.

"Like what?" Seamus said. "That everyone wants you dead for stealing the schoolmarm?"

"I don't know as I like how you call her lady. It doesn't sound respectful enough. Call her ma'am. Or Mrs. Frost. One more lady and I will shoot you."

Ernestine smiled. "I like how you stand up for me," she said, and pecked Frost on the cheek.

To Seamus's amazement, the most feared pistolero in the territory blushed. "I wish I was drunk," he said.

"Why?" Jeeter Frost asked.

"So I could laugh without being shot."

"You might be shot anyway, laugh or no laugh." Jeeter gnawed on his lower lip, then declared, "We have us a predicament here, Ernestine. We can't let this hombre go or he'll run to the sheriff and tell where we are."

"The solution is simple," Ernestine said. "We fix it so he can't run to Sheriff Hinkle."

"It is nice we think alike," Jeeter said. "Do you have a sharp knife I can borrow? I should do it quiet-like. A shot would wake the other boarders."

"We don't need to kill him, dearest."

"We don't?"

Ernestine went to the dresser, opened a drawer, and came back with a scarf. "We tie him and gag him. By the time he is found, we will be long gone."

Jeeter Frost winked at Seamus. "See why I married her? Brains and beauty, both. What more can a man ask for?"

"A bottle of whiskey," Seamus said.

"A rope would be better, though, for tying him," Jeeter mentioned to his new bride.

"I am afraid I don't keep rope handy. I work with children, not cows." Ernestine moved to the dresser yet again. "I do have scissors. We can cut the scarf into strips. They will work as well."

"Whatever you say, Mrs. Frost," Jeeter teased.

Seamus did not resist. Not with the Missouri Man-Killer covering him and plainly itching for an excuse to put lead into him. The schoolmarm bound his wrists behind his back, and she did a thorough job, too, tying the knots so tight, his circulation was cut off.

"You are a woman of many talents," Jeeter Frost complimented her after giving her handiwork a tug. "Next you will be telling me that you can break broncs."

"I am good for more than reading and writing," Ernestine said proudly. "You will find I can hold my own. Now let me finish packing."

Jeeter watched her every movement as a puppy might watch its master. "Look at her. She is sunrise in a dress. How did I ever get so lucky?"

"Are you sure you don't have some whiskey?" Seamus asked. "A flask will do."

"We forgot to gag you."

Ernestine was folding her unmentionables. "I will attend to the gagging in a minute, handsome. I need to pack in case someone else shows up and we must depart in a hurry."

"Always one step ahead," Jeeter said to Seamus. "She thinks she can keep me out of trouble and I am beginning to think she can."

"I wish I had someone to keep me out of trouble," Seamus Glickman said.

Chapter 22

Ernestine Frost hurried out the rear of the boarding-house. Behind her came Jeeter, puffing from the weight of her carpetbag. "I am so proud of you," she told him.

Jeeter grunted. The carpetbag was not as heavy as the packs containing her books, which he had already loaded on the horse he had rented from the stable. But it was heavy enough that he would gladly drop it and leave it if Ernestine would not become upset.

"You didn't kill him," Ernestine said. "You had the opportunity but you refrained from squeezing the trigger."

Jeeter had never really considered shooting Glick-man. Not when the shot was bound to draw people, and more law. But he did not mention that to her.

"It shows that you can change," Ernestine said. "That you are not the rabid killer everyone else thinks you are."

"I'm not rabid," Jeeter said.

"I know you are not, my love," Ernestine sweetly declared, and held the gate open for him. "You have proven that my trust in you is not misplaced."

"I'm glad." Now that they were man and wife,

Jeeter naturally wanted to make her happy. But it surprised him considerably that she was so giddy over a trifle.

"I can't wait to get settled somewhere and start our new life together," Ernestine gushed. "Won't it be wonderful?"

"Wonderful," Jeeter echoed as he lugged the carpetbag to the packhorse. "The important thing now is not to be seen riding out of town. If we are seen we will head west to throw them off the scent and swing north later."

"Maybe I should talk to the sheriff," Ernestine said. "Let everyone know I am with you because my heart is swelled with love, and not because you took me against my will."

"That deputy we left tied up in your room knows the truth," Jeeter said. "He will tell the sheriff."

"And all will be well!" Ernestine smiled and clasped her hands and raised her eyes to the starry sky. "Oh, thank you, Lord, for preserving us!"

Jeeter glanced skyward, and frowned. An oversight on his part had occurred to him. He had never asked her feelings on religion. "Talk to God much, do you?" he asked, trying to make the question sound perfectly innocent.

"No more than most, I would imagine," Ernestine said. "The Lord is my shepherd. I shall not want."

"Have you ever read the Bible?"

'Not all the way through, I must confess. But I have read most of it, in snatches, at one time or another. We can read it together nights now that you have learned to read."

Jeeter could think of something he would much

rather do at night than read, but again he held his tongue. "I admit I don't know a lot about it. But something a parson said once has stuck with me. It is the truest thing I ever heard and it explains a lot."

"A parson? You must attend church, then. This is a side to you I did not expect."

Jeeter could not recall the last time he was in God's house. The parson had sat next to him at a restaurant and gone on and on about the Almighty and the soul.

"What did he say that so impressed you?"

In the process of tying a knot, Jeeter answered, "That God sends his rain on the just and the unjust."

Ernestine waited, and when he did not say anything else, she said, "That's it? That one quote?"

"It's enough," Jeeter replied. "It is everything."

"I am not sure I understand. There is a lot more to the Bible than that. It overflows with truth."

"None of the other Bible sayings I have heard made a lot of sense to me," Jeeter said. Particularly the one about turning the other cheek. If he had taken it to heart, he would have long since been dead. "But that one did."

"Don't you worry," Ernestine said. "We will read the Bible together and I will explain everything that needs explaining and it will all make sense." She paused. "But why that one quote more than any other?"

"Ever seen a baby that has had its brains dashed out? Or come upon a woman who has been staked out and raped? Or a man who has been tortured by Apaches?"

"Good Lord, no."

"I have. And that there rain business is why I can sleep at nights," Jeeter said.

"How can—" Ernestine began, and turned. Spurs had jingled in the alley. A man was coming toward them. He wore a high-crowned Stetson and tin gleamed on his shirt. "Oh no!" she whispered.

Jeeter had heard the spurs, too. His Lightning was in his hand, close to his leg, as he came around the packhorse. "Evening," he said with a smile. "What can we do for you?"

"Good evening." The man doffed his hat to Ernestine. "I am Deputy Powell. I am looking for Seamus Glickman and I wonder if you folks—" Powell stopped. "Hold on. Aren't you the schoolmarm, ma'am?"

"She was," Jeeter said, still smiling, and clubbed the deputy above the ear. Once, twice, three times he struck. At each blow Powell staggered. Powell tried to draw his revolver, but it was still in his holster as he oozed to the ground and lay twitching and groaning. Jeeter hit him one more time to shut him up.

"Oh my!" Ernestine breathed. She never did like violence, and this churned her stomach. "Did you have to be so brutal?"

Jeeter was examining his Colt. It appeared none the worse for the clubbing. "He is still alive."

"That is something, I suppose," Ernestine said without much enthusiasm. Here they were, barely married an hour, and already he had tied up one man and beaten another. Lawmen, no less. "I just hope this is the end of it."

Jeeter shoved the Lightning into his holster. "Mount

up. We better light a shuck before someone else shows up."

"Are you sure you don't want me to talk to the sheriff?"

"Not after what I have done to his deputies, no."

"We don't want a posse after us, do we?" Ernestine envisioned her new husband in blazing battle against superior numbers, and shuddered. She did not care to be a widow so soon after becoming a wife.

"They will come after me anyway," Jeeter said.

"I can set things right. Don't you want that?"

"What I want is for us to go on breathing," Jeeter said. "Now, are you my woman or are you not my woman?"

"I said I do, didn't I?"

"Then do as I say and climb on this horse." Jeeter held the reins for her. "We can be long gone by the time this law dog and Glickman are found."

Confused and hurt, Ernestine mounted. "I hope you are not one of those husbands who likes to boss his wife around."

"I am not," Jeeter assured her. "But I will be bossy if I think we will live longer."

"You are off to a fine start."

Jeeter put a hand on her leg. "Trust me. Please. Folks have been thinking bad things about me all my life. I have found that the best way to deal with their misguided notions is to avoid them."

"My mother taught me that honesty is the best policy," Ernestine imparted.

"Honesty is fine and dandy," Jeeter said, "so long as it does not get you dead."

*   *   *

"It is all your fault, big brother," Verve Larn said. "You told us it would be safe to come here."

The four Larn brothers were sitting at the bar in the Tumbleweed, a seedy saloon frequented by those who liked their saloons dark and rarely visited by the law. The owner had spent a good many years behind bars and was friendly to those who had done the same or might end up there.

Stern Larn took a swig straight from his bottle and wiped his mouth with his sleeve. A minute ago, out on the street, there had been a lot of shouting and running around. Then a man had rushed into the saloon and loudly informed the owner that Crooked Creek Sam had been found murdered.

Now Stern said quietly so only his brothers heard, "They don't know it was us who done it. Quit your frettin'."

The man who had rushed in was not done. Puffed up with the importance of his news, he practically hollered, "And that is not all! The schoolmarm has been taken!"

"Taken how?" some asked. "Taken sick?"

"No, no," the man said. "She was stolen."

"Someone abducted the schoolmarm?"

"Hold on to your hat," the man said. He had saved the best tidbit for last. "Word is, the hombre who stole her is Jeeter Frost."

"The hell you say."

Everyone in the saloon began talking at once, some asking questions, others divesting themselves of opinions about the character of any man who would stoop so low as to steal a schoolmarm.

A man at a table near the Larns stood up to say,

"I have done my share of deeds I am not proud of, but I would never stoop to stealin' a woman."

Happy Larn snickered and whispered to his brothers, "Listen to him. Shows how much he knows. We've stole women before. Remember that filly with the red hair? She sure was a wildcat."

"It was a shame you strangled her," Cordial Larn said.

Happy Larn shrugged. "She shouldn't have riled me like she done. She had only herself to blame."

Men were converging on the bar to hear more from the bearer of sensational tidings.

"I told you we had nothin' to worry about," Stern Larn reiterated. "We can finish up and ride on whenever we are of a mind."

"What say we join the posse?" Verve Larn proposed. "It ain't every day we get to hunt a jasper as famous as Jeeter Frost."

His brothers stared at him as if they had never seen him before, and Stern said, "I have heard some lunkhead notions in my time, but that beats all. The idea is for us to fight shy of the law, not rub elbows with it."

"It might be fun," Verve insisted.

"You go if you want," Cordial said. "And if anyone recollects seein' you down toward Crooked Creek and asks if you had anything to do with the death of Crooked Creek Sam, you can tell them shootin' him was fun, too."

"Forget the damn posse," Stern snapped. "We have business in Coffin Varnish the day after tomorrow. Or have you forgotten?"

"I ain't forgot nothin'," Verve said. "I will be there with the rest of you. Kin comes before all else."

"A family is like a chain," Stern said. "All the links have to be strong or the chain will break."

"Dang, that was well put," Happy said. "You have a way with words."

"Enough rotgut and I can babble with the best of 'em." Stern smirked, then soberly told Verve, "But I was serious about the chain. You are one of the links. You must always be there for those who share your blood. Kin is more important than anything."

"I know that."

"Then let's not hear any more foolish talk about posses and such," Stern said. "We have killin' of our own to do. Those Haslett boys would like nothin' better than to put windows in our skulls."

"That is only fittin'," Happy said, snickering, "since I can't wait to put windows in theirs."

"I wish there were more of us than there are of them," Cordial said. "Four against four is too fair."

Stern Larn nodded. "I have been thinkin' the same thing. We need an edge and I figure I have come up with one." He smiled. "We get to Coffin Varnish before they do and lie in wait for them."

"Shoot them from ambush?" Happy said. "The people in Coffin Varnish might not like that."

Verve snorted. "They invite folks to kill one another, they shouldn't be particular about how it is done."

"I never said it had to be *in* Coffin Varnish," Stern Larn said. "We can lie in wait for the Hasletts just outside of town. Pick them off with our rifles before they can get off a shot."

"You are a man after my own heart," Verve said.

"I like the idea as much as you do," Cordial said,

"but there was mention of permits, which means we have to get permission from somebody."

"That's right," Happy said. "If we don't do it right, we are liable to have the law after us."

Stern Larn sat back. "Only if the law knows it was us. What if we shoot the Hasletts and skedaddle? We can be halfway to Denver before anybody comes after us."

"The only one who knew about the feud is Crooked Creek Sam," Verve mentioned, "and he won't be tellin'."

"Let's put it to a vote," Stern said. "Do we bother with a permit or do we do this the way hill folk have been killin' one another since the dawn of creation?" He held up his hand. "I will start. I vote for ambush."

"For ambush," Verve said, squirming in his chair.

Happy Larn added his say. "Ambush."

That left Cordial. He endured their stares while re-filling his glass and then emptied half of it at a gulp.

"Well?" Verve prompted.

"I am a Larn, ain't I?" Cordial said. "I am as strong a link in the chain as any of you."

"Good." Stern Larn rose. "Finish your drinks and let's fan the breeze. We have us some killin' to do."

Chapter 23

Seamus Glickman had pounded his boots on the floor for so long and so hard, his feet were throbbing welters of pain. He pounded them several more times, wincing as his ankles protested with agony, and listening intently for someone to call out and demand to know what all the ruckus was about. The other boarders had to hear. But no one yelled; no one came. He sagged, his chin on his chest.

As soon as Jeeter Frost and the schoolmarm left, Seamus had started pounding. That was a good twenty minutes ago. His ankles were tied, and Frost had secured his arms to the bottom of a bedpost, but he could still move his legs. Not that it had done him any good.

For the umpteenth time Seamus pushed against the gag with his tongue. It would not move. Frost had wedged it fast and tied a smelly bandanna over his mouth to keep it in place. *Damn him to hell!* Seamus thought. Damn them both, the shootist and the schoolmarm. Seamus did not care if Prescott was a woman. She deserved to be strung up by her thumbs and horsewhipped.

Seamus had been doing some pondering while he

pounded and he had come to a decision. He was through with the law. Wearing a badge paid well but not well enough to justify being buried before his time. Jeeter Frost holding that Colt on him had been a revelation. Frost could easily have shot him. Seamus suspected that if not for the schoolmarm, that is exactly what Frost would have done.

Seamus had always appreciated the fact that wearing a badge entailed risks. He knew a lot of lawmen were bucked out in gore. But knowing it in his head and experiencing it were two different things. Now that he had actually and truly stared death in the face, Seamus did not like death's expression.

The question was: Should he stay on until Hinkle's term of office was done with or should he quit right away? He was mulling it over when steps sounded in the hallway and someone shook the door.

"Open up. This is the sheriff."

Seamus slammed his boots on the floor and gurgled as loudly as he could gurgle.

The next instant the door resounded to a powerful blow. The jamb splintered and in burst George Hinkle, his shoulder lowered, his revolver in hand. "Seamus! You're alive!" Hinkle produced a folding knife and made short shrift of the strips of shawl. "I was worried," he said as he cut. "We found Powell out in the alley. Jeeter Frost pistol-whipped him."

The instant his hands were free, Seamus yanked on the bandanna and pulled out the gag. Spitting and coughing, he swallowed a few times to lubricate his throat. "That damned Frost got the drop on me."

"You are lucky all he did was tie you up," Sheriff

Hinkle said. "Powell about had his head half split open."

"Then Frost and the schoolmarm got away?" Seamus stiffly rose and sat on the edge of the bed. He was going to tell Hinkle the truth about Ernestine Prescott, but he had to endure another fit of coughing.

"That poor woman. There is no telling what she has had to endure. Everyone in town is stirred up. I asked for twenty volunteers to form a posse and had to turn forty away."

"There is something you should know," Seamus said.

"Whoever saves her will be the talk of the territory," Hinkle went on. "I intend for that to be us. She is my ticket to better things. To being appointed a federal marshal."

"What are you on about?"

"I don't intend to be a county sheriff forever. This badge is a stepping-stone, like everything else in life." Hinkle came over and clapped Seamus on the shoulder. "I tell you that if we save the schoolmarm, we can rise as high as our ambition takes us."

"We?"

"Don't you have a hankering to move up in the world? Wouldn't you like to be a federal marshal, too? The schoolmarm has done me the biggest favor anyone ever did, and she doesn't even realize it."

"What if she is with Frost because she wants to be with him?" Seamus casually asked.

"Don't be ridiculous. She is being forced. We have the word of the justice of the peace. Besides"—Sheriff Hinkle grinned—"you wouldn't want to spoil my chance at the federal job, would you?" He paused. "Now, what is it you wanted to tell me?"

Seamus thought of how Ernestine Prescott had helped cut the shawl into strips and done some of the binding while Frost covered him. He thought of how she had pulled the wool over everyone's eyes, how she had been seeing Jeeter Frost behind the town's back, as it were, and now the entire town was worried about her welfare and her virtue when she was as safe as could be and had probably lost her virtue some time ago.

"Well?" Sheriff Hinkle prodded.

"I can't rightly recollect," Seamus lied. "Maybe it will come to me later."

"In that case, fetch your horse and whatever supplies you think you will need. The posse heads out in half an hour."

"Do you still want me to lead it?"

"Why wouldn't I? That is, if you are up to it."

"I want to set eyes on the schoolmarm again more than anything," Seamus said. So he could slap her and thank her for her part in his humiliation.

"I am sending Jack Coombs with you," Sheriff Hinkle said.

"That old coot? What for?"

"He is the best tracker in these parts," Hinkle said. "Maybe the best tracker alive. Once the sun is up, call on his talents. It would not surprise me if you are back here tomorrow night with Frost in handcuffs and the schoolmarm singing your praises."

The posse proved to be the usual mix of citizens, notable among them Lawrence Fisch, the son of the president of The First Bank of Dodge City, who also happened to be the president of seven other banks

built in towns along the railroad's right-of-way. Others
included store clerks, a blacksmith's apprentice, Texas
cowboys who had arrived in Dodge two days ago with
a herd, a butcher, a gambler, and the last person in
the world Seamus expected to join a posse. Gigging
his mount over, Seamus said as much.

Frank Lafferty was scribbling on a pad by the light
from a nearby window. "The schoolmarm has been
kidnapped and you wonder why I want to go along?
This will make headlines across the country."

"So you are not in this for her, you are in this for
you." That was more like the Lafferty Seamus knew
and disliked.

"Don't get me wrong. I hope we find her alive
and well."

"But it will be better for your career if she is vio-
lated and dead," Seamus said. "I think I will talk to
the sheriff and have him refuse you permission to go
along."

"He can't," Lafferty said smugly. "Haven't you ever
heard of the First Amendment? I have a right to be
on this posse, more right than anyone else."

"You are a human coyote. Real coyotes feed on
animal carcasses. You feed on the carcasses of people,
like you did the Blights and Paunch Stevens. All so
you can puff yourself up and fill your poke."

"Why, Undersheriff Glickman, how perceptive of
you," Lafferty said. "Imagine, someone wanting to
make money. Or wanting to further their career. I
suppose you have no desire to do either?"

"I hope we catch up to Jeeter Frost and he puts a
slug in your head," Seamus said.

"Spoken like a true lawman."

Seamus reined to the front of the posse and swung his arm to signal they should move out. As they passed the Comique he gave a wistful sigh. He could be eating a thick steak smothered in onions and drinking fine wine. Instead, he was venturing off across the prairie after a vicious killer and a wayward schoolmarm. If he wasn't real careful, it could be that Lafferty would get to feed off another death: his own.

They rode in silence for over an hour.

Jeeter Frost held to a trot until he was sure no one was after them. Then he slowed to a walk. It was folly to exhaust their mounts until there was a definite reason to do so.

Not one word from Ernestine the whole time. She was acting strange, Jeeter concluded. Ordinarily, he liked quiet. He had been alone for so long that quiet was a natural condition. But now that he had someone, her silence ate at him like the sting of rancid vinegar. He took it for as long as he could. Finally, shifting in the saddle, he blunted asked, "Are you still mad at me?"

"Over what?" Ernestine asked.

The suggestion that he might have given her more than a single cause to be mad astounded him. "About me slugging that deputy. What else could it be?"

"Well, there is your bossy disposition," Ernestine said. She never had liked being told what to do. She had a mind of her own and was perfectly willing to exercise it.

"But we had to light a shuck!" Jeeter protested. "If we had hung around Dodge, I would be behind bars by now."

"Perhaps. Perhaps not," Ernestine said. "I am not so certain your attack on the deputy was warranted."

"It sure as hell was," Jeeter said.

Ernestine's already ramrod-straight back became straighter. "I will thank you not to take that tone with me. Nor use that kind of language. Honestly. We have only just been married, and here you are, displaying some disturbing tendencies."

Jeeter felt a funk coming on. "You knew who I am and what I have done when you agreed to be mine."

"I agreed to be your wife, not your property," Ernestine clarified "As for the other, you led me to believe that if we wed, you would put that life behind you and start anew."

"And I will," Jeeter said, "just as soon as we reach somewhere safe."

Ernestine glanced at his darkling profile. "Why not turn over the new leaf here and now? Forsake the old ways? Unbuckle your Colt and put it in your saddlebags."

"Why don't I dig my own grave while I am at it?" Jeeter rejoined. "Or didn't you hear the part about somewhere safe?"

"You can be terribly facetious at times, do you know that?"

Jeeter had no idea what the word meant, but it did not sound like something he wanted to be called. "I do what I have to in order to survive."

"You bring that up a lot. But I am talking about your attitude toward me," Ernestine said. "You have taken to treating me as if I am ten years old."

"That's just silly," Jeeter said. "Who better than me knows you are a growed woman?"

"Grown," Ernestine amended. "And the answer is no one. You are my first and you will be my last. My heart is yours for as long as you want it, and when you do not want it anymore, I will not give it to anyone else."

Jeeter relaxed a little. "You still care for me, then?"

"Now who is being silly?" Ernestine retorted. "Or do you consider me so fickle as to let a little thing like pistol-whipping that deputy come between us?"

"A man never knows with women."

"You will find me as constant as the sun and the moon in my affection for you," Ernestine said. "But always remember. Unlike some women, whose brains are ruled by their bodies, I am the opposite. My body is ruled by my brain and will continue to be so for as long as I endure."

"Even if I have to pistol-whip someone else someday? Or be forced to shoot somebody?"

"You have me by your side now," Ernestine said. "I will see to it that you do not find yourself in situations where violence is called for. It will be my wifely duty to guarantee you never again spill a drop of human blood."

"You are taking a lot on your shoulders."

"You don't want me to try?"

"Hell, Ernestine," Jeeter said, and then, "This marriage business is new to me. I can't change my ways as I would change clothes. It will take time. But I give you my solemn word that once we are shed of Kansas, I will tread softly on your account."

"There is no time like the present," Ernestine insisted. To her, he was merely being stubborn.

"You don't know what you are ask—" Jeeter

stopped and twisted halfway around. "Did you hear that?"

"Hear what?"

"Hoofbeats. Someone is following us."

Ernestine swiveled and listened, but the only hooves she heard were those of their own mounts. She suspected her new husband of trying to change the subject, and grinned. "You are making it up."

Jeeter rose in the stirrups and peered hard into the night behind them. It took a few seconds for what she had said to sink in. "Why in God's name would I do that?"

"I will be grateful if you do not test the Almighty's patience by taking him in vain," Ernestine said.

Jeeter was beginning to wonder about her. She had a knack for taking everything he said the wrong way. Most of the time he did not mind because it was over trifles. But now their lives were at stake. Or at least his, since the good citizens of Dodge thought he had stolen her. He drew rein and she followed his example.

"Why did you stop?"

"Can you hear them now?" Jeeter asked.

Consternation crept over Ernestine. Distant and faint came the unmistakable drum of horses, moving fast. "How did you hear them?" she marveled.

"When you have ridden the wild country as long as I have," Jeeter said, "it comes natural."

"Who do you think it is?"

"Who else? It is the posse. And if they think I will let them get their hands on me, they have another think coming."

Chapter 24

Ernestine Frost was in a bewildered frame of mind. She had lived her entire life without once witnessing an act of violence. Which suited her fine since she always regarded violence as an act of last resort. To her way of thinking, any dispute, any difficulty, could be resolved by talking it out. That was all it took. A little talk and a sincere wish by the parties involved to settle things amicably.

Then she married Jeeter Frost. Since her wedding she had held a lawman at gunpoint and helped bind him, then watched as another lawman was beaten senseless.

Now this.

Ernestine had never been particularly squeamish. She was not one of those who fainted at the sight of blood. Once she had come on the scene of a mishap involving a wagon that overturned and crushed the driver. She had seen the man's crumpled form, seen shattered ribs sticking from the man's pulped chest, and been unmoved. So it was not the grisly aftermath of violence she abhorred as much as it was the idea of violence itself.

By rights she should object to Jeeter inflicting more. But she was in a quandary. She had pledged herself to him, promised to be the best wife she could be, to stand by him through thick and thin. She should stand by him now and do as he wanted, but when he told her his plan, she balked.

"I refuse."

"I am your husband. You are supposed to do as I ask."

"How many wives are asked to do what you want me to do?" Ernestine pointed out. "You overstep the boundaries."

Jeeter stifled his exasperation. He reminded himself that she was new to this sort of life. "Are you saying there are limits to your love?"

"I most definitely am not!" Ernestine replied, flustered by the suggestion. "When you give someone your heart, you give them all of you."

"I gave mine to you," Jeeter said.

Ernestine was confounded by how adroitly he had turned her argument against her. "And I to you!" she said more shrilly than she intended.

"Then why won't you do it?"

"Men could die," Ernestine said, thinking that would settle it.

"*I* could die," he rebutted. "Would you rather have that?"

Choked with emotion by a mental image of him lying on the plain shot to pieces and covered with blood, Ernestine said, "No, never." And knew she had lost.

"Right here will do, then," Jeeter said. "Remember,

do it when they are twenty yards out. Remember to drop flat when the lead starts flying. Don't worry about me. I can take care of myself."

"Can't we avoid them? It is night. It should be easy."

"If we don't do it now, we will have to do it later," Jeeter said. "I would rather we had the edge than they did."

Ernestine bowed her head. "I pray God will forgive me." She heard him take the packhorse and go off into the dark, and she had never felt so frightened as she did waiting there alone for the posse to catch up. She prayed they would not find her. She prayed they would pass her to the east or the west, but it was not to be. The pounding of hooves grew louder, ever louder, and when it was loud enough to match the pounding in her veins, she climbed down, held firmly on to the reins, and called out, "Who is there? What do you want?"

The riders came to a stop. For a while there was silence and then a youthful voice asked, "Was that a female?"

"Yes," answered someone in a harsh tone.

"Shouldn't we answer her?"

Ernestine could just make them out, a knot of men and horses close enough to hit with a flung stone. "Who are you? What do you want?" she repeated, giving them the chance to say they were not the posse and were not after Jeeter and her.

"Who is askin'?" the man with the harsh voice demanded.

"I asked you first," Ernestine said. "If you are a gentleman, you will answer first."

"I ain't no gentleman," the man snapped. "Who are you? Are you alone? What in hell are you doin' out here?"

Ernestine probed the night for Jeeter. He would not wait long to spring his surprise. She must talk fast. "Tell me you are not out to harm anyone. Tell me you are not out to kill."

There was a gasp, and another voice said, "Did you hear? How does she know?"

"It is not natural," said yet another man. "Maybe she's not real. She could be a haunt."

"I don't want to tangle with no spook!" exclaimed the youngest.

"Shut up, all of you!" the harsh one commanded. "She's not no haunt." He raised his voice. "You're not no haunt, are you, lady?"

"I am not sure what a haunt is," Ernestine told him, "but I am flesh and blood just like you. Now please. Who are you? Who do you intend to kill?"

"The party we are after should have been planted long ago," the man said. "If ever there was a case of deservin' to die, this is it."

They had to be referring to her Jeeter. Ernestine took a step, pleading, "Ride off! Now! Before it is too late! Oh, I beg of you! Ride for your lives!"

"What are you talkin' about, damn it?" the man growled, and then, almost in the same breath, "Wait! You're the schoolmarm! The one the whole town is stirred up about!"

"We found her?" the young-sounding one said.

By then Jeeter Frost was close enough. He had slunk on foot in a loop that brought him up from the rear, and he had his Colt Lightning out when he came to the first of them. He pressed the muzzle to the man's spine and blew the backbone into splinters. At the shot the man cried out and flung forward over the saddle, spooking his mount, which bolted. Instantly, Jeeter sprang to the second rider, jammed the Lightning low against the man's side, and squeezed off another shot. The slug, angling upward, tore through the man's innards and burst out between the sternum and the clavicle. The man was dead before his body started to fall.

Whirling, Jeeter aimed at the belly of a third and put a slug into it. The logical thing to do was finish him with another shot, but there was a fourth rider to deal with, and the man was wheeling his mount and unlimbering a revolver while cursing a mean streak. Jeeter aimed for the neck since a neck shot nearly always killed outright or slowed them enough that they were easy to dispatch, but with the rider moving and with the dark his aim was off and the slug caught the rider in the side of the head, which worked just as well.

Jeeter turned, thumbing back the hammer. The man he had shot in the belly was clinging to the saddle horn, ink that was not ink spreading down his leg and over his saddle. Jeeter raised the Lightning.

"Why us?" the man asked hoarsely, his voice quavering. "Why in hell did you do this to us?"

"You should have left well enough be," Jeeter said.

"But—"

Jeeter shot him between the eyes, a nice shot that made up for missing the other one's neck. The man pitched from the saddle and the horse ran off. Jeeter did not try to stop it. They did not need another horse.

In the quiet that followed, Jeeter commenced reloading. He thought they were all dead until the one he had shot in the spine groaned and went on groaning. He went over. The man was on his back, paralyzed, unable to move anything but his lips. Out came flecks of blood.

"You done killed me."

"That was the general idea."

"You are him, aren't you? Frost?"

"I am him."

The man was fading, his face ungodly pale. "You are a hellion. But if I have to die, it might as well be someone famous who kills me."

Jeeter squatted and remarked, "You are the politest hombre I ever shot. I would like to remember your name. What is it?"

"Happy," the man said, and smiled, and died.

The eyes bothered Jeeter. He reached down and closed them.

"Did I hear correctly?" Ernestine asked. She had come up behind him. "He told you that he died happy?"

"You should not look at this," Jeeter said, unfurling and facing her. "It ain't fitting."

"Isn't," Ernestine said. "And I was the bait, wasn't I? If I don't have the right, who does?" She went from body to body, glad the dark hid the worst of it. "Only four? I thought the posse would be bigger."

"They must be spread out," Jeeter said. "Groups of them across the prairie, the better to catch me. Which is why we can't dawdle."

"Four lives snuffed like candles," Ernestine said softly. "Tell me how you feel, if you don't mind."

"I am glad it was them and not me." Jeeter sought sign of more riders out on the benighted sea of grass, but he might as well have peered into the depths of a well.

"That is all?"

"What else is there?" Jeeter said. "It was them or me and as long as I am breathing it will not be me."

"I must say," Ernestine commented, "this is a night of revelations. You are more than the man I thought you were."

"Is that good or bad?" Jeeter asked. Her attitude was grating on him. She could nitpick a thing to death, this woman.

"I honestly don't know yet," Ernestine admitted. It was all too new, too disturbing. She glanced at the dead man at their feet. "Why isn't he wearing a badge?"

"Eh?" Jeeter looked, and shrugged. "Most sheriffs don't have a lot of badges to pass out. They swear in those who join, and that's enough."

"Do we bury them?"

"Only if you want the rest of the posse to catch me," Jeeter said. The shots were bound to bring them. He clasped her hand and started toward his mount and the packhorse, but abruptly stopped and turned around. "Where is my head tonight?" Quickly, he bent and searched the dead man's pockets.

"What are you doing?" Ernestine asked, although she had guessed. But she was too horrified to admit it.

"They might have money on them." Jeeter found several coins, and chuckled. "Look here. A half eagle and some half dimes. I will treat you to a meal in Coffin Varnish."

"I will not eat food bought with stolen money," Ernestine said.

"Taking from a corpse isn't stealing," Jeeter argued. "A corpse can't own anything."

"Your logic never fails to astound me. Next you will say this wasn't murder since they were out to murder you."

"Self-defense, I call it. It is their fault for coming after me. If they had let me be, they wouldn't be lying here."

Ernestine gazed at the other bodies. "They were only doing what they thought was right. The people in Dodge City think you have abducted me. This is what comes of you not letting me explain the situation to them."

"You want me behind bars, is that it? Say so now and we can part company with no hard feelings." Jeeter moved to the second man.

Stunned, Ernestine said, "How can you say that with our vows so fresh? Is that all I am to you? The same as a new shirt?"

Jeeter sensed the answer was important to her. He stopped frisking and met her gaze. "You are everything to me, and I want you by my side the rest of my born days."

"Then forget playing the vulture and let's ride," Ernestine said, adding as an afterthought, "Please."

"Fetch your horse," Jeeter said. He figured that would buy him time to finish searching, but her animal was only a few yards away. He gave her a boost, then did something he would never have done if he had been by himself: He walked away from dead men and the money they had on them.

"Are you upset with me?"

"Why would you think that?" Jeeter smiled to hide his feelings. Sometimes talking to her was like playing poker; he had to wear a poker face so she would not guess the truth.

"A woman has her intuition. You are not one of those who wears his sentiments on his sleeve, but you give enough away with how you talk and act." Ernestine smiled. "I am sorry if I nag you."

"I don't think that." Jeeter had told another falsehood. He was about to say more, but his keen hearing had detected the distant drum of more hooves. A lot more.

"What is it?"

"More of the posse, just like I reckoned," Jeeter said. "Enough jabber for a spell. We have to fan the breeze."

Fan it they did, at a gallop for a quarter of a mile, then a canter, then a walk. By then Jeeter could no longer hear their pursuers, and so long as he couldn't hear them, they did not pose an immediate threat.

"What if they follow us all the way to Coffin Varnish?" Ernestine asked.

"It will just be too bad for them."

Ernestine shook her head. "Why must you always talk like that? Why are you always so ready to kill?" She did not understand. She just did not understand. He had so many good traits, yet he shot people as if he were squashing flies. What was she missing that would explain it? she asked herself.

"I like breathing," Jeeter said.

"It is more than that. It has to be."

Jeeter pondered long and hard but still could not

think of a way to satisfactorily explain to her. Then squat shapes and a few lights hove out of the gloom to the north. "Coffin Varnish," he said.

"How far behind would you say that posse is?" Ernestine wanted to know. It was beginning to look to her as if her marriage would be one of the shortest in history.

"Far enough," Jeeter Frost said. "Don't you worry. When they get here they are in for a surprise."

Chapter 25

Chester Luce was having the most wonderful dream.

He was the governor of Kansas. He lived in a stately mansion and had servants to wait on his every whim. He was driven everywhere in a fine carriage. When people saw him, men doffed their hats out of respect and women gave him the sort of look that showed they were interested in getting to know him better. Best of all, he had a secretary. Her name was Helga. She bore a remarkable resemblance to Filippa Anderson, only she wore clothes that were much more revealing than the plain dresses Filippa always wore.

In his dream Chester had invited her to a private supper, just the two of them eating by candlelight. He had dismissed the servants. By coincidence, Adolphina had gone off to Wichita to attend a conference on the growing role of women in government.

Chester had just poured a glass of red wine for his guest and was savoring the tantalizing fragrance of her perfume when someone had the audacity to pinch his nose.

In his dream Chester was perplexed. He could not understand why his nose was being pinched. Nor could he see who was pinching it because they were standing behind him and had reached around to do the pinching. He was about to demand they cease and desist when he woke up with a start and realized with a greater start that his nose *was* being pinched. In real life he could see who was pinching it by the light of a lamp held by a woman who stood in the doorway of his bedroom.

"You!" Chester Luce blurted, whispering.

"Me," Jeeter Frost said quietly, and let go of his nose. "I woke you rather than your missus, but I can wake her, too, if you want me to."

Chester glanced over. They slept in separate beds. Adolphina insisted on that. She did not like being touched while she slept and he occasionally, and quite by accident, brushed her with a leg or a knee, which always woke her and resulted in a tirade about the evils of the flesh. Chester had not objected when she proposed the idea. His wife was a big woman, and she liked to sprawl out, making it hard for him not to touch her. For the first year of their marriage he had curled into a corner and tried his best to stay there. Unfortunately, once he was asleep, his body had a mind of its own.

"Do you want me to?" Jeeter asked when the mayor did not reply.

"No. Please. Let her sleep." Chester slowly sat up and adjusted his nightshirt. "How did you get into my house? What do you want? Who is that woman with you?" He asked all his questions softly so as not to wake his wife, who at that moment started to snore loud enough to shake the walls.

Jeeter glanced at her in annoyance. He never had liked people who snored. Once, down in San Antonio, he shot through the wall of his hotel room because the snoring of the man in the next room woke him up. He had not meant to hurt the man, only to wake him so he would stop snoring. But damned if the slug didn't catch the man in the leg. It woke him up, sure enough, and set him to squalling. Jeeter barely made it out of the hotel a step ahead of the law. "Come with me," he commanded.

Ernestine preceded them down the hall. She was amazed at how Jeeter had barged into the house as if it were his. Unlike Dodge, where the people knew enough to lock their doors at night, the back door had not been latched.

"I repeat," Chester said when they stopped out of earshot of the bedroom. "What are you two doing here? What is the meaning of this?"

"I figure you owe me a favor," Jeeter said.

"So you come into my house uninvited at—" Chester stopped. "What time is it, anyway?"

"A little after two, I think. I don't own a watch so I can't be sure."

"In the *morning*? My God, man. What was so important that you couldn't wait?"

"The favor," Jeeter repeated. "I want you to get it right. If you mess it up, it will be just too bad for you and your dust devil of a town."

The threat was cold water in Chester's face. He remembered the Blight brothers, and that journalist, and the reputation of the small man standing in front of him, and he blanched. "Perhaps you would be so kind as to explain," he said in his most diplomatic manner.

"A posse is after me. When they get here, you are

to say you haven't seen any sign of us," Jeeter instructed.

"A posse? From where? What have you done?"

"From Dodge," Jeeter said.

"My least favorite place in all the world," Chester said. Even more so after the hard time the sheriff's office was giving him over the notice and its aftermath.

"Then you shouldn't have any objection to lying to them," Jeeter said. "That, and you are a politician."

Chester chose to overlook the slur. "What did you do to get a posse after you?"

"Not much," Jeeter said. "The important thing is that they don't find me. If they do, I will have to do more of what I have done."

"You are being evasive," Chester said, and when Jeeter put his hand on his Colt Lightning, he quickly added, "Not that I will make an issue of it. Although I fail to see how this constitutes a favor."

"It's simple," Jeeter said. "I heard about what you've done. How you invite folks here to kill, for money. All because of me shooting those brothers that day. That's the favor."

"Ah. Which brings us to the pretty young lady," Chester said. He was stretching the truth. She was not really all that pretty, or all that young.

"She's my wife," Jeeter revealed.

"You don't say." It never occurred to Chester that a man-killer would have a woman tucked away somewhere. "I am pleased to meet you, Mrs. Frost."

"Thank you," Ernestine said. "My husband has told me about you. We are in your debt."

"Nonsense. Consider it a gesture of goodwill."

"You will do it, then?" Jeeter asked.

"Did you doubt I would?" Chester rejoined, when what he really wanted to say was, *Do I have a choice?* "When do you expect the posse?"

"It depends on if they find the bodies or not and take the time to bury them," Jeeter said.

"What is this about bodies?" Chester's goodwill evaporated like dew under a hot sun. "You have killed again?"

"Relax. They were from Dodge."

"Was it self-defense?" Chester envisioned being arrested for harboring a murderer. There went his governorship, his mansion, his servants, his delightful personal secretary.

"Sort of," Jeeter said. "You can go back to bed now. It will be a few hours yet."

Inwardly quaking at the image of himself behind bars, Chester absently asked, "Where will you be?"

"In your kitchen."

An invisible knife sank into Chester's gut, and twisted. "What?"

"In your kitchen," Jeeter said again. "My wife is going to put coffee on so we can stay awake. If your wife wakes up, tell her you have guests and not to raise a fuss."

Chester could not imagine telling his wife anything. Suggesting, yes, so long as he suggested tactfully. "There is an empty house down the street. I can take you. You would do better to stay there."

"Here," Jeeter insisted. "It is the last place the posse would expect."

"What if they come in?" Chester said. "What if they spot you? Think of the consequences."

"I am thinking of my wife and what is best to keep her safe," Jeeter said.

Ernestine felt a rush of warmth. Here was more proof of how deeply he cared.

"I will do what I can to help you," Chester said, wishing they were anywhere but in his house.

"I thought you might."

Jeeter Frost had a lot to do, too.

First he installed his new wife in the kitchen and left her to make coffee while he led their horses down the street toward the livery. Halfway there he stopped. The livery was one of the first places the posse would check. Three weary horses were all the incentive they needed to search the town from end to end.

Jeeter scratched the stubble on his chin and pondered. One of the abandoned buildings was an old feed and grain. It was big and spacious and empty. He led the horses around to the back. As with many feed and grains, there was a wide door where farmers had loaded their wagons. The door was open a few inches. Rusty hinges creaked as he opened it all the way. The area where the wagons pulled in was solid earth, not a wood floor. He brought the gruella and the other two horses inside and tied them so they could not stray off. He did not strip the saddles or the packs. He might need to get away in a hurry.

Jeeter felt bad about that. The gruella was tired and needed rest, and he never mistreated the mouse dun if he could help it. Patting its neck, he said, "I will feed and water you as soon as I can. I promise."

He went out, closed the door, and walked around to the street. He was congratulating himself on his

cleverness when he glanced down. It was too dark to
see hoofprints, but he knew they were there. A good
tracker could tell they were recent and follow them
straight to the feed and grain.

Jeeter did not know if the posse had a tracker with
them, but he never took chances, yet another reason
he had lasted as long as he had. He hastened to the
general store, found a broom behind the counter, and
came back out. He was brushing at the dust when
a large pig came out of a vacant yard and squealed
inquisitively at him.

Jeeter had a brainstorm. "Stay right where you are,
pig," he said, and ran back into the general store.
Saratoga Chips were exactly what he needed. When
he ran back out, the pig was rooting along a fence.
He opened the chips and held one out. "Here, pig.
Try one of these."

Pigs would eat most anything, and were always hungry. It was why they were called pigs, Jeeter reflected,
as he held the chip under the pig's nose. It sniffed a
few times, grunted a few, and chomped, nearly biting
Jeeter's fingers.

"Like that, do you?" Jeeter grinned and backed into
the street while holding out another chip.

The pig took the bait.

After that the rest was easy. Jeeter had only to walk
back and forth over the prints his horses had made,
the pig following him like a little lamb, until a multi-
tude of pig prints overlay the horse tracks.

It would have to do, Jeeter told himself. Pig prints
were less obvious than the swipes of a broom. He
gave the pig the last of the chips and hurried into

the general store, being sure to bolt the front door after him.

The aroma of brewing coffee made Jeeter's mouth water and reminded him of how hungry he was. He was delighted to find a plate of toast and jam waiting for him.

"I thought you might like something to eat," Ernestine said.

"You are a fine wife," Jeeter complimented. "When we get to California, I will do my best to do you proud."

Ernestine sat at the other end of the table and buttered a slice of toast. "Do you trust the mayor to do as you want?"

"I reckon he had reason to oblige us," Jeeter said, and patted his Colt.

"A word from him to the posse and you could face the gallows," Ernestine mentioned. She had been thinking about it while she made the coffee and the toast. "I would rather not have any husband of mine hanged."

"We will listen at the kitchen door," Jeeter said. "We will hear if he says anything."

"Not if he whispers."

Once again Jeeter marveled at how she thought of everything. "What do you suggest?"

"One of us should hide in the store, close to the front door," Ernestine proposed. "In the corner by the dry goods is a table with bolts of cloth on it."

Jeeter had seen the table. He could unravel a few of the bolts, enough so the cloth hung over the edge and hid him. "I like it. I like it a lot."

"You be careful," Ernestine said. "If they see you, you will have to fight your way out."

"Some wives wouldn't care half as much."

"I am not them. I took you for better or worse. At the moment it is more the latter than the former, but we will have plenty of the former if we can put the latter behind us. Just don't shoot anyone if you can help it."

"For you I will try real hard," Jeeter said. Reaching across the table, he placed his hand on hers. "I am sorry. This is not much of a wedding night."

"It is different, I will say that for it," Ernestine said. "I will have something to tell our children and our grandchildren."

The idea of kids jolted Jeeter. The life he had led did not lend itself to dreams of a family and a home. But now both were very real prospects. Him, a father! Bouncing a baby on his knee. Teaching his son to fish and hunt and use a gun. That last gave him mental pause. The way of the gun was hard and brutal. His son deserved better. His son should have a quiet, peaceful life. His son should be able to walk the streets without fear of being shot in the back.

"You have a strange look," Ernestine said.

"What do you want our son to be when he grows up?"

"I haven't given it any thought," Ernestine admitted. "I suppose I would like for him to be well-to-do, and happy. Happy, most of all."

"Happy is important," Jeeter agreed. He had spent so much of his life alone and unhappy.

"I like how you think ahead," Ernestine said. "We

have not had a baby yet, yet you are looking out for
its welfare."

"I wish—" Jeeter began. But he did not get to say
what he wished. For just then hooves thudded outside
in the street. A voice was raised and the thudding
came to a stop.

The posse had arrived.

Chapter 26

Seamus Glickman was not in a good mood. He thought it would be simple. Ride hard, overtake the shootist and the schoolmarm, and bring them back to Dodge City. That was how it should have gone. But his posse was not able to ride as hard as he wanted. Almost from the moment they left Dodge, he had to hold them back. All because of one man.

Jack Coombs was drunk. The old scout was fond of liquor, so much so that he practically walked around with a bottle glued to his mouth. Dodge residents were accustomed to seeing him stagger down streets, bouncing off hitch rails and walls. They thought it comical.

Not Seamus. Drunk and disorderly was a misdemeanor, but he took it as seriously as murder. It helped that he always received a share of the fine imposed. Arresting four or five drunks a night was always a profitable enterprise.

Had it been up to him, Seamus would not have invited Jack Coombs along. Granted, Coombs was once a top army scout, but that was years ago. Coombs had long since given it up. His age was a factor. Creaking joints and aching muscles took a toll on a man, especially when he spent most of every day in the saddle.

Another factor, a bigger factor as far as the army was concerned, was Coombs's drinking. It got so he could barely sit the saddle when he rode out on patrol. So the army let him go and Jack Coombs drifted. From town to town and saloon to saloon he wound his inebriated way, until, somehow or other, he ended up in Dodge. And in Dodge he stayed. In Dodge there were often cowboys willing to buy an old scout a drink and listen to his tales of yesteryear. Coombs also earned drinking money by sweeping out stores and shoveling manure when he was sober enough to handle a shovel.

At the moment, Jack Coombs could barely handle a set of reins. Every now and then he swayed, and just when Seamus was certain the old fool would pitch from the saddle, Coombs righted himself and kept riding.

After the sixth or seventh time, Seamus lost his patience. Slowing to a walk, he snapped, "Why in hell did you come along, old man?"

Jack Coombs had gray hair and skin that in certain light appeared almost as gray. He was worn and weathered and wrinkled. He smelled of old leather, which might be due to the frayed buckskins he had not washed since Adam knew Eve, and might be him. "I beg your pardon?" he said politely in that cracked voice of his.

"You heard me," Seamus said in disgust. "You should be back in Dodge sleeping your latest binge off, not out after a killer and a kidnapper."

"The sheriff needed a tracker."

"The sheriff has a hole in his head," Seamus countered. "In your condition, you couldn't track a Conestoga if you were tied to the tailboard."

"That was mean," Coombs criticized.

"It is the truth and you know it," Seamus said. "Do us all a favor and head back. I will tell Hinkle you came down sick. There will be no hard feelings."

Jack Coombs tugged at the scraggily gray wisps that hung from his chin. "I reckon I will stick with it."

"Damn you, you are slowing us down."

"I will help plenty once the sun comes up and I can track," Coombs said. "Just you wait and watch."

"Sunrise is hours away yet," Seamus noted. "You can't stay in the saddle that long."

"In my prime I could go three days without rest or food," Coombs said. "The white Comanche, folks called me."

Seamus sighed. "You are no more a Comanche than I am the Queen of England. And in case you have not made use of a mirror lately, your prime was as many years ago as you have wrinkles."

Coombs sniffed and looked away. "You think you are clever but you are not. Those like you always think they are so clever, but they bleed the same as everybody else."

"Was that a threat?" Seamus bristled.

The old scout snickered. "You said it yourself. In the condition I'm in, I couldn't stomp a flea. So I'm hardly likely to threaten a fire-eater like you."

"Keep it up, old man."

"Why must you pester me? I have never done you no hurt," Jack Coombs said.

"You are an aggravation I do not need," Seamus told him. "You were inflicted on me against my wishes."

"I can track," Coomb said.

Part of Seamus urged him to let it be, but he couldn't. "What is going to happen come morning when you start to dry out? You will be a wreck. How much tracking can you do when the shakes strike?"

"One bridge at a time," Coomb said, and then stiffened and rose in the stirrups. "That feller you sent on ahead is on his way back, and he is riding hell-for leather."

Seamus gazed to the north. All he saw was grass and dark. All he heard was the sigh of the wind. "You are loco. I don't see or hear anything."

"You will in a bit," Coombs said. "Maybe I do have whiskey oozing out my pores, but I still have the ears of a wolf and the eyes of an eagle."

"You are lucky if you have the ears of an earthworm," Seamus said.

"Shows how much you know. Worms don't have ears."

Seamus sighed again. If being stupid was ever made a crime, the scout would be one of the first thrown behind bars. He was about convinced he should have two posse members escort Coombs back to Dodge, by force if need be, when his horse pricked its ears and snorted, and a few seconds later he pricked his own ears, and swore.

"So the old man was right," Frank Lafferty said. He had been behind them the whole time, listening.

"Don't you have anything better to do than listen to others talk?" Seamus irritably demanded.

"I am a journalist. Listening is what I do best."

The rider Seamus had sent ahead was Lawrence Fisch, the son of the president of the First Bank of Dodge City. For the posse Lawrence, always one to suit his clothes to the occasion, had donned new store-bought overalls, boots with big Mexican spurs, a flannel shirt more suitable for winter, chaps, of all things, a high-crowned Stetson that could pass for a butte, and not one but two nickel-plated Remingtons he had never fired a day in his life. "You will never guess!" he breathlessly declared as he reined to a halt.

"I won't even try," Seamus said. "What has you so flustered?"

"Bodies," Lawrence Fisch said. "Bodies everywhere."

"What? Where?"

"Between here and Coffin Varnish. About a mile or more, as the grouse flies."

That was another thing about the banker's son that got Seamus's goat. Lawrence Fisch had a habit of mangling figures of speech. "As the crow flies," he amended. "And you saw these bodies with your own eyes?"

"Would I have raced like hell to tell you if I hadn't?" Lawrence rebutted. "My horse nearly stepped on one. It was prancing and acting up, and then I smelled the blood. God, the blood."

"Did you see Jeeter Frost or the schoolmarm?"

"No. Just the bodies. Strangers, although I have the feeling I have seen them around Dodge."

"Show us," Seamus directed. Shifting in the saddle, he bellowed at the posse members, "Dead people ahead! Keep your eyes skinned!"

To the creak of leather and the ratchet of rifle levers

being worked, the posse broke into a trot. Seamus was in front next to Fisch, Coombs, and Lafferty right behind them.

The bodies resembled peculiar dark humps until Seamus got close. He came to a stop and the others followed suit, then came up on either side so they could see the bodies, too. Bodies were always interesting. Bodies were something to talk about because people were always fascinated by them.

Seamus dismounted and was again imitated.

"Anyone know who they were?" Frank Lafferty asked as they went from one dead man to another.

"I do," Seamus said. He had encountered the Larn brothers a few times in Dodge. They were from a hill clan in the South, and they were not to be trifled with. But someone had more than trifled. Someone had blown the four of them to hell and back.

A fire was kindled. Not much of a fire since they were using grass for fuel, but it was enough light for Seamus to establish that the Larns had been ambushed. "This one was shot in the back," he noted.

Always seeking facts, Lafferty asked, "Who could have done this?"

"It seems pretty obvious to me," Seamus said. "Jeeter Frost."

"But why?" Lafferty asked. "What were these men to him? What motive did he have?"

"I can't begin to guess," Seamus said, then went ahead and guessed anyway. "Maybe they heard about the schoolmarm and were trying to save her. Maybe Frost didn't want them telling anyone they had seen him and her. Hell, maybe he killed them for the thrill of it."

"Do you think he would do a thing like that?" Lawrence Fisch asked.

"Who knows why killers kill?" was Seamus's retort. "Anyone who would run off with a schoolmarm has to be one mean son of a bitch." He felt a twinge of conscience at saying that. He was the only man there, the only person in all of Dodge City, who knew that the schoolmarm had run off with Frost willingly. But it was too late for the truth.

"Do we bury them, Sheriff?" a Texas cowboy inquired. "Or leave them for the buzzards?"

"We are Christians, aren't we?" Seamus said. When, in truth, he could not remember the last time he set foot in a church. But an idea had occurred to him. If he delayed the posse, if he contrived to slow them enough, Frost and Prescott might get away. And despite Sheriff Hinkle's grand notion about using the fame garnered from arresting Frost to become a federal marshal, Seamus was of the opinion that it was best for everyone if the clandestine lovers escaped. The only jinx in the works was Jack Coombs, but Seamus could deal with him later. Then another posse member rained on his parade of thoughts.

"What do we bury them with? We didn't bring shovels or picks and this ground is too hard to use our hands."

"We can wrap them in blankets and take them with us," Jack Coombs suggested. "Have them buried in Coffin Varnish."

For a drunk it was a damn good idea. Seamus scowled. He would have to do something about Coombs soon. "We'll do that. Put the bodies on horses that aren't skittish. Do it right and wrap them good and tight."

It was half an hour before they were under way again. Seamus had to pretend to be in a hurry without actually being in a hurry. When they were about ready he sent the rich kid, Lawrence Fisch, on ahead again, inwardly chuckling at the lunkhead's attire.

Seamus noticed that Jack Coombs sat in the saddle a little steadier than before. The liquor was wearing off. Pretty soon Coombs would be as sober as the rest of them, and sober the man was as good a tracker as any who drew breath. Seamus couldn't have that. He couldn't have that at all.

Eventually Coffin Varnish reared in the distance. Fisch came riding back to inform them the town was quiet and peaceful and everyone appeared to be asleep although there were a few lamps on. "We will disturb everyone if we go riding on in."

Seamus liked that, though. He doubted Frost and the woman were there, but if they were, the more noise the posse made, the better the chance Frost would hear and avoid them. So he rode at a gallop, and when they neared the outskirts, he bellowed, "Stay alert, men! That killer could be anywhere!"

A nice touch, Seamus thought. He brought them to a stop in front of the general store, and it was not long before a light glowed and the door tinkled and the mayor, in his nightshirt, peeked out.

"I say. What is the meaning of this? Some of us are trying to sleep."

Seamus dismounted and brushed dust from his clothes. "Remember me? We are on official business. Law business. We are after Jeeter Frost."

"He has stolen the schoolmarm," a posse member said.

"And we have bodies," Jack Coombs piped up.

"My word!" Chester Luce declared. "Give me a minute to get dressed and I will be right out."

"Take five if you need to," Seamus said generously.

Frank Lafferty came over to him. "Shouldn't we search the town? Go from building to building and turn it upside down?"

"Down the street is an Italian family with kids," Seamus said. "You want to scare them half to death?" He indicated the eastern horizon. "No, it will be daylight soon enough. We will search then, when it is safer." He added with secret glee at the extra delay, "We have the bodies to bury first."

"When it is light I can track," Jack Coombs said. "It won't take us long to catch them then."

That was exactly what Seamus did not want to happen. He leaned against the hitch rail until the mayor reappeared, fully dressed.

"How may I be of assistance?"

"We need shovels to dig with," Seamus said. "Coffee, too, to keep us awake. We have been in the saddle all night."

"I don't have room for all of you in the store," Chester said. "But there is plenty of room over to the saloon. I will wake Win Curry."

Seamus could have hugged him. "And the shovels?"

"Oh, those I have. You can borrow a few I have for sale. Just don't scrape them up if you can help it."

Jack Coombs glanced at Seamus. "You are forgetting to ask him the most important thing." To the mayor he said, "Have you seen any sign of Jeeter Frost and the schoolmarm?"

"I have been in bed all night," Chester replied. "Unless he marched into my bedroom and stuck a gun up my nose, I doubt it."

Seamus laughed. "Bring the shovels. Any picks you have, too. Then you can go wake Curry." He stared across the street at the saloon. There was the solution to his problem. "I can sure use that coffee." But it was not coffee he was thinking of.

Chapter 27

Adolphina Luce did not like to get up early. She always did, to order Chester to fix breakfast, but she always went back to bed as soon as she was done eating. She would stay there until she absolutely had to get up. She liked to lie and slowly let life seep back into her until she had enough energy to rise and do whatever chore needed doing. So she was mildly miffed at the commotion her husband was making so early, and then more than mildly miffed when he came into the bedroom to dress and informed her a posse had shown up, and explained he must attend to them in his official capacity as mayor, and for her not to bother herself but stay in bed and sleep.

There were days when Adolphina would just as soon he had not been elected. He was always scooting off to do this or that, yet often as not she found him at the saloon. But she only had to remind herself his being mayor was a stepping-stone to greater things to temper her annoyance.

On this particular morning Adolphina tried to get back to sleep and couldn't. Her mind would not shut down as she wanted. The curse of having a keen brain, she lamented. Because the truth be told, she *was* the brains of their marriage. Were things left up to him, they would be in the poorhouse.

The sun was barely risen when Adolphina reluctantly rose, donned her robe, and padded down the stairs to the store. Her husband was not there. She went to the front window and saw men loitering in front of the saloon.

"It figures," Adolphina said aloud. Leave it to men to come up with an excuse to drink. She turned and shuffled down the hall to the kitchen. She was surprised the lamp was lit. She was even more surprised to smell the aroma of coffee and food. But neither matched the surprise she felt when a pistol barrel was flourished in her face.

"Not so much as a peep, lady. I am Jeeter Frost and you will do as I tell you."

Adolphina had never seen the man-killer, but she had heard him described. She was not the least bit intimidated. "What are you doing in my house?" she demanded.

"Having breakfast," said a spindly woman by the stove. "Would you care to join us, Mrs. Luce?"

"Who are you?" Adolphina snapped. "Are you with this brute?"

"That I am," Ernestine Frost said sweetly. "Here. Let me pour you a cup of coffee and I will enlighten you."

Adolphina listened in horror to the schoolmarm's tale. How anyone in her right mind could wed a nasty speck of bile like Jeeter Frost was beyond her. The only conclusion she could come to was that the poor woman was delusional. Or desperate. Adolphina could understand the latter. There had been a time when

she had feared she was fated to go through life unat-
tached. She was no blushing romantic. When she
looked in the mirror she saw a big ox of a woman,
and few men liked to marry oxen. Then along came
Chester, who had never been with a woman in his life
but took it into his silly little head that she was the
one for him.

Adolphina never could figure out why. Chester
could do better. Not a smarter woman, certainly, but
better looking. Yet he courted her. She had pretended
not to be interested, which only increased his ardor,
such as it was, all the while assessing his prospects.
As a lover he made a great lump of clay. He not only
did not know what to do; he was scared to death to
do the little he knew. She'd had to encourage him,
which, granted, did not take much. It never did with
men. A woman batted an eye and a man was all over
her. A pretty woman, at any rate.

As a businessman Chester was so-so. He had a head
for accounts and numbers, but not necessarily a sharp
head. His best asset was, ironically, his sunny disposition. Chester was friendly with everybody. He always
had a ready smile, a nice comment. Ideal traits for,
say, a politician.

It was Adolphina who goaded him into his political
career by filling his head with visions of the greatness
that awaited him if he would do as she wanted. He
gave in. He always gave in. But all had not gone as
she planned. Instead of flourishing as Dodge City
flourished, Coffin Varnish withered on the municipal
vine. Forcing her to work doubly hard to catapult
Chester to higher office.

Now, sitting there listening to the schoolteacher

prattle on, Adolphina had another of her marvelous inspirations.

"So you see," Ernestine said, bringing her story to a close, "Jeeter and I are very much in love. He did not kidnap me. I want you to tell people that after we go. I want everyone to know."

"Amazing. Simply amazing," Adolphina declared.

"Love is like that," Ernestine said.

"No. I meant it is amazing that a wonderful woman like you has taken up with a slug like him."

"Hey, now," Jeeter Frost said.

Ernestine shared her husband's reaction. "There was no call for that unseemly remark, Mrs. Luce."

"Oh, don't get me wrong, dearie," Adolphina said. "I am sure you adore him. I adore my husband, too. But let's face it. Neither is worth much."

"Hey, now," Jeeter Frost said again.

Adolphina ignored him. In a very short while he would be of no consequence. She was going to dress and get the small revolver her husband kept in the nightstand. She would disarm the killer and hold him for her husband to turn over to the posse so Chester would get the credit. Word would spread of how he saved the schoolmarm. Were he to run for higher office, he would be a shoo-in. She became aware that the schoolmarm was talking to her.

"Do you hear me?"

"I am sorry, dearie," Adolphina said. "I was distracted. What did you say?"

"I do not appreciate your insults. My husband might not be much in your eyes, but he is everything in mine."

"They say love is blind and they are right." Adolphina patted the other woman's hand. "You are living proof. But don't take what I say personally. I have your best interests at heart."

Jeeter had been over by the door watching down the hall, but now he stepped to the cabinet that contained the pots and pans and selected a large frying pan.

"You confuse me, Mrs. Luce," Ernestine said.

"Only because you are new to this," Adolphina told her. "You are thinking with your heart and not your head. If you were thinking with your head, you would realize your husband is not much of a catch and you would be better served if you were shed of him."

Ernestine gasped. "How can you say that?"

Adolphina was only trying to spare the woman's feelings for when Frost was taken into custody. "Be honest with yourself and with me. If your husband were a pickle, he would be at the bottom of the barrel."

By then Jeeter was next to the kitchen table. "Pickle this," he said, and swung the frying pan. It connected with the side of the big woman's head with a satisfying *thunk* and she folded over the table.

"Jeeter, no!" Ernestine squealed. "What did you do that for?"

"If people don't want to be hit over the head with frying pans, they shouldn't call other people pickles."

"Is she dead?"

Adolphina groaned.

"No," Jeeter said, and hit her again. He did not use all his strength, as much as he wanted to.

"Oh, Jeeter," Ernestine said softly.

"I didn't kill the sow." Jeeter set the pan on the counter. He clasped his wife's hands, pulled her out of the chair, and embraced her. "I won't let anyone, man or woman, try to break us apart."

"She was only trying to—" Ernestine stopped and stared at the slumped form on the table. Spittle was dribbling from a corner of her mouth. "To be honest, I don't know why she was being so mean."

"From now on, no one speaks ill of you," Jeeter said. "Not where I can hear. Not if they want to stay healthy."

"My protector," Ernestine said.

Winifred Curry was not in the best of tempers. He made money selling liquor. He did not make money selling coffee. Coffee he supplied for free, and so far the posse had downed two pots and Undersheriff Glickman had just asked him to make another.

"It is for a good cause," Chester said when Win swore.

"I don't see you making any," Win criticized. "And what good cause would that be?"

"We are helping the minions of law and order."

"We?" Win said. "When you make a batch, then you can say we. For now it is me, myself, and I, and I wish they were drinking whiskey and not Arbuckle's." He went through the door in the back into his living quarters.

Chester Luce grinned and walked over to the table occupied by the undersheriff, the journalist, and the old scout. "Mind if I join you gentlemen?" he asked, pulling out an empty chair.

"Why did your friend have that sour face when I asked him to make more coffee?" Seamus asked.

"We woke him too early," Chester said. "He is always a grouch when he does not get his sleep."

"I could use some," Lafferty said, and yawned. "The coffee isn't helping as much as I hoped."

Seamus glanced at Coombs. "How are you holding up, Jack? You sure do fidget a lot."

"I am wide awake."

"You don't sound happy about it."

"I am awake and sober," Jack Coombs said. "There is nothing to be happy about."

Seamus masked a smile by taking a swallow of coffee. He had observed how the tracker kept gazing at the shelves behind the bar and licking his lips. "That's right. You are not used to being sober, are you?"

"Don't remind me."

"The sun will be up soon," Seamus said. "Then you can start tracking. A few hours in the heat and dust and you will forget all about whether you are sober or not."

"I suppose," Coombs said, with about as much enthusiasm as if he had been told he was to have a spike driven through his knee.

"I hope we can take Frost alive," Lafferty said. "An interview with him would be carried by every newspaper in the country."

Chester asked, "Is that all he is to you? A story?"

"That is all anyone is to me," Lafferty said. "Dead or alive he is news, but alive I can milk it more."

"How about you?" Chester asked Glickman. "What is he to you?"

"A pain in the ass," Seamus said.

Jack Coombs was gazing at the long row of bottles again, his expression a mix of longing and pain. "It was downright dumb of him to kidnap the schoolmarm. It is the first dumb thing I ever heard tell of him doing."

"You don't call killing people dumb?" Lafferty asked.

"Not if they give cause," Coombs said. "In the old days we did not make the fuss over it that folks make today. Sometimes it had to be done and that was all there was to it."

"In the old days there was no law," Chester mentioned.

"You say that as if it was bad," Jack Coombs said. "But the less law there is, the more freedom you have. I miss those old days. The days when a man could do what he wanted without a tin star looking over his shoulder."

"You mean drink?" Seamus said. "A man has always been able to drink as much as he wants."

"I could use one now," Lafferty said. "But we might have a lot of riding to do and I don't ride well when I have had liquor."

"I will treat myself to a bottle when this is over," Seamus said. "There is nothing quite like the warm feeling you get when whiskey goes down your throat."

"Quit talking drink," Jack Coombs said.

"Sometimes I will have rye or scotch, but neither holds a candle to the best whiskey," Seamus went on. "I could sip on a bottle all day and all night and not miss eating food." He almost laughed when the old scout trembled and wiped a sleeve across his mouth. "Yes, sir. Good whiskey is better than a good woman or just about anything else any day."

"Is there such a thing as a good woman?" Chester responded without thinking.

"You should know," Lafferty said. "You are the only one at this table who is married."

"There are good women, then," Chester said. He stared at the bottles. "Hell, I could use a drink right now myself."

Seamus rose and went around the bar. He selected his favorite label of whiskey, forked several glasses with his fingers, and returned to the table. Setting one of the glasses in front of the mayor, he proceeded to open the bottle so he could pour.

"What are you doing?"

"You said you wanted a drink."

"I said I could use one," Chester said. But when the glass was half-full, he raised it to his lips and gratefully sipped. "Mmmm. Nice."

Seamus poured one for Lafferty and one for himself and made it a point to set the bottle near Jack Coombs. He swallowed and made a show of smacking his lips. "This here is fine whiskey."

"I suppose one wouldn't hurt me," Lafferty said, and indulged. "You are right," he told Seamus. "It goes down smooth."

Just then Winifred Curry hurried from the back and over to their table. "I am plumb out of coffee," he said to Chester. "You will have to get a can from your store."

"Me?" Chester said.

"Who else?" Win smiled. "It is for a good cause. You are helping the minions of law and order. Isn't that right, Sheriff Glickman?"

"What? Oh, sure," Seamus said. He was only half listening. His main interest was in Jack Coombs.

The old scout was chugging whiskey straight from the bottle.

Chapter 28

Chester Luce was not smiling as he started to cross the street from the saloon to his store. He could count on one hand the number of times in his life he had given something away for free. Chester would be damned if he would provide free coffee for the posse. He would get a can of Arbuckle's, but he would present Glickman with a voucher and demand payment. If the amount on the voucher was more than the amount he paid for the can, well, that was commerce.

The bell over the door tinkled. Chester debated on waking Adolphina and decided against it. Asleep, she could not cause him trouble. With luck she would stay in bed until noon and by then the leather slapper and his lady friend would be long gone.

Chester moved down the center aisle. He came to the shelf with the Arbuckle cans and kept walking. He would check on his uninvited guests in case they needed anything. Better to keep them happy and content until they left, he reasoned.

The kitchen door was closed. Chester knocked and opened it. Smiling, he began, "Is every—" Then he stopped, frozen in astonishment at the sight of his wife sprawled half across the table with blood trickling from a gash in her temple. "Adolphina?"

In a rush of insight Chester divined what had happened. His wife had woken up and come down to the kitchen. She had stumbled on the killer and the schoolmarm, and the killer had killed her.

"Dear God!" Chester blurted. Sorrow seized him, sorrow so potent his head swam and he had to put a hand on the table to stay on his feet. "Adolphina!" he cried. He could not bear to look at her. Turning, he stumbled from the kitchen and sagged against the hall wall.

As strange as it seemed to other people, he had cared for that woman. She had not been much to look at. She had the temperament of a bull. But she had a shrewd head on her broad shoulders and she had stuck by him through good times and rough, and he had, by God, cared for her.

A bleat of sadness escaped him. Although he resented her bossiness, he had relied on her guidance. He could always count on her to have their mutual best interest in mind.

Belatedly, Chester realized her killer and the schoolmarm were gone. Snuck off, no doubt, intending to slink out of town before their foul deed was discovered. Not while he drew breath! Straightening, he hastened down the hall and through the store to the front door. He started to open it, and paused. He must collect his thoughts and do it right. He would rush into the saloon. He would say he had stumbled on Jeeter Frost and the schoolmarm in his store, and seen Frost kill his wife with his own eyes. The posse would be quick to spread out and search for them.

Chester hoped they killed Frost. Or, better yet, took him alive so he could hang. Frost would deny murdering Adolphina, but it would be Frost's word against his. The schoolmarm might side with Frost, but Chester would say she was not in the room when Adolphina was killed, and anyway, no one would believe her once they found out she had run off with Frost and not been abducted.

Chester opened the door and bolted out, only to stop short.

Four riders had drawn rein near the posse's horses and were staring at the bodies wrapped in blankets. To the east the sky was brightening, and Chester could see the four were lanky and dirty and had bulging Adam's apples. Scruffy sorts, bristling with weapons. More riffraff passing through, he judged.

"Hold on there, mister," said the oldest of the four in a distinct Southern drawl. "We would like a word with you."

"I am in a hurry," Chester said.

"You can take the time to be civil," the man said, an edge to his tone. "Who might you be?"

Chester introduced himself, stating proudly, "I am the mayor of Coffin Varnish, and I have urgent business in the saloon."

"I am Abe Haslett. These are my brothers, Jefferson, Quince, and Josephus." The three nodded in turn. "We have business, too. With you. But it can wait."

"Before you scoot off," Jefferson Haslett said, "do you mind tellin' us who these dead folks were?"

"I was told they are the Larn brothers," Chester replied, and was taken aback by their shock.

"The devil you say!" Abe Haslett declared.

"The Larns!" Jefferson exclaimed.

"How in hell?" asked the youngest, Josephus.

"Who could've done it?" wondered the last, Quince.

Chester thought he understood. Glickman had mentioned something about the Larns being from the South. These Hasletts were from the South, probably their friends. "Did you know them?"

Abe Haslett nodded, his gaze glued to the bodies. "I should say we did. Their families and ours go back a long ways."

"Whoever killed them has deprived us," Jefferson said.

"I am sorry to hear that," Chester said. "Now, if you will excuse me." He could imagine them getting worked up, and he did not want to be the brunt of their anger. Skirting their mounts, he was almost to the batwings when they opened and out stepped Lawrence Fisch, the son of the president of the First Bank of Dodge City.

"Who are those fellows you were talking to?" Fisch asked.

"Friends of the Larns," Chester said. "Good friends, as upset as they got when I broke the news."

"You don't say?"

"Southerners," Chester added, and went to go on by, but Fisch was blocking the doorway.

"Just what we need. More Southern trash. My father does not think much of Southerners and neither do I."

"What's that about the South, sonny?"

Chester had not heard Abe Haslett dismount and come up behind him. The man moved as quietly as a cat. He did not like the glint in Haslett's dark eyes, but young Fisch did not seem to notice.

"My father says you are a bunch of poor losers," the banker's son said. "He was in the South right after the war."

"This pa of yours," Abe said. "He is a Yankee, I take it?"

"He was born and raised in Indiana," Lawrence Fisch said. "He did not fight in the war, though. He was and has always been a businessman."

"I fought in the war," Abe said. "I wore the gray with pride."

"Good for you," Lawrence Fisch said.

Abe Haslett colored. "This pa you keep mentionin', he was in the South, you say? Right after the war? And he was in business?"

"Your ears work at least," Lawrence replied.

"That would make him a carpetbagger," Abe Haslett said. "One of those vultures who preyed on us when we were down, buyin' land cheap and such so they could fill their pokes."

"Now, you hold on," Lawrence bristled. "My father is always fair and honest in his dealings."

"Sure he is, boy," Abe said with thick scorn. "He is a stinkin' Yankee carpetbagger and you are the son of a stinkin' Yankee carpetbagger."

Chester thought he should say something. "Please. Let's not provoke one another. There is no call for this."

"There is plenty of call," Abe Haslett said, and motioned at his brothers. "My kin and me hate Yankee carpetbaggers. Our family, our friends, lost land and valuables to the scum."

"You better not mean my father when you say that," Lawrence Fisch said.

"If the shoe fits, boy. He is a Yankee and he was a carpetbagger, so that makes him scum the same as the rest."

"The hell you say, you damn Reb," Lawrence said angrily, and put his hands on his nickel-plated Remingtons.

"You just made the biggest mistake of your life, pup," Abe Haslett said, and went for his own hardware.

Minutes earlier, in the bedroom of Chester and Adolphina Luce, Ernestine Frost pried herself from the man she had married and dreamily asked, "Did you just hear a bell?"

"All I hear is my heart pounding in my chest," Jeeter told her. It had been his idea to come upstairs. They could not see the street from the kitchen and he wanted to keep a close eye on things and note the posse's comings and goings. Ernestine had refused to stay in the kitchen alone.

"What if this poor woman wakes up? She will be mad as can be and will take it out on me."

"She won't wake up for a month of Sundays," Jeeter had responded. But he let Ernestine come. The bedroom was small but nicely furnished and smelled of pleasant odors. They had not made it to the window, though. Halfway across, Jeeter took her in his arms and kissed her as he had hankered to kiss her ever since they said their I do's. She had the softest lips, this woman. One kiss was not enough. They had kissed and kissed and kissed some more, until Jeeter thought his chest would explode. "I didn't hear no bell and I am a better hearer than you."

"I am sure I did," Ernestine insisted.

"Maybe it was a wedding bell," Jeeter joked.

"Oh, you." Ernestine grinned. "You are superbly wonderful, do you know that?"

Jeeter wished he could stand there forever with his arms around her waist and that loving look in her eyes. "I have been called many things but never wonderful."

"Any woman would be proud to call you hers."

Jeeter knew better. "The only female I want is you, so it has worked out right fine."

Ernestine giggled, then said tenderly, "Each moment with you is a moment of discovery for me."

"Discovery?" Jeeter repeated.

"I learn truths about myself I never realized," Ernestine explained. "You bring me out of myself."

"Is that a good thing?"

"It is a very good thing," Ernestine assured him, and tilted her face to be kissed yet again.

Jeeter would gladly have obliged her, but at the juncture hooves clomped in the street. "Hold on," he said, and darted to the window. Cautiously parting the curtains, he peered down on four dark silhouettes and their mounts.

"Who are they?" Ernestine whispered at his elbow.

"Maybe more of the posse showing up late."

"Oh Lord. There must be a couple of dozen. We can't let them find us, Jeeter. I will die if anything happens to you."

Jeeter smiled at her. "I ain't about to be bucked out in gore now that I have you."

"But there are so many," Ernestine fretted. "We should leave. Now. Before we are found out."

"You worry too much," Jeeter said. "The safest place to be is right under their nose."

Ernestine crooked her neck around. "I just heard the bell again."

Jeeter heard voices. He looked outside. The mayor was talking to the four newcomers. "Did he just come out of the store?"

"That's what that bell was!" Ernestine exclaimed. "The one over the front door."

"Then he has seen his wife," Jeeter guessed, and lowered his hand to his Colt Lightning.

Placing her hand on his, Ernestine pleaded, "No shooting! Please! There are too many of them."

"He will warn them."

"Let's just go," Ernestine urged. "Let's sneak out the back and get our horses and leave Coffin Varnish before they find us."

"You want me to tuck tail and run?"

"It is not running. It is avoiding trouble," Ernestine answered. "Besides, didn't you tell me that you left Dodge to avoid the Blight brothers? This is no different."

"I didn't have you then."

Puzzled, Ernestine asked, "How am I a factor?"

"No man likes to show yellow in front of his sweetheart," Jeeter said. "I would as soon go down with my guns blazing as be a coward in your eyes."

"That you could never be," Ernestine said. "Didn't that penny dreadful call you the Missouri Man-Killer and the Terror of the West? You instill fear in others. They do not instill fear in you."

Jeeter had never thought of it quite like that. "I reckon my reputation does make others a mite skittish." Not that it caused the Blights to think twice about tangling with him.

"We must go before the posse puts your reputation to the test," Ernestine said, and pulled on his arm.

Jeeter glanced back out the window. The mayor had moved to the saloon and was talking to someone under the overhang. Jeeter dipped at the knees but could not see who it was.

"Please," Ernestine said. "For my sake if you won't do it for your own. I do not care to be a widow so soon after becoming a wife."

Jeeter wavered. The window was a good vantage point. He could shoot anyone who tried to cross to the store. But he could not stop the lead from flying, and two dozen guns was a lot of lead. Ernestine might be hit. "All right." He gave in. "We will do it your way."

"Thank you," Ernestine said, and kissed him on the cheek. "You are doing the right thing."

Hand in hand they descended the stairs to the hall and were a few steps from the kitchen when all hell broke loose.

Chapter 29

Chester Luce saw it. He saw Lawrence Fisch jerk at his nickel-plated Remingtons, but the revolvers were not quite clear when Abe Haslett's pistol boomed. Fisch staggered against the batwings and looked down at a hole in his shirt over his sternum, a hole that had not been there a second ago.

"You have killed me, you son of a bitch."

"Not yet," Abe Haslett said, and shot him again.

As shouts and yells erupted in the saloon, Lawrence Fisch slowly turned. He swatted at the batwings and shouldered on through, crying, "Help me, someone! I am done for!"

Chester was only a step away from the Southerner. He did not want to draw attention to himself, but acrid powder smoke tingled in his nose and before he could stop himself, he sneezed.

Abe Haslett looked at him, and the muzzle of Haslett's six-shooter swung in his direction. "Somethin' on your mind?"

"Only that he is part of a posse," Chester said, "and they are liable to take exception."

"A what?"

The other Hasletts had dismounted and were running toward the saloon. They stopped when Abe Haslett whirled and bellowed, "I just shot a John law! Take cover!"

Chester dived under the batwings. He rolled and collided with something that should not be there. For an instant he was nose to nose with Lawrence Fisch. Their eyes met just as the spark of life faded from Fisch's. It made Chester think of Adolphina, dead in their kitchen, and he squawked in terror.

Strong hands gripped him by the arms and hauled Chester erect. He was surrounded by posse members, foremost among them Undersheriff Glickman, who snapped, "What in hell happened? Who shot Fisch, and why? Is Jeeter Frost out there?"

"It was a Haslett," Chester said. "There are four of them. Rebs. Friends of the Larns."

"But why shoot Fisch?" Seamus was thinking of how mad George Hinkle would be, to say nothing of the boy's father.

Over at the window the butcher's helper said, "They are shucking rifles from their saddles and taking cover. It looks like they mean to shoot it out with us."

"But *why*?" Seamus said. He was after Jeeter Frost and only Jeeter Frost. "This makes no kind of sense." He grabbed the front of the mayor's coat. "You were out there. Why, damn it?"

"They don't like people who don't like Rebels," was all Chester could think of to say.

Out in the street a rifle cracked and the windowpane splintered but did not shatter. Win Curry dashed from behind the bar, saying, "Stop them! They are shooting my saloon!"

Chester tore his gaze from Lawrence Fisch. "My wife is dead, too. Jeeter Frost is to blame."

"What?" Seamus said, unsure he heard correctly.

"He killed her in our kitchen," Chester elaborated. "I think he beat her to death."

"You *think*?"

"It must have been a terrible way to go. Better if he had stabbed her with the butcher knife or chopped her with the meat cleaver."

"Hold on." Too much was happening too fast for Seamus. "Are you saying Frost has been in Coffin Varnish this whole time? Is he with the schoolmarm? Why were they in your kitchen?"

"What does anyone do in a kitchen?" Chester evaded the question.

Another shot struck the window. The pane dissolved in shards, and Abe Haslett bellowed, "Poke your heads out and we will give you the same! We won't let you take us in, do you hear?"

Seamus's confusion grew. "Why would we want to arrest them?" he asked no one in particular. "Someone tell me what in hell is going on."

"I wish I could," a store clerk said. "But someone would first have to tell me."

"I hate this stupid town," Seamus said.

Chester heard that. "You can't blame Coffin Varnish. This is Dodge City's fault. Dodge got the railroad and we didn't."

Seamus was fit to slug someone. "So now the railroad is involved? Why not throw in prairie dogs and George Custer?"

"You are talking nonsense," Chester Luce told him.

That did it. Seamus hit him, as fine a punch as was

ever thrown, flush on the point of the mayor's dumpling chin. Chester Luce went down and did not stir once he hit. Seamus stalked to the window, and careful not to show himself, hollered, "This is Sheriff Glickman! You will account for yourselves and your antics!"

"This is Abe Haslett! You ain't takin' us in, you hear, tin star?"

"Why in hell would we want to?" If Seamus were any more confused, he would swear he was drunk.

"You don't fool us!" Abe shouted. "We know you know about Crooked Creek Sam!"

Seamus began to think the entire world had gone insane. "Crooked Creek Sam Hoyt?"

"You figured out we were in on his killin'," Abe yelled. "Us and the Larns. That's why you did the Larns in. But you won't do us like you done them. No siree!"

"They say they had a hand in murdering Crooked Creek Sam?" Seamus said, more to focus his thoughts than anything else. "Those and the four dead ones we found? Am I getting this right?"

"The countryside is overrun with cutthroats," a posse member remarked.

Seamus was still putting the mental pieces together. As near as he could tally it, he had four killers—dead killers—in accidental custody, and four more killers were out in the street with the intention of waging war on his posse. "This is a hell of a note."

"What do we do?" the blacksmith's apprentice asked. He was young and stocky and had more muscle than hair.

"What do you think we do?" was Seamus's rejoinder. "We shoot the hell out of them."

*   *   *

Thunder revived Adolphina. Crashing thunder in the distance, she thought. But she did not open her eyes or stir. Her head hurt too much. She struggled to remember why and it came back in a wave of pain and anger; that damned rascal Jeeter Frost had walloped her with her own frying pan.

Rage galvanized Adolphina into sitting up. Almost instantly she regretted it as spikes of pain tore through her. Her head felt ripe to burst. Groaning, she touched her temple and stared at a drop of blood on her fingertip. "The weasel. The miserable weasel."

Thunder rumbled again, only now Adolphina recognized it for what it was: gunfire. She looked about her, then rose and gazed down the hall. The killer and the schoolmarm were nowhere to be found. "Miss Prescott?" she called out. "Are you there?"

Reassured by the lack of a reply, Adolphina moved toward the front of the store. The din in the street was nearly nonstop now. She figured the posse had spotted Jeeter Frost and the runt was being shot to bits. "Nothing would please me more," she said aloud.

The store was dark, yet to be lit by the glow of the rising sun. Adolphina crept to the window and eased onto her knees. A wretched-looking man was crouched behind a water trough near the store, firing a rifle at the saloon. But it was not Jeeter Frost. She did not know what to make of it. Suddenly lead thudded into the wall, and she ducked down. No sooner did she do so than more shots, from the saloon, struck the window. Three holes appeared, along with a hairline crack.

Adolphina remembered how much that window cost

her and Chester. Anger bubbled within her. "The fools!" she fumed, and rose. Heedless of the danger, she yanked the door wide and bawled, "Watch your shooting over there! You are hitting my store!"

The man behind the water trough glanced around in surprise. He abruptly heaved erect and sprang toward her.

Adolphina did not know what he intended, but she was not about to let him in. She slammed the door, or tried to. He hit it with his shoulder, the impact bashing the door against her, and she teetered on her heels. Although she recovered her balance almost immediately, the harm had been done. He was inside, his back to the wall, his rifle leveled.

"That wasn't very nice, you tub of lard."

"I beg your pardon?" Adolphina said. She was prickly about her size. It was not her fault nature had not endowed her with a shape men found more appealing.

"Trying to close the door in my face," the man growled. "You could have gotten me killed."

"Leave these premises this instant, whoever you are," Adolphina demanded.

The man snorted. "That is not about to happen, lady. Me and my brothers are in a tight, and I figure you are our salvation. I am Abe Haslett, by the way."

"My condolences to your mother," Adolphina said.

Abe Haslett glowered. "Makin' me mad ain't too smart."

"What is all this shooting about? I was told a posse is in town. Am I to infer you and the posse are at odds?"

"They want us for a killin' but I will be damned if

they will treat us to a strangulation jig," Abe said. "Which is where you come in."

"I am afraid I do not understand," Adolphina admitted.

"There are too many of them and not enough of us. We could light a shuck, but they would be after us in no time. So I aim to make good our escape by holding you over their heads."

"You are no gentleman."

"Dire straits play hell with manners, lady. But don't fret. We won't harm you if you don't give us cause."

Adolphina was outraged. She clenched her fists and suppressed an urge to pummel him senseless.

The firing in the street had about tapered off; only a few shots were coming from the saloon. Abe Haslett turned his head toward the doorway but did not show himself. "Law dog! Can you hear me over there?"

"I hear you!" Undersheriff Glickman responded.

"I have a woman here!" Abe yelled, and looked at her. "Who are you, anyhow?" After she told him, he hollered, "Mrs. Luce is her name! Unless you want something unpleasant to happen to her, you and your men will lay down your guns and let us ride out."

"First Frost, now you!" Seamus Glickman shouted. "Whatever happened to chivalry? Did it die with the knights?"

"What in hell is he talkin' about?" Abe asked Adolphina.

"I will thank you not to use foul language in the presence of a lady," Adolphina instructed him. "If you insist on hiding behind my skirts, at least be polite about it."

"You are wearing a dressin' gown, not skirts," Abe Haslett said. "And on you it is more like a tent."

"There you go again. You have a foul mouth."

Abe's dark eyes glittered. "You just don't listen, do you? Female or no, I will not abide slurs."

"Being called a tent is hardly a compliment."

"All right," Abe said. "I will desist if you will behave. Once me and my brothers are in the clear, I will let you go with no hard feelin's. Do we have a deal?"

"You have the rifle," Adolphina answered.

By now the firing had completely stopped. Abe cupped a hand to his mouth and bawled, "Jefferson! Quince! Josephus! Are all of you still with me!"

"I am here, brother!"

"Alive and kickin'!"

"I got nicked but I am fine!"

Abe smiled. "Stay put while I show our prize. Then we will be on our way, and good riddance." He wagged his Winchester. "After you, if you please, and do not think of running or my trigger finger might twitch."

"You would shoot a woman in the back?" Adolphina asked.

"Back or front makes no never mind to me," Abe told her. "Now out you go. Keep your hands where I can see them, and don't speak unless I say you can flap your gums."

"I hope I get to spit on your grave," Adolphina said, but she moved past him and out under the brightening sky of dawn. A golden arch crowned the eastern horizon, and down the street a pig, unperturbed by the gunfire, was astir.

"And you call yourself a lady," Abe criticized, following her out and crouching so she shielded him from the shooters in the saloon. "Do you see her?" he yelled. "I am no bluff."

Chester Luce appeared in the shattered saloon window. "She is my wife! You had better not harm her!"

"You have my sympathy, mister," Abe called out. "As for the harmin', that depends on the cooperation we get." He raised his voice. "Did you hear that, law dog? Do I have your word we can ride out?"

"You have it," Seamus Glickman replied. "And I will be delighted the day I officiate at your hanging."

"Kansans sure are bloodthirsty," Abe said. Then, "Brothers! We must make ourselves scarce while we have this whale to bargain with."

"That does it," Adolphina said, and turned. "I have borne all the bad manners I am going to."

Abe pointed the Winchester at her bosom. "You will turn back around and behave, damn you."

"I am not a whale," Adolphina said.

"You are no guppy, either."

Between the pain from the gash in her temple and her fury, Adolphina's head was pounding. "You are as yellow as your teeth. I have half a mind to take that rifle from you and wrap it around your neck."

"There will be hell to pay if you try," Abe Haslett warned.

"Hell it is, then," Adolphina said, and reached for his Winchester.

Chapter 30

"I can't," Ernestine Frost said.

Jeeter Frost had led the horses out and was holding hers so she could mount. The thunderous din in the street was added incentive for them to fan the breeze, but now his new bride had paused and was staring back at the rear of the general store. "What is it you can't?" he asked.

"I can't leave yet," Ernestine said. "I have to go back and check on her."

"You do not," Jeeter said.

"We left her lying there over the table. We don't know if she was alive or dead." Ernestine shook her head. "It is not right. We can't go riding off without doing what we can for her."

"The cow brought it on herself."

"Please be nice," Ernestine scolded. "If you don't want to go, even though it was you who walloped her with that frying pan, then I will go myself." She started to walk off but he grabbed her arm.

"Hold on. Hear that shooting? I am the one who has to go." Jeeter turned her toward her mount. "You climb on and wait for me. I won't be long."

"We are man and wife now," Ernestine said. "We should go together."

Jeeter decided that if he was to wear the britches in their marriage, he must put his foot down on occasion. This was an occasion. "No. Please. Lead is flying all over the place. I don't want you taking a stray slug." He cupped his hands for her use as a step. "I will run in quick, splash water on her face to bring her around, and run back to you. We can be gone in five minutes."

"You are so sweet," Ernestine said, and permitted him to give her a boost. He handed her the reins and gave her the reins to the gruella and the lead rope to the packhorse.

"In case they spook," Jeeter said. Drawing his Colt Lightning, he retraced his steps to the general store. When he saw the kitchen was empty, he smiled. "The sow is all right." He could return to his new bride.

From the front of the store came voices. The sow's, and another's. It might be some of the posse, Jeeter guessed, and she might be telling them about him and Ernestine. He had to find out. Stalking down the hall, he warily slunk to the counter. The front door was open. Out in the street men were hollering. Something about a woman being used as a hostage.

It was none of Jeeter's business. He should go. But Ernestine might ask if he had seen the Luce woman with his own eyes, and he could not lie to her. He would never lie to her. Feeling supremely stupid, he cat-footed to the front door, and was momentarily stupefied.

Adolphina Luce had hold of the muzzle of a Winchester. The other end was held by a man Jeeter had never seen before. Even as he set eyes on them, the rifle went off. The lead tore into Adolphina's chest and ruptured out her back. Recoiling in shock, she let go and said, "I didn't think you would do it."

"You dumb cluck!" the man snapped. "Don't blame me. It went off when you pulled on it."

From the saloon came a loud wail, *"Adolphina!"*

Jeeter had not liked the woman. He felt no regret when her thick legs folded and she keeled over. He had no cause to linger and was turning when the man with the rifle also turned—toward the store.

"Who the blazes are you?"

Jeeter was keenly aware the muzzle was pointed at him now, and he never could stand having guns pointed at him. "Drop your rifle," he commanded.

"Like hell."

"Suit yourself," Jeeter said, and shot the stranger between the eyes. He backed away but had only gone a few steps when a younger man with a rifle materialized beside the twitching body.

"Abe! Abe! Who shot you?" The younger man glanced into the store. "It was you, you son of a bitch!" He started to raise the stock of his rifle to his shoulder.

"The hell with you, too." Jeeter sent a slug into the man's forehead. Ordinarily he liked to know who he was killing, and why, but these two had brought their rash ends on themselves. He continued to back up, past shelves crammed with merchandise, his Colt fixed on the doorway, and it was well he did.

Two more men appeared. By their features they were related to the first two. They did not bandy words but sprayed lead, working the levers of their Winchesters as rapidly as they could.

Jeeter dived behind shelves crammed with dry goods. Pieces of merchandise and wood slivers from the shelves rained around him. He scrambled along the bottom until he came to the end near the wall. The shelves were about a foot wide, six of them spaced evenly from bottom to top. The top came within several feet of the ceiling.

Jeeter kicked folded blankets aside and began climbing. He had maybe thirty seconds before the pair came in. Dishes fell and crashed. A box of silverware made a terrible racket. He reached the top and clung flat on his belly, his breath caught in his throat. The pair were bound to have heard the stuff fall. If they reasoned out where he was, they would drop him like a sitting duck.

Another moment, and the two men were at the aisle end of the shelves, rifles at the ready, sweeping the barrels back and forth.

"Where did he get to, Jefferson?" one asked.

"I don't know," the other said. "But he can't have gotten far, Quince. He's as good as dead."

They were not too bright, these boys. They advanced between the shelves, looking right and left and left and right but not up. Never once up. Jeeter shot the one called Jefferson in the top of the head and the one called Quince in the face when Quince glanced at the top of the shelves.

Jeeter reloaded. Always reload right away; that was one of the most important rules, along with always kill with the first shot and never rush your aim if you had the time not to. He did not climb down until he had six pills in the wheel, and he held on to the Lightning as he descended.

He must get to Ernestine. But he had only taken three steps toward the back when feet thudded in the street and shadows flitted across the window.

Someone wailed in torment and cried, "No! No! No!"

"You in the store! This is Undersheriff Glickman! You will come out with your hands empty and up or we will come in with our hands filled and our guns spitting lead!"

"Oh, hell," Jeeter Frost said.

Seamus had never seen a woman shot. Killing a female just was not done. No surer way of being invited to be the guest of honor at a hemp social existed, unless it was stealing a horse. He should be shocked. He should be outraged. But he felt nothing, nothing at all. That he had not liked the mayor's wife had a lot to do with it, he reckoned. Still, he felt he should feel *something*. The mayor certainly did.

Chester Luce cradled his wife's head in his lap and bawled. He was not ashamed to show his grief. He held her and rocked back and forth and the tears would not stop.

Half the posse was spread out on either side of the general store. The rest covered them from the saloon. Three of their number had fallen to the rifles of the Hasletts, but that left plenty to end it.

Seamus was not about to go charging in. Too many had already died. That, and he was puzzled. He had seen Abe Haslett shoot Adolphina Luce. Then someone had shot Abe Haslett. Another Haslett had rushed to Abe's side, and he had been shot, too. The remaining pair had charged into the store, there had been more shots, and now silence. "What the hell is going on?" he asked himself.

A posse member by the name of Winston was peeking in the window.

"Anything?" Seamus asked.

"A pair of legs sticking past a shelf. They aren't moving. I don't see anyone else."

"Who can it be?" Frank Lafferty asked. He was on his knees behind the water trough, scribbling. "Who is in there, you think?"

"How the hell should I know?" Seamus grumbled. The schoolmarm's so-called abduction had turned into a bloodbath. He had nothing to do with any of it, but he would bet his bottom dollar that Sheriff Hinkle would hold him to account. It wasn't fair. It just wasn't fair.

"We should rush whoever it is," Winston said. "All of us at once so they can't pick us off." He gave Seamus a pointed look. "That is what I would do if I was in charge."

Seamus had about taken all the stupidity he was going to take. "Refresh my memory, Winston. What is it you do at the Oriental?"

Winston scrunched up his mouth and shifted his weight from one foot to the other. "You know very well what I do."

"I want to hear you say it," Seamus said harshly.

"I wash dishes."

"You clean other people's slop off of plates and bowls, and you think you can run this posse better than me? Very well. Go rushing on in there if you want, but you do it by your lonesome."

Winston muttered something, then said loud enough to be heard, "That isn't what I suggested. I suggested all of us at once."

"So that many more of us can be shot," Seamus said. "A fine lawman you would make. Stick to your pots and pans."

Lafferty was peeking over the top of the trough. "I want to know who is in there. Who we are up against. Unless I miss my guess, he has killed four people."

"He did us a favor shooting the Larns," Seamus said. But the journalist had a point. It would help to know. Keeping his eyes on the door and window, Seamus hunkered beside Luce. "Mayor? Who is in your store?"

Chester was still weeping. He could not stem the tears. They flowed over his round cheeks and down his double chin. Only vaguely was he aware that someone was speaking to him.

"Mayor Luce!" Seamus gripped his wrist and shook it. "Snap out of it, damn you! I am sorry about your wife, but I have more lives to worry about than hers."

Tearing his gaze from Adolphina, Chester blinked and coughed. "That was unkind of you."

"Who is in your store?" Seamus persisted.

"You never did like her. We could tell by the tone of your voice and your eyes. You looked down your nose at her, just like all the rest."

"What are you babbling about? This is not about her. It is about whoever is in your store. You must have some idea."

Chester sniffled and wiped his nose with his sleeve. He was stalling so he could flog his sluggish brain. It had to be Jeeter Frost, but he would be damned if he would tell the lawman that. "You should not have treated my wife so poorly."

"Will you stop with your wife? She is gone and good riddance. I need to know who is in your store. You said something about Frost earlier. Is it him?"

"Did you just say good riddance?"

"I am losing my patience. The sun is almost up. Soon this street will be an oven."

Chester gently eased Adolphina to the ground. Her face, never all that pretty, was less so in death. But it was the face of the one person in the world who had loved him. "She deserves a decent burial."

Seamus began to wonder if the mayor's mind had cracked. "Who said anything different? Forget about her for a minute and focus on our other problem."

Chester focused on his store. Correction, on Adolphina's and his store. He had done most of the work but it was theirs, together, and now she was gone. Without saying a word he rose and strode past Glickman and in through the doorway.

"Wait!" Seamus cried, and lunged, but he was a shade too slow. His back to the jamb, he demanded, "What do you think you are doing?"

"Shouldn't we go after him?" Winston asked.

"Shut up, dish soap," Seamus snapped. He started to go in but drew his leg back. Whoever had shot the Larns might feel as unfriendly toward the law. "Mayor Luce! Get back here!"

Chester ignored him. He stepped over a spreading pool of scarlet and on past the last of the shelves to the counter. Skirting the pickle barrel, he moved behind it. From where he stood he could not see the door or the window and the posse could not see him. He took a silver flask from a drawer, opened it, and swigged.

"I am sorry about your wife." Jeeter Frost was crouched at the end of the counter.

"Thank you," Chester said.

"I got here too late to save her." Jeeter did not mention hitting her with the frying pan.

"They don't know it is you in here," Chester said. "Not for sure."

"It would be nice if they could go on thinking that," Jeeter said. "Have they sent anyone around back yet?"

"Not to my knowledge."

"The dandy in charge isn't much good at this."

"Seamus Glickman," Chester said.

"That's him," Jeeter said. "My wife and I tied him up back at her boardinghouse, but he must have come after us." One eye on the front of the store, Jeeter sidled along the counter to Chester. "Listen, I can't stay. As soon as they think of it they will send someone to watch the back door to keep me from getting away. I have to be gone by then and now is as good a time as any." He held out his hand. "I thank you for your help and wish you the best. Again, I am sorry about your wife. Now that I have one of my own, I know what it would mean to me to lose her."

Chester was touched. "I hope you and the schoolmarm have a good, long life," he said. "As for the posse, I will do what I can to delay them so the two of you can get away."

"You would do that for us?"

"For my Adolphina," Chester said. "She and I once had what you two have. I will delay them out of respect for her."

They shook hands, and Jeeter Frost smiled. "I was wrong about you. You are more of a man than I reckoned." He hurried off.

"Good luck," Chester said. Turning, he made for the gun case over against the north wall. He was grinning as he opened it.

Glickman and the posse were in for a surprise.

Chapter 31

Seamus waited five minutes by his pocket watch. Then his patience ran out. Cupping his hand to his mouth, he shouted, "Mayor Luce! What have you found in there?"

Chester did not reply. He had taken out a pair of Colts. Not new but used, a pair he had received in trade for merchandise back before Coffin Varnish went to hell in a handbasket. From the bottom of the case he had brought a box of ammunition and now he was loading the second six-shooter. He had never shot a gun before, but he was confident he could keep the posse out there long enough for Jeeter and Ernestine to escape. It served the posse, and especially Seamus Glickman, right, Chester reflected. Had they not shown up, the gun battle with the Larns would not have taken place and Adolphina would still be alive.

"Mayor Luce!" Seamus hollered. "Why don't you answer me? What is taking so long in there?" The posse members were looking at him expectantly, all except for Lafferty, who was hunched over behind the water trough, scribbling as if any moment the world would end.

Chester hefted a Colt in each hand. They were

heavier than he thought they would be. He tried twirling one and nearly dropped it.

"Mayor Luce?" Seamus tried again. "If you can hear me, get down. Lead will soon be flying every which way." He cocked his Merwin and Hulbert. "Are you ready, gents?" he whispered to the others. They did not appear ready. They looked nervous as hell.

Winston cleared his throat. "Are you sure it is smart to go charging on in there? Whoever killed those Larns must have killed the mayor, too."

"Weren't you the one eager to go rushing in a few minutes ago?" Seamus said in contempt.

"Too many have already died," another man remarked. "I would rather we don't get added to the list."

Their timidity rankled Seamus. "We have a job to do and we will damn well do it. On the count of three, in we go." He paused. "One."

Chester Luce heard every word. He had crept to within ten feet of the front door, and now he extended both his arms across a shelf lined with folded pants and shirts. He aimed at the center of the doorway, thumbed back the hammer of the right-hand Colt, and fired.

Seamus swore he heard a slug buzz past his ear. Crouching, he spotted a plume of gun smoke. The killer had given himself away. He snapped off a shot, then ducked back.

Chester saw a pile of pants jump as if alive, and winced at a searing pain in his side. *He had been shot!* It was so preposterous that he glanced down at a spreading stain on his shirt to confirm it. Suddenly his delaying tactic was not nearly as amusing. "I will be damned," he said to himself.

When there was no outcry or return fire, Seamus risked another look. He made out a vague outline behind the shelf but could not see who it was for all the clothes. "You in there!" he bellowed. "Give up while you can!"

Chester giggled. A silly thing to do, him just being shot, but the whole situation was silly. Here he was, he had never harmed another soul in his life, and he was buying time for the most notorious killer in the territory. What kind of sense did that make? he asked himself. To make it even sillier, Glickman had gone and shot him.

Then Chester peered past the pants and out the front door and beheld his wife lying dead and cold in the street. Suddenly he did not feel like giggling. Suddenly he was boiling mad. All he ever wanted was to make a success of the town he helped found. But no. Dodge City destroyed any hope Coffin Varnish had. Dodge City had killed Coffin Varnish. Now that he thought about it, Dodge City had killed Adolphina, too. "Damn Dodge, anyhow," he said aloud.

"Did you hear something?" Seamus asked his men. He had, but then he was next to the open door.

"What was it?" Lafferty inquired from the safety of the water trough.

"A voice," Seamus said. He leaned out, wondering if it had been the person behind the clothes.

Chester frowned when his view of Adolphina was unexpectedly blocked by the head and shoulders of the undersheriff. By the very man who, in Chester's estimation, was most to blame for her untimely passing. A man from *Dodge*, Chester fumed, and fired both revolvers.

Seamus cried out as lead tore through his shoulder. He went down on one knee, then immediately threw himself clear of the doorway so he would not be shot a second time. Gritting his teeth against the agony, he realized he had dropped his revolver. Hands seized him, and he was half-carried, half-dragged over to the water trough and deposited next to Lafferty, who reluctantly made room.

"How bad it is, Sheriff?" a cowboy asked.

"If you die can I have that fancy revolver of yours?" Winston inquired.

Seamus would love to shoot him with that fancy revolver. Instead, he said, "This is what we get for not doing our job. If we had rushed him like I wanted a minute ago, I wouldn't be shot."

"First you didn't want to rush, then you did," Winston said. "If anyone is to blame, it is you for not making up your mind."

"There is no predicting being shot," a clerk added.

"One of you go fetch the rest from the saloon," Seamus commanded. "I have had enough. We are ending this and getting me to a sawbones." He was not bleeding a lot, which was a good sign, but he had to watch out that infection did not set in. More people died of infected gunshots than from actually being shot.

"Fetch everybody?" Winston said.

"And while you are at it, send two or three around to the back so the bastard can't get away." Seamus realized he should have thought of that sooner.

Deputized citizens scurried to obey. Seamus twisted and dipped his hand in the water trough. The water was lukewarm and had a smell to it that discouraged him from splashing it on his wound.

Lafferty was writing away, and grinning. "I can see the headlines now! Gun battle in Coffin Varnish! Undersheriff Glickman shot! Is there any chance you will die?"

Seamus examined his shoulder. The slug had gone clean through and missed most blood vessels and the bone. "I expect to live."

"That is too bad."

"How is that again?"

"We would sell more papers if you died."

"It would please me no end if you were kicked in the head by a horse," Seamus said.

"Don't take it personally," Lafferty said. "I would be tickled pink if it was Wild Bill Hickok who was shot."

"Hickok is already dead. He was shot in Deadwood a few years ago."

"He was? Well, that was before my time. To me, you are the story, and although you are not anywhere near as famous as Hickok and never will be, you will have to do."

The batwings were flapping. The rest of the posse was hurrying from the saloon.

Seamus eased up high enough to sit on the edge of the water trough. Several men were keeping an eye on the store window and the doorway.

"Men," Seamus began when they were all gathered, "I have good reason to suspect that Jeeter Frost is holed up in that store. We are going to rush him. Or, rather, you are, since I can't hardly rush anything in the shape I am in."

From out of the group came a muttered "How come only us? Your legs still work fine."

"Who said that?" Seamus demanded, and when no one responded, he swore. "Where is your sense of duty? Of civic pride? You are sworn to uphold the law, and that should count for something."

"Only if the upholding doesn't get me killed," another man said.

"As a posse, you would make a fine sewing circle," Seamus chastised them.

"We fought the Hasletts, didn't we?" Winston retorted. "You could at least give us our due."

Seamus slowly rose, his shoulder a welter of pain. "What I would like to give you is a good swift kick in the britches. But if you won't do this without me, then by God I will show you that one of us has sand!"

That was when a revolver boomed over by the saloon, followed by a whoop and a holler. Jack Coombs came from under the overhang, a nearly empty whiskey bottle in one hand, a smoking revolver in the other. "Where is he? Where is the coyote we are after?"

"Oh, hell," Seamus said.

The old scout staggered toward them, swaying as if he were on the pitching deck of a sea-tossed ship. "I am a hellion born and bred! I can lick my weight in wildcats and spit my weight in nails!"

Winston's brow puckered. "Did he just say spit his weight in nails? What does that mean? I have never heard it before."

"I doubt he knows," Seamus said. At the scout he

snapped, "Jack! Go back inside the saloon. Your help isn't needed."

Coombs chugged another mouthful of red-eye, then let loose with a remarkable imitation of a Comanche war whoop. "You need killing done, I am your man! I have killed Apaches! I have killed Sioux! I have killed Crows!"

"Aren't the Crows friendly?" someone asked.

"I have killed a few white men, too," Coombs boasted. "Scalawags like this Jeeter Frost. Outcasts and ruffians. Riffraff and vermin. Scum and then some."

"He is almost poetical when he is drunk," Winston said.

Lafferty was running out of paper. He flipped a sheet to write on the other side, and glanced at the general store as he flipped. He noticed that everyone was staring at Jack Coombs. Not one person was watching the store. Which explained why he was the one who blurted in astonishment, "Will you look at that!"

Everyone turned.

Chester Luce was framed in the doorway. He had a long-barreled revolver in each hand and a dark stain on his shirt that could only be one thing. His pudgy frame was perfectly still except for the quivering of his thick lips.

"Mayor Luce?" Seamus said.

Jack Coombs was almost to the water trough. "What has gotten into that ball of butter?"

"Butter, am I?" Chester yelled shrilly. "My wife never thought I was butter! She called me her little hamster!"

Seamus needed a drink. He needed a drink badly. "If I am not dreaming, I should be."

"You are butter, all right," Jack Coombs said to Luce. "A bufflehead, too, or you would not be standing there holding pistols I wager you do not know how to use."

"Oh, don't I?" Chester said, and shot the scout in the chest. Pivoting, he shot a second posse member and then a third, both too stunned to react in time.

"He is killing everyone!" Winston the dishwasher cried, and was jarred onto his heels by a slug that removed most of his left eye and part of his nose.

Lafferty, scribbling in a frenzy, bawled, "Somebody do something!"

Chester pointed both revolvers at the water trough. "Do you know what I hate more than Dodge? Nothing. And all of you are from Dodge, so I hate all of you more than I hate nothing."

"He has gone plumb crazy!" the butcher's helper exclaimed.

Seamus thought so, too. A wild gleam lit the mayor's eyes. But there was little he could do, unarmed and wounded. "Drop those pistols, Mayor Luce!"

Chester did no such thing. He walked out into the sunlight, firing with each step. It was true he had never handled a revolver before, but he did not need to be a marksman to hit the posse. They were packed close together and only a few yards away and they could not scramble fast enough to avoid the lead he flung at them. Shot after shot after shot, until he came to the trough, and Seamus Glickman. Smiling, he pointed a revolver at Glickman's face. "You are the one I want to kill the most. You are the one to blame for Adolphina."

"What in hell are you talking about?" Seamus demanded. "I didn't shoot your wife. Those Larns did."

"You are from Dodge," Chester said, and squeezed the trigger. The metallic click brought a frown. "Damn. This one is empty. I had better try the other." He raised his other pistol.

Seamus stared his demise in the muzzle. He should do something, he should defend himself, but his limbs would not work. All he could do was blurt, "Damn you, Luce. You are a pitiful excuse for a mayor."

That was when Jack Coombs reared up off the ground with a bowie knife in his hand. His chest was covered with blood and blood was trickling from both corners of his mouth, but he had enough life in him to bury the bowie to the hilt in Chester Luce's ribs. More blood bubbled from the old scout's mouth as he gurgled, "You killed me and now I have killed you!" Cackling, he expired in a limp heap.

Chester had never felt such pain. But it was only for an instant. Then his chest seemed to explode, and his last sight as his legs gave way was Adolphina, lying so close that he flung out an arm and clasped her lifeless fingers in his. "I am coming to join you, my love. We are shed of Dodge at last." He gasped once and was still.

Lafferty jumped up from behind the trough. "Did you see? Wasn't it glorious? My readers will eat it up."

"Someone hand me my revolver," Seamus Glickman said, "so I can shoot me a journalist."

Epilogue

Jeeter Frost was never caught.

Dodge City hired a new schoolmarm. As for the old one, about six years after her disappearance, a rumor spread that Ernestine Prescott had been spotted in California, and was happily married to a small man who ran a tavern.

Seamus Glickman quit his job as undersheriff. He went back East, to Philadelphia, and lived with his sister for a while before opening a shop that specialized in the finest of clothes for men.

Sheriff Hinkle was reelected but did not go on to become a federal marshal. He made no mention of Jeeter Frost or the schoolmarm in his campaign speeches.

Frank Lafferty worked first in Denver and later in San Francisco. He was a leading journalist of his day, even if, as his critics pointed out, his journalism pandered to those with prurient interests. He also wrote penny dreadfuls, his most popular entitled *Chester Luce, Shootist Supreme*.

As for Coffin Varnish, within a year it was just another ghost town.

The Andersons, Dolph and Filippa, moved to Minnesota. They loved the bitter cold and deep snow. It reminded them of home.

The Giorgios received a letter from Italy and sailed for Naples, never to be heard from again.

Placido and Arturo returned to their village in Mexico. They were happy to be back among people who, as Placido put it, were not loco.

Winifred Curry saw to it that Chester and Adolphina were properly buried. He even paid for headstones—small headstones—from the money he made when he put their bodies on display. A dead mayor was a novelty. A dead woman was a sensation. He estimated three-fourths of the county came to view them, at a dollar a view.

"A writer in the tradition of Louis L'Amour and Zane Grey!"
—*Huntsville Times*

National Bestselling Author
RALPH COMPTON

NOWHERE, TEXAS
THE SKELETON LODE
DEATH RIDES A CHESNUT MARE
WHISKEY RIVER
TRAIN TO DURANGO
DEVIL'S CANYON
SIX GUNS AND DOUBLE EAGLES
THE BORDER EMPIRE
AUTUMN OF THE GUN
THE KILLING SEASON
THE DAWN OF FURY
DEATH ALONG THE CIMMARON
RIDERS OF JUDGMENT
BULLET CREEK
FOR THE BRAND
GUNS OF THE CANYONLANDS
BY THE HORNS
THE TENDERFOOT TRAIL
RIO LARGO
DEADWOOD GULCH
A WOLF IN THE FOLD
TRAIL TO COTTONWOOD FALLS
BLUFF CITY

Available wherever books are sold or at
penguin.com